Guy Adams lives in Spain, surrounded by rescue animals. Some of them are his family. He isn't a spy, but he is a boy, so naturally he's always dreamed of being one.

Having spent over ten years working as a professional actor and comedian, eventually he decided he'd quite like to eat regularly, so switched careers and became a full-time writer. Nobody said he was clever. Against all odds he managed to stay busy and since then he has written over twenty books.

Praise for Guy Adams:

'*The Clown Service* is fun and rips along like the finest episode of the old *Avengers* series' *The Independent on Sunday*

'I just couldn't put it down ... highly recommended' FantasyBookReview.co.uk

'*The Clown Service* is a great beginning to what could become a classic series. Guy Adams has all his pieces in place, and ably demonstrates what he can do with them. If the dark gods of publishing – and his audience – so decree. ... one of my top three reads of the year' SFSite.com

Also by Guy Adams:

Torchwood: The House That Jack Built
Torchwood: The Men Who Sold The World
Kronos
Hands of the Ripper
Sherlock: The Casebook
Countess Dracula
The Clown Service

GUY ADAMS

THE RAIN-SOAKED BRIDE

DEL REY

3 5 7 9 10 8 6 4 2

First published in the UK in 2014 by Del Rey, an imprint of Ebury Publishing
A Random House Group Company
This edition published in 2015

The Random House Group Limited Reg. No. 954009

Addresses for companies within the Random House Group can be found at
www.randomhouse.co.uk

A CIP catalogue record for this book is available from the British Library

Penguin Random House is committed to a sustainable future for
our business, our readers and our planet. This book is made from
Forest Stewardship Council® certified paper.

MIX
Paper from
responsible sources
FSC® C018179

Printed and bound in Great Britain by Clays Ltd, St Ives plc
ISBN 9780091953171

To buy books by your favourite authors and register for offers visit;
www.randomhouse.co.uk
www.delreyuk.com

From the other side of St Isaac's Square, a driver beats his horn twice in quick succession. It echoes like a musical sting from a trumpet, bouncing around the buildings of St Petersburg. Toby Greene, a man who is doing his very best to appear relaxed, nearly jumps out of his skin at the sound.

'A little on edge, old thing?' asks the voice in his ear. 'Do try not to scream in panic at every bit of traffic noise.'

'It's all right for you,' Toby mutters, straightening his bow tie, keeping his lips still and his voice only just loud enough for the mic to pick up. 'The worst thing that can happen to you this evening is that you get a parking ticket.'

August Shining, Toby's superior, leans back in the driver's seat of his hire car, looks through the windscreen at the young officer's retreating back and smiles. 'This is true. But you'll be fine. Probably.'

'Thank you for your confidence.'

Toby continues to walk, tugging the sleeves of his dress shirt from within the cuffs of his dinner jacket, wanting to wear it well.

'The name's Greene,' chuckles August in his ear, 'Toby Greene.'

'You don't walk into the lobby of the Astoria in jeans and a T-Shirt.'

'I don't walk *anywhere* in jeans and a T-shirt. Now stop talking, someone will hear you.'

'Maybe they'll be of more help.'

Toby looks up at the illuminated dome of St Isaac's cathedral as he crosses the street and walks towards the hotel entrance. The Russians treat God well, he thinks; they grant him five-star accommodation and shower him in opulence.

He steps through the doors of the Astoria and fixes an affable smile in place. Everywhere he looks, people are serious. The staff are earnest, the guests, as is the way with wealthy travellers, are looking for something to disapprove of. His smile makes him unusual. In his experience, however, people suspect a man with a big grin on his face of little but being drunk. People will remember the emotion but little else.

The foyer is a mixture of gold and cream. As much an embodiment of a luxurious heaven as the cathedral across the road. Gold drapes shimmer. Chandeliers glitter. The veined marble floor tiles sprout upwards into pillars. It's like walking into an ostentatious oyster.

Toby ignores the reception desk and moves straight through to the bar.

He nods at a girl mixing cocktails as if he knows her well and takes up residence at a small table near the exit, his back very carefully aimed towards a large and raucous group of Russian men in the far corner. He doesn't need to face them, he can watch them in the mirror that hangs behind the bar.

'Party in full swing?' asks Shining.

Toby doesn't reply, he's smiling at the waiter who has come to his table enquiring after his order.

'Go on,' says Shining. 'Ask for a vodka Martini. I promise not to laugh.'

'Gin and tonic,' Toby orders in impeccable Russian. Languages are his strong point. He has an excellent ear.

'I'll make the call,' Shining informs him, and Toby leans back in his chair, glancing around, smile in place. Just a wealthy idiot, nothing to see here. He glances at his watch and shoots the occasional look towards the foyer as if waiting for someone. In his ear he can hear Shining talking on his mobile.

In the car, the old man has poured himself a cup of coffee from a flask and is making a very passable imitation of being an angry guest.

'I can't relax with all the noise,' he is saying. 'I like a party as much as the next man but I swear I just heard someone screaming and that's nobody's idea of fun.'

Toby can't hear the response of the hotel receptionist but he can imagine their unctuous tones, their promises to deal with the situation at once.

A couple of minutes pass and a stressed manager appears. This is good. This is according to plan. The man looks towards the loud party in the corner, takes a breath, attempts to look stern and walks over. Toby watches him in the mirror as he draws the attention of the alpha male of the pack, a hirsute beast in a suit so shiny Toby suspects he could comb his hair in its reflection. Toby knows this man. His name is Bretzin, he is the 'Brigadier'

3

of the St Petersburg brigade of the Bratva, Russia's organised crime syndicate. The hotel manager is right to look scared – Bretzin has killed people before now for no greater irritation than spilling his drink. In London, Toby had read this man's file and for a moment, just a moment, wondered if they weren't biting off more than they could chew.

The manager is walking a delicate line. The Rock on the phone has forced him to face up to a Hard Place and he is deeply uncomfortable. There is a lot of deferential nodding and his body language makes it clear he would love nothing more than to run away. He cannot. He stands by his duty, passing on the complaint even as the intimidating man wears him down. Toby has no doubt that the Bratva pays the hotel well to be able to use their private suites but the Astoria is a hotel of distinction and can only turn a blind eye for so long.

Eventually, Bretzin nods, making no attempt to hide his disgust at being forced to act. The manager walks away so quickly he's almost running.

Bretzin speaks into the ear of one of his men, passing on a set of orders. This is one of Bretzin's *boyeviks*, or 'warriors'. A loaded gun. The man puts down his drink without a hint of complaint, gets to his feet and makes his way towards the exit.

'Any luck?' asks Shining.

Toby reaches into his pocket, takes out his mobile and pretends to place a call.

'Hi,' he says, still speaking Russian and getting to his feet. 'Yeah, that should be fine.'

He takes some money from his wallet and leaves it on the table next to his half-finished drink.

'I'm on my way now,' he says, following the Russian out of

the bar and towards the lifts. 'Shouldn't be a problem.'

He hangs back slightly, pretending he has trouble hearing the other person on the line, letting the Russian get into the lift first. Access to the private suites is only possible via a key card and Toby doesn't have one. Of course, he knows a man who has. If he enters the lift too quickly the man may try and force him to leave, insisting that he's only heading to the top floor. He has to get this just right. Like so much in life, espionage is all about the timing.

The Russian has entered his key card and pressed the button for the top floor. Toby moves again, grabbing the closing door of the lift and forcing his way in. The Russian tries to complain but Toby presses the button for the fourth floor, one beneath the suite level, smiles distractedly at the Russian, and continues with his phone call.

'I know,' he shouts, 'I know. It's just about getting them onside. Hopefully, if we sit back they'll do the hard work for us and we can reap the benefits.'

'Are you actually talking to me?' Shining asks in his ear.

'Not really,' admits Toby, turning his back on the Russian and watching the floor numbers click upwards on the display above the control panel. All the time he keeps his head low so that the camera in the roof doesn't get a clear shot of his face.

He continues talking. White noise. An irritation but not a threat.

As the lift passes the second floor, he spins around and punches the Russian in the throat. It's a dirty blow but Toby isn't of a mind to worry about such things. The Russian drops forward and Toby brings his knee up into the man's face. He steps over him, slips the phone into his jacket pocket, grabs the

Russian's head and twists hard. There is an unpleasant crunch. It has taken Toby four seconds to reduce the population of the elevator to one.

'Are you all right?' Shining asks.

'Fine. Clock's running.'

'Understood.'

From this moment on Toby is in serious danger. He can hope that nobody saw him kill the Russian on the security camera, they can't be monitoring all the feeds all the time. Likely it will be footage that will be consulted after the fact. But he can't *know* that. Worst-case scenario: the alarm bells are already ringing.

The lift stops at the fourth floor. Toby glances out. The corridor is empty.

The doors close again and the lift continues to the private suite.

Toby takes the Russian's gun, a heavy and ostentatious .45. Typical gangster swagger, Toby thinks. The dead man's world is all about size and volume, every shot fired is an act of violent PR. He checks the safety catch then tucks it in the waistband of his trousers, damn thing won't fit in any of his pockets but his training tells him to hold on to it, better to have too many weapons than not enough, it's there in reserve should he need it.

He removes his own gun from the holster beneath his arm. It's a subcompact pistol, easy to conceal but concealment doesn't mean a damn thing once you've fired it so he'll have to do his best not to. He cocks it and returns it to the holster.

He lifts the Russian to his feet. He's so heavy, Toby isn't quite sure he's going to manage but he finds his balance, standing directly behind him as the lift doors open out onto the private suite.

6

'Grigory?' a voice asks, confused by the sight of his colleague.

Toby shoves the dead Russian forwards, jumping over him and launching himself at the man who has been left to babysit.

Gangsters are slow, Toby tells himself, they don't have the paranoid training. It takes them a few seconds to react and that's his window. That's his opportunity.

There is nearly too much space between them, the gangster has had time to draw his weapon as Toby reaches him. But not time to aim it.

Toby grips the man's wrist and forces it upwards, using the momentum he has built running across the room to send them both falling backwards onto the deep red carpet. Toby throws his weight into it, driving his forearm down onto the man's windpipe as they hit the ground. The babysitter's eyes bulge and his mouth splutters spit onto Toby's cheeks. He keeps up the pressure, forcing himself down while still holding the gun out of harm's way. Finally, the babysitter stops moving.

Toby gets to his feet.

'All this exercise,' says Shining in his ear. 'You'll be aching tomorrow.'

'Hope so,' Toby replies.

'If your back is still towards the lift, the main bedroom is ahead of you,' Shining continues. 'To your left is a bathroom and an adjoining corridor leading to the second and third bedrooms.'

The room is ludicrously large, filled with old-fashioned opulence. The sort of decadent soft furnishings that ooze their comfort at you. The paintings on the walls are contrastingly modern, explosions of colour and form, mood rather than content.

Toby quickly drags the two bodies out of immediate view. He hopes that he'll be long gone before anyone else comes up here, but if he's wrong about that then it would be better were his handiwork not obvious the moment the lift doors opened. He might need every second he can get in order to react.

As he's dropping the heavier of the two men behind a sofa there is the flush of a toilet and the sliding door of the bathroom peels back to reveal a third man tucking a pink silk shirt into the waistband of his showy suit pants.

He stares at Toby who is already running towards him. The man looks to the left to where he's left his gun on a glass-topped table. He is turning towards it as Toby hits him, sending them both through the doorway and into the bathroom.

Toby isn't so lucky this time. The gangster keeps his balance, pushing back and shoving him against the floating sink which smacks him in the small of the back, hitting the concealed .45 with a loud crack and sending a jolt of pain down his legs.

Toby swings two punches. The gangster avoids the first and nearly the second, it glances off the side of his head with insufficient force to do any good. Toby grips the man's shaven head as he's lifted up and backwards, then slammed down onto the sink which shatters beneath his weight.

As he falls, a shard of glass cuts into his back and he can't restrain a cry of pain.

In the car outside, Shining spills his coffee but he knows better than to say anything. Toby needs to concentrate, the panicked questions of his superior won't help.

Toby lets himself go limp, then lifts up his legs and kicks out, sending his attacker barrelling backwards. The man hits the side of the bath and loses his balance, reaching out for the shower curtain, desperate to steady himself. Toby keeps moving, taking the only advantage he's likely to have.

He pushes the man who topples into the bath, pulling the curtain down after him. The man kicks out but Toby forces his legs apart and then up, keeping the man's equilibrium off. Toby grabs the legs, turns, forcing the man face down inside the bath, his hands slapping against the porcelain, trying to get purchase. Toby flings the legs away and then grabs the man by the back of his collar and slams his face down against the metal of the taps. There is a wet cough and the plughole fills with blood and spit. Toby repeats the move, making sure he keeps his own balance, the last thing he wants to do is fall in the bath on top of the man. He needs to keep his advantage. He needs to be the one in control.

The man doesn't die easily. He thrashes desperately, only too aware that he's seconds from never moving again unless he can somehow turn his situation around. He catches Toby with his right leg, sending him toppling across the room. The man is just pushing himself up in the bath, his face a mess of blood, when Toby returns, the stolen .45 in his hand. He beats the man with the handgrip, hammering at him until he drops again, landing as a dead weight in the bath.

Toby staggers back and sits down on the toilet.

'OK?' Shining asks, his voice hesitant.

'I'm fine.' He touches his back which is hot and wet, blood mingling with sweat and making his shirt cling. 'Pretty much.'

He gets up, reaches into the bath to check the man's pulse. Satisfied, he steps back out of the bathroom and closes the door behind him.

'This is taking too long,' Shining warns him.

'I know.'

He moves to the bedroom and pulls open the door.

There are three women in the bed. A blonde, a brunette and a redhead. All the flavours, he thinks, angry at the man who has left them here, hollow and brittle, waiting for his return. Human beings reduced to dolls. He tries to maintain his cold mood; anger is only likely to make him sloppy. They look at him with confused, doped eyes. The brunette gets most of Toby's attention.

'She's here.'

'Excellent.'

He holds up his hands in a placatory gesture. 'I'm here to help,' he tells them. 'I'm going to get you out of here, but we have to be quick.'

They look on in confusion. Struggling up out of the bed linen. He reaches into his pocket and pulls out a small case containing a syringe, sealed needles and a vial of liquid.

The blonde, a bruise under her left eye the vague shape of France, offers him an enthused look when she sees the syringe. His heart sinks. She hopes he's going to offer her a different type of freedom, the only escape she's known for far too long.

'This will help clear your head,' he explains, talking to the dark-haired girl he's come here for. 'It'll help.'

She shakes her head as he fills the syringe. Despite the drugs in her system she's still a fighter. It's a wonder they've let her live so long.

'Please,' he insists, holding her down, feeling lousy as he fights against her struggling. 'It's for your own good.'

How many times has she been told that over the last few years? He tries not to think about that as he injects her.

He lets her go and changes needles to repeat the dose on the others.

By the time he's finished, the brunette is clearer-headed. The adrenaline won't last long, he knows, but for now he has her.

'Who are you?' she asks.

'Doesn't matter,' he says. There's no way he's giving her his name, not in front of the other two. He steps back into the main room. 'We need to be moving.'

He presses the button for the lift.

'Not going,' says the redhead, her voice still sluggish. 'If we run, they'll only come after us.'

'That won't be a problem,' Toby explains, unhooking his cummerbund and flipping it over. He peels back the silk and pulls out a thin strip of explosive. 'They won't think there's anyone to come after.' In truth, they won't care enough to look too closely. The Bratva will be far too concerned about which rival gang has attacked them to worry about the fate of three prostitutes. These women were disposable, though he isn't going to tell them that. 'You need to put on some clothes.'

As the women dress, stumbling around in quiet confusion, he places the explosive in predetermined points. This is careful physics. Too much and the risk to innocents will be unacceptably high, not enough and they'll have wasted their time. He removes the detonator from his jacket pocket and sets it for five minutes. That will be time enough.

'They won't think anyone was interested in rescuing you.' As he says this he realises how awful it sounds and regrets it but the clock is already ticking. 'They'll think this was just a rival gang making waves. They'll be thinking about retribution, not you. You can vanish, start again.'

The lift chimes and he spins towards it, his pistol in his hand. The doors open, the lift is empty. He pulls a chair from next to a writing desk and drags it over. Holding the doors open, he stands on the chair, reaches inside and stretches up to disable the camera. He doesn't want anyone to know who left this suite.

'Get in,' he says. He suspects it's their conditioning more than anything else that has the blonde and the redhead running into the lift. They're used to doing as they're told. 'You need to run,' he explains, beckoning for the brunette who's still hanging back. 'Keep your heads down for a while and you should be safe.'

Something occurs to him. He dashes over to the body of the gangster he killed in the lift and removes the man's wallet. He opens it. Loads of cash. Showy bastard. He throws the wallet to the blonde. 'Share it. It'll get you a train ticket.'

He turns back to the brunette, glancing at the detonator. Four minutes.

'Come on! We need to go.'

'No,' she says, cold and simple.

'Tell her who you are,' says Shining in his ear.

'How would that help?' he replies. 'She's never met me.' He pleads with her. 'We haven't time to argue, please, we need to go.'

Behind him the lift chimes again and he turns to see the doors closing.

'Wait!' he shouts, but the redhead has stabbed the button for the foyer and she isn't interested in hanging around.

'Fuck!' Toby shouts as the doors close and the lift begins to descend. He looks to the timer as it continues to count down.

'What's happening?' asks Shining.

'Two of them have left without us,' Toby explains, stabbing the call button for the lift, wanting to bring it back up as soon as it's free.

'How long have you got?'

Toby looks to the timer on the detonator. 'Three and half minutes. Enough.'

'Disconnect it.'

'No, it'll be enough.'

'Disconnect it.'

'No.'

'Who are you talking to?' the brunette asks.

'A friend,' he replies, tapping at his ear. 'Now, as soon as the lift comes back we won't have long. I need you to do exactly as I tell you.'

'That is what men always say.'

He ignores that. The lift has reached the ground floor. He presses at the button again, pointless but unable to help his impatience.

Eventually, it begins to climb back up again. He glances at the detonator. Three minutes. Plenty of time. It's fine. It's all fine.

'Ready?' he asks her as the lift passes the fourth floor. 'We go right down, walk straight out of the hotel and my friend is waiting in a car outside. We don't hesitate. We ignore everyone. We just walk.'

He looks at her and she gives a vague nod. That will have to do.

The lift arrives. The doors open. Toby has his gun in his hand but, once again, the elevator is empty and all is well. 'Get in,' he says, pushing her forward.

As the elevator descends, he finds himself counting down along with the detonator. Two and half minutes ...

Just before the doors open, he replaces his gun and straightens the .45 in his waistband. He checks his appearance in the reflective metal wall of the lift. He'll pass muster. In a perilously short cocktail dress that has seen better days, his companion is likely to raise the odd eyebrow but they'll move quickly. No time for questions. Straight out to the car. Drive to the docks. Go home.

The doors open and the foyer is a hive of activity. A group of people arriving clutter the reception desk, bellboys run around loading luggage and trying to be invisible. The entrance to the bar is suddenly filled with the party of gangsters, having drunk their fill. They are heading towards the lifts, towards Toby and the girl.

'Keep your head down,' he says, grabbing her by the shoulder and manhandling her towards the exit. Just young lovers out for a night on the town.

'Son of a bitch,' the woman says, spitting the words as if they're poisoned food in her mouth. He feels a tug at the waistband of his trousers and he realises she's taken the damn gun.

'No!' he says but it's far too late, she's pointing the gun towards the gangsters and firing.

The foyer becomes a chaos of noise and panic as the sounds of the gunshots echo off the walls. He sees the girl's target, Bretzin of course, spasm as two bullets hit him, one taking off the side of his head, the other punching a hole in his throat. His companions are quick to respond and all of a sudden the room is filled with armed men and people screaming.

'What's going on?' Shining shouts in his ear.

'Get moving!' Toby replies, grabbing the girl by the arm and running towards the door even as the gangsters try and aim their guns. They don't know who they're aiming for and that's the only thing that saves Toby and his companion, forcing their way through the panicked bystanders as everyone tries to take cover.

The girl tries for one more shot and that's nearly the end of them. The bullet goes wild as she's pulled across the lobby but it identifies them as the enemy.

'Stupid,' shouts Toby, snatching the gun from her and slamming her through the exit with more force than he will later be comfortable with. He's angry and panicked. He sees their escape vanishing, their chances evaporating with every step.

'He had to die,' she tells him as they emerge onto the street.

'He may not be the only one,' he replies, looking towards the headlights of August's car as his partner accelerates towards the hotel. People on the street are looking around in confusion, alarmed by the gunshots and not knowing which way to run. August has to swerve the car to avoid a couple who run out into the road, wanting to put some distance between themselves and the hotel.

Armed pursuit appears in the hotel doorway. Out in the open, Toby has no idea what else he can do but get in the first shot. He removes the subcompact from his holster and fires. Shattering the glass in the door and hitting two of the gangsters.

The car screeches to a halt next to them.

'Quickly!' August shouts, throwing open the door.

Toby pushes the girl towards the back, still keeping his eye on the hotel exit. A gunshot rings out and knocks a hole in the passenger window. If August hadn't been bent over, opening the door for Toby, it would likely have caught him too.

Toby returns fire but there are too many of them, he knows that he doesn't stand a chance if they focus their aim on him. He has no cover and his death is so certain to him that he feels calm as he grabs the car door and turns to climb inside. At least they got her out, he thinks, waiting for the bullet that will end his life, at least it's over for her.

Which is when the private suite erupts, a blossoming of light in the night sky and a compression of air that claps like the wrath of God.

Toby gets in, unable to believe the good fortune of the timing. The car screeches off up Voznesensky Avenue.

Shining checks the rear-view mirror as he turns left to drive back past the cathedral. 'They're still coming,' he says, 'it takes a bit more than blood and thunder to shake off the Bratva.'

Toby turns in his seat, trying to get a clear view of the road behind but August has taken the corner now and there's nothing to see.

They drive past the cathedral, turning left again as they cut back towards Senate Square and, beyond it, the English Embankment. They're drawing back past the hotel now, still smouldering on the other side of the cathedral.

'What went wrong?' Shining asks.

'Someone felt the need for revenge,' Toby replies, glancing towards the girl in the back. 'She shot Bretzin.'

'Good for her,' Shining replies, changing down so he can turn onto Senate Square.

'But not for us.'

'He deserve it,' she says in English from the back seat.

'No question,' Toby replies. 'I just hope it doesn't stop us getting out of here with our heads attached.'

The traffic is in chaos. Many cars have pulled to a halt, responding to the explosion that has lit up the St Petersburg sky. Shining is aware that he's drawing attention to them by driving so quickly but can only hope to put a bit of space between themselves and any pursuit.

He doesn't manage it.

'They went the other way,' he says, stabbing a finger at the mirror where a black BMW is speeding towards them. 'They must have guessed we'd have to cut back on ourselves.'

'Or there's enough of them to take a punt that we might have done,' Toby replies, turning back to the girl. 'Keep your head down.'

The BMW, having spotted them ahead, accelerates, weaving past the slow traffic to draw up behind them. Toby can see one of the passengers leaning out of the window and aiming a gun towards them.

'Brace yourselves,' he shouts as a pair of shots ring out, neither hitting them.

Toby sees the girl turning in her seat to look through the window.

'Don't,' he says, reaching back and tugging at her arm. 'Just keep your bloody head down.'

Shining swerves in the traffic, cutting from one lane to the other, weaving through the cars and trying to keep them a moving target. He tugs his phone from his jacket pocket, concentrating on the road ahead, and tosses it to Toby as the shooter in the car behind fires again. There is the terrifying sound of pierced metal then a crack of glass as a bullet hits the rear window.

'Andrei,' Shining says. 'Evac. Plan B.'

Toby nods and presses the call button. After a few seconds the call is answered, the car still speeding along Senate Square.

'Andrei?' Toby asks, 'we need you to do your thing. Black BMW on our tail. Can you handle it?'

There's a raucous stream of Russian expletives from the phone and Toby hangs up.

'He can handle it,' he says, turning back to the girl. 'You need to hold on tight.'

Shining keeps his foot on the accelerator as the water and English Embankment appears ahead of them.

In the car behind, Sergei Usoyan, a young *shestyorka*, the bottom rung of the Russian Bratva, tries to retain his aim as Albert, the driver, weaves around a stationary truck.

'Just shoot them,' suggests Semion, from the back seat.

'What do you think I'm trying to do?' Sergei replies, taking another shot and blowing out one of the car's brake lights.

There is a flash of light from the pavement, as if someone has turned a searchlight onto the road and, for a moment, the occupants of the car can't see a thing.

'What now?' asks Albert, fighting to keep control, only too aware that he is driving blind.

The light is gone as suddenly as it appeared and he slams on the brakes as they approach the junction with English Embankment. Ahead of them, the car they're pursuing makes no effort to slow down. It surges straight ahead, shooting through a gap in the traffic.

'They're not turning!' Semion shouts. 'You must have hit the driver.'

'Yeah,' says Sergei. He knows he didn't, but he'll take the credit if it's on offer. Something like that is your passage up the ranks.

The car sails straight across the road, mounts the pavement, hits the low wall and vaults towards the Bolshaya Neva river. For a moment it's flying through the air, its undercarriage torn lose by the impact. Shattered concrete and bricks trail behind it. Then it curves down and falls out of sight. A moment of silence then a plume of water shoots upwards as the car hits the river.

Albert ignores the blaring horns of other drivers as he cuts slowly across the road, pulling up alongside the hole in the wall. They get out, running to the wall and looking out onto the river where the impact has sent great circular waves out across the frothing surface of the water.

Sergei raises his gun but Semion knocks it away. 'Not now,' he says, 'the place will be crawling with police any second. They're dead. Job done. Let's get out of here.'

They run back to the car, Sergei laughing. 'I got the bastard! You see that? I got him!'

The BMW turns back up Senate Square, Albert sticking his finger up at the complaining traffic. 'What's wrong with the fuckers?' he says. 'You'd think they'd be more interested in someone taking a nosedive into the river.'

'People don't give a shit about one another these days,' says Semion, seemingly without a trace of self-awareness. 'Makes you sick.'

They drive back the way they came, not sparing a glance for the young man standing on the pavement who watches them go past. If they had, they might have noticed the strange way he was staring at them. Maybe they would even have noticed the large flashgun he puts back in a case before wandering off through the park.

Half an hour later, and a mile or so down the road, three people ascend the gangplank of the cruise liner *Oriana*.

'Well, Mr and Mrs Somerset,' says Shining, speaking Russian

for the girl's benefit. He hands out their fake passports. 'I hope you enjoy the rest of your honeymoon. Don't mind me, your gracious uncle, I'm just so glad you didn't mind inviting me along.'

Toby looks at the girl. 'Don't worry, I'll be sleeping on the floor. It's only a cover story.'

She shrugs, looking at her face on the passport. 'I don't sound like a Caroline.'

'You'll stay in your cabin until we get back to Southampton,' says Shining. 'Isn't that what all honeymooning couples do?'

She just stares at him. 'I don't understand. I am grateful, but ...'

'Working with August is always confusing,' admits Toby. 'You get used to it.'

'But they just stopped following,' she says. 'Why?'

'A friend of mine,' says Shining.

'He has a lot of friends,' adds Toby.

'He has certain skills,' continues Shining.

'They always do,' adds Toby.

'He makes people see what he wants them to.' Shining acts as if Toby hasn't interrupted, these are two men who have spent long enough together that they have a habit of talking at the same time. 'Remote hypnosis. He can create brief, shared illusions. Andrei is invaluable whenever I'm in St Petersburg, though it takes a lot out of him. He'll be sick for a week thanks to us.'

'You're talking crap,' she insists, scowling at them. 'Why do you treat me like a child?'

'We certainly don't mean to,' says Shining, taking her hand, 'and crap is subjective. You'll get used to it. We're not your average espionage department.'

Toby starts singing 'Send In The Clowns' and chuckling. She throws him a disgusted look.

'I think you're trying to make a fool of me,' she says. 'Don't. Too many men have made a habit of that.'

Toby stops singing, his face now completely serious. 'I know. That's why we had to come for you. I understand. It seems unbelievable. I was just like you a few months ago, I didn't understand any of it. You get used to it. If there's one thing you can accept, it's this: we look after our own.'

'But I don't even know you!'

Toby nods and she is struck by the look of deep sadness on his face. 'I know, and that's my fault. But listen, Tamar, I'm sorry you had to wait so long but you're free now. You're safe.'

'Safe?' Shining smiles. 'For now. Give it time ... Things in the Clown Service rarely stay safe for long.'

SIX MONTHS LATER

CHAPTER ONE: THE TEST

Baekdu Mountain, Baekdudaegan, Korean Peninsula

The Changhe Z-11 helicopter veered over Heaven Lake, buffeted by the high winds that always rage around the peak of Mount Baekdu, and prepared to descend.

Its sole passenger looked out through the window, gazing down on the brilliant, shining surface of the frozen caldera lake. The ice showed a distorted reflection of the helicopter as it passed. It was stretched thin, then fat, like a customer in a fairground hall of mirrors.

Local myths claimed that the lake was home to monsters. The passenger smiled at the thought. He knew all about monsters.

It was also claimed as the birthplace of Kim Jong-il. The Korean Central News Agency had added one last piece of deific splendour to the dead dictator's legend when it claimed that the ice had split with a deafening crack at the moment of his death. The passenger knew all about the power of legend too.

They came to a shaky landing on an area of flat ground away

from the tourist areas and the passenger stepped out, barely able to stand in the wind.

'You are lucky we didn't end up in the lake,' said the pilot. 'This is not a good place to fly.'

'I have a feeling our host likes to make things difficult,' the passenger replied, removing a data tablet from his jacket and checking the GPS information. 'As well as keeping this so close to the border he can deny us later. We need to head down towards the forest,' he said. 'About a kilometre or so.'

'I'll stay here,' the pilot said. 'I'm paid to fly you, not keep you safe from bears.'

The passenger shrugged. 'I don't think it's the bears I'll be worrying about.'

He began to descend the mountain, tucking the data tablet back into his coat to keep his hands free.

As he worked his way down through the rocks towards the tree-line a few feet below, he cursed his clients' frequent desire to arrange meetings in inhospitable places. What was wrong with a civilised restaurant or pleasant bar? He suspected they chose these places as a test of his character, something he found insulting and childish. He didn't have to prove himself, his work spoke for itself.

It took him half an hour to reach the forest, by which time he was sweating despite the low temperature.

He took a moment to check the coordinates again before setting off towards the compound his tablet assured him was located a short distance to the east.

He wasn't in the least surprised when, shortly after, he found himself surrounded by troops, emerging from the trees, their automatic rifles trained on him.

'I am expected,' he said, speaking English. To hell with them, he decided; if they didn't understand him that was their lookout. 'And if I was going to have an escort it would have been nice to have it earlier.'

The commanding officer grunted at him, checking his face against a photo he pulled from the pocket of his jacket. It didn't match, obviously – the passenger made a point of never wearing his real face to a rendezvous. To do so would risk blowing years of cover.

'If you want me to prove who I am,' the passenger suggested, 'I'm only too happy to do so. Considering my mood, though, you might want to take it as read. If I were to offer an example of my credentials, I can't guarantee you would all survive it.'

'Let him through,' called a voice from further into the trees.

An older officer appeared, his uniform marking him out as several ranks above the rest of the men.

He walked unsteadily towards the passenger. The stiffness of his limbs suggested arthritis and the Englishman noted one of his eyes was quite blind, a white, useless thing that appeared to have been boiled.

'We are cautious,' the old solider said, in heavily accented English. 'This is not how we do things.'

'Outside help?' the passenger asked. 'Nothing to be ashamed of. My skills are rare. In fact, I'd go as far as to say I don't know of another contractor in my line of work.'

'This is true. And yet it is … uncomfortable.'

'So is standing out here. Can we maybe carry on our conversation somewhere a little warmer?'

The old soldier nodded and the party retreated back into the woods, the passenger held at their centre, quite aware of the suspicious eyes and itchy trigger fingers that surrounded him.

The compound was only five minutes away. A rough collection of shacks that had clearly seen better days. The old soldier noticed the look of distaste on the passenger's face.

'We abandoned this place years ago,' he explained. 'But it serves our purpose today.'

Walking past the barbed-wire fences and along the overgrown mud track, the passenger was led to a central hut. The old soldier waved at the rest of the soldiers, commanding them to stay outside.

Inside there was no more furniture than a table, two chairs and a small log burner that was already alight. On the table there was a wooden crate and, beckoning for the passenger to take a seat, the old soldier reached into it. He pulled out a thin, card folder which he dropped onto the desk, then a half-bottle of Cheongju, a Korean rice wine that the passenger detested. He chose not to mention the fact as the old soldier placed two glasses on the table and poured him a measure. 'It warms the bones quicker than the fire,' the old soldier said, draining his own glass in one and then replenishing it. This was a man who liked to maintain a distinct level of liquid warmth, the passenger decided.

'Is that for me?' he asked, pointing at the folder.

'It is,' the old soldier agreed, 'but first I have been asked to witness proof of your abilities.'

The passenger frowned at that. 'I don't think you want to do that.'

The old soldier shrugged. 'It is my orders.'

The passenger sighed and got to his feet. 'My reputation is well earned. I am not used to performing auditions.'

'I understand. I am sure the high fee we are offering for your services will more than compensate for any personal insult.'

The passenger looked at him and, for one pleasing moment, he noted that the old soldier looked afraid. 'It is not about personal insult. What I do is dangerous, and not just to me. I cannot be held responsible for your safety.'

The old soldier nodded sadly and drained his rice wine. 'Why do you think they sent me? I am old. My usefulness is done. I have nothing left but medals. If my family could eat them, then perhaps they would be worth the efforts it took to earn them.'

'You are looking death in the face, old man,' the passenger explained.

'I've been doing that for years,' the old soldier conceded, pouring himself more Cheongju. 'You are to demonstrate your abilities. The test is simple. If you are able to take this,' he tapped the folder, 'and walk out of here alive, my masters will consider the contract accepted.'

The passenger looked out of the window. The troops outside had encircled the hut, their rifles raised.

'Stupid,' the passenger said, closing his eyes and beginning to mutter under his breath. He spoke for no more than thirty seconds, then sat down at the table and took a sip of his drink. It made him wince.

'You find it distasteful?' the old soldier asked.

'The drink,' the passenger replied. 'The rest is just business as usual.'

Outside, the screaming began.

CHAPTER TWO: THE RAIN

a) The Laurels, Kempton, Bedfordshire

Sir James Lassiter lay awake, staring into shadows.

His sleep had been uneasy for days. This wasn't unusual. The heavier his workload, the harder he found it to turn his mind off at the end of each day. It had been his custom to self-medicate with a decent brandy and hope for the best. Tonight, even the alcohol hadn't settled his mental chatter and he lay there in the dark wondering if there was really any point to him staying in bed.

He felt his wife stir next to him and turned to look at her sleeping face. She wore a blindfold, used to his sitting up in bed reading past the time she wished to sleep. With her mouth open and her arms splayed out on the covers, he decided she looked like someone who had been executed by a rifle squad. The thought was enough for him to finally give up on sleep. He got out of bed, doing his best not to disturb her. He stuck his feet into his slippers, pulled on his dressing gown and shuffled out onto the landing.

He moved towards the stairs, pulling the belt of his dressing gown tight and wondering if another brandy might be the ticket. He decided not. He checked his watch: it was half past three in the morning. He would only end up waking with a heavy head in a couple of hours. He had an early start and the last thing he needed was to make his brain even more sluggish. Perhaps some cocoa, or even a snack. At least his wife, being asleep, could hardly add her bitter seasoning to a round of sandwiches. She was always complaining about his damned waistline, as if he wasn't old enough to do whatever he liked.

He switched on the kitchen light, wincing slightly in the brightness. Damn place was like a hospital operating room, all white tile and chrome. His wife would insist on the shiniest things.

His mobile phone was sat charging on the sideboard and he glanced at it, as was his habit. Things were better when they couldn't get you at every hour of the day and night, he thought, but the habit was well ingrained by now, he was always to be found dangling at the end of a 3G signal.

He'd received a text message. The number wasn't one he recognised. He swiped a finger at the touchscreen so he could read it. The entire message was a string of bizarre graphics, no letters he recognised. Some kind of stupid error in the software he imagined, staring at it.

As if to prove him right the phone screen suddenly cracked. In surprise he dropped it to the floor where it clattered on the tiles.

'Bloody thing,' he muttered, shaking his hand. It felt burned, as if the phone had suddenly heated up while he had been holding it. Maybe it was some kind of fault with the battery?

Outside it began to rain.

He stooped down to pick up the phone, tapping at it carefully in case it was still hot. It wasn't.

He'd have to submit a claim for a new one. An irritating faff. Maybe he could call Sonia in the morning and see if she could bring him one to use in the meantime. As much as he hated the thing, he could barely function without it.

The screen was blank now, no doubt irreparably broken by the fall or the sudden heat.

He put it back on the sideboard and moved to the window, trying to decide what to eat.

He looked out on the garden he had paid a fortune to have landscaped. A prim collection of box hedging and ornate borders. He considered it sterile but his wife liked its austere lines.

The moon was three-quarters full, its light turning the garden into a black and white picture, or a gothic engraving. He looked at the shadows beneath the ash tree that bordered the lawn, absurdly convinced that he could see someone standing there, staring at the house. Ridiculous. What would someone be doing stood out there on a night like this? Even burglars would stay at home in their beds when the rain was as heavy as this.

The rain.

Even though the noise of it filled his ears he realised there was no sign of it beyond the glass. Which was ludicrous.

He pressed his face to the window. It must be a trick of the light, he decided. Of course it was raining, it was lashing down, the noise was echoing around the house.

Outside the garden was still and impossibly dry.

Ludicrous.

He moved out of the kitchen into the darkness of the hallway and drew to a halt at the sight of a woman stood utterly still by the front door. The sound of rain was loud now and, as the woman walked towards him, he felt his toes grow wet.

'Ellen?' he asked, shocked at the sight of her. But it wasn't his wife. She was still sleeping soundly in the bedroom above. She would remain so, right through until morning when she would come downstairs to find the body of her husband lying on the kitchen floor, soaked to the skin.

b) Skirmett Road, Cadmoor Wood, Buckinghamshire

As her husband forced the only thing he truly cared for along the country road, Rachel Holley leaned back in the passenger seat and wondered what the hell had attracted her to him in the first place. She considered herself fair and easy-going by nature, the sort of person who generally sought to find the best in people, but, try as she might she could find nothing in Leonard Holley that wasn't loathsome. There must have been a point, she assured herself, all those years ago, when he had been a different man. She couldn't have been so blind, could she?

'I wish you wouldn't bloody sulk,' he said, dropping the car into second in order to traverse a tight bend.

She stared out on the open fields around them, pale shadows in the moonlight, and imagined running across them, free from this boor of a man.

'I'm not sulking,' she said. 'I'm exhausted. I thought we were going to stay in a hotel.'

'Why waste the money?' he said. 'It's only an hour or so's drive and I'm still on New York time.'

'I wish I were.' For that matter, she wished she were still in New York. On her own.

'Can't win with you,' he said. 'Usually I'm frittering away taxpayer's money; now, when I try and save a few quid, I'm being unreasonable.'

'I didn't say that, I just said I was tired.'

'You always bloody are these days.'

And why might that be? She wondered. *Did you ever think about that?*

Living with Leonard was a constant game of bickering. Of turning a blind eye to affairs, financial misdealing and any one of a number of things for which she kept expecting to see her face shoved on the front of a tabloid. Some men went into politics out of a sense of power, some actually hoped to do some good, others, like Leonard, were just always keeping an eye out for the easy con. She was a prisoner in a Fleet Street hack job waiting to happen and she was sick to death of it. Whenever the subject came up, at those times when her patience ran dry and she determined to leave, he would always beg her to reconsider, to think of his career, a career – he would never fail to remind her – that kept her in the lifestyle she enjoyed. In the end she would stay, not through selfish greed but rather because she was too weak to make the move. He would beat her down with his arguments and she never had been any good at confrontation. She would back down and, for a week or two, he would be especially nice to her. Then, once enough time had gone by, he would return to normal and she would be left hating herself even more than him, disgusted at her own inability to stand by her convictions and walk out on their marriage. Then she would think of the disapproval of her parents, the inevitable loss of the few friends she had gathered through Leonard's social circle, and the threat of public attention as the papers scrutinised their divorce. No doubt one of them would find a willing mistress to make famous for a day.

It all just felt impossible and she hated it.

'I haven't slept for nearly a whole day,' she said. 'I can't help being tired, can I?'

'Should have napped on the plane like I said. But then you never listen to common sense.'

'I can't sleep on planes ...' She let her reply peter out. Why was she bothering to argue? She was exhausted, the last thing she needed was to get into an argument. She went back to her silence.

In his pocket, his mobile phone beeped a text alert. 'God's sake,' he said. 'Who's that at this hour?'

'Want me to check?' she asked, happy to have something to distract them from their cross words.

'No.' He looked panicked. 'I'll do it.'

'You're driving.'

'Barely.'

He fished the phone out of his pocket, casting her a nervous glance. He thinks it's one of his lovers, she realised. At that moment she could have punched him, the pathetic little man.

Keeping one eye on the road, the car barely moving, he looked down at the phone and grunted.

'What is it?' she asked, unable to resist making the situation more awkward for him if it was another woman.

'A jumble,' he replied. 'Something's wrong with it. Not even words. Fuck it!'

He dropped the phone, shaking his hand as if stung. He

shuffled in his seat, writhing as if he had just dropped something dangerous into his lap.

'What?' she asked.

'Get it!' he shouted. 'The phone, bloody thing burned me.'

The windscreen of the car suddenly filled with rain and Leonard swore. 'Brilliant, just what I need on top of everything else.'

He turned on the windscreen wipers of his beloved Mercedes and slowed to a crawl. 'I can barely see a thing,' he said. 'Where did this come from?'

She had a light sweater folded across her lap and she used it like a glove to pick up the discarded phone, holding it carefully. Then, as she realised it wasn't even hot, took it in her other hand.

'It's stone cold,' she said.

'I tell you it burned me!'

'The screen's cracked.'

'There, I told you there was something wrong with it. Bloody thing.' He blew on his fingers and then stamped on the brake.

'What now?' she asked, staring through the windscreen.

It was lucky they had barely been moving, she realised. The road ahead dropped into a steep hill and below them, distorted by the rain, she could see a woman stood at the very edge of their headlights.

'Silly cow,' said Leonard, pulling on the handbrake. 'I could have run right into her. What's she doing wandering up the road at this hour?'

Rachel peered through the wet glass, trying to look at the woman in the road. She was dressed entirely in white, black hair clinging to her pale face as the rain beat down on her.

Leonard beat the horn, making Rachel jump.

'For God's sake, Leonard, I think she knows we're here.'

'Then why doesn't she shift out of the bloody way?'

With a frustrated roar, he disengaged his seat belt and opened the door. 'She'll soon bloody move if I have anything to do with it.'

'Leonard, she probably needs help.'

'She soon will do.'

He got out, slamming the door behind him, slipping on the wet tarmac as he headed down the hill towards the woman.

'Leonard!' Rachel shouted. The man was impossible. She undid her own seat belt. Rain or no rain she was determined that whoever that was down there shouldn't have to feel the full force of her husband's temper.

She was opening the door when the handbrake clicked off and the car began rolling down the hill.

She grabbed at it, in panic, the passenger door swinging open as the gradient pulled it forward. The rain poured in on her, as she fought to lift the handbrake. It wouldn't move.

'Leonard!' she shouted, her voice sounding absurdly weak against the roar of the rain. 'Leonard!'

She looked up just in time to see the surprised look on his face as he turned, slipped on the wet road and then vanished beneath the wheels of his beloved car.

Of the woman in the road there was no sign.

c) South Wimbledon Tube Station, Merton High Street, London

Five o'clock in the morning and Sonia Finnegan wished she was anything but awake as she trudged along. The road offered sluggish commercial traffic, most of the shops were closed except for the cab company where a bored-looking Sikh sat in front of his radio and dreamed of his bed. A van dumped bundles of today's papers outside the newsagents, the driver lost within the sounds of his iPod, tinny drum rhythms seeped out from the earbuds like water from a leaking pipe.

London never truly slept but, like any city, it hit an early morning lull, the winter darkness draped across it, chilly and inhospitable, where the only people still moving feel adrift in their own worlds.

Sonia was no different as she ran through the programme for the day ahead and wondered whether Sir James was going to be in a good mood or not. He was a good employer, better than many she'd worked with, but he was a man of moods, most especially at times like this and she considered it important to try and second-guess them. She hadn't got where she was today without being able to anticipate the needs of those she worked with. It was, as she often told her three-year-old son, her superpower. He tried to look impressed when she told him this but made no bones about the fact that it would be way cooler if she were able to be invisible. In a way, she tells him, that's exactly what she is.

She entered South Wimbledon Tube station, offering a distracted smile at the bored-looking guard in the booth who was staring into his flask of coffee as if it held the secret to happiness.

She pressed her Oyster card against the reader, passed through the barrier and made her way down the escalator to the platform.

There was no one else there. She wasn't surprised. The only people travelling into London at this time were people aiming for trains or planes. It would be another hour or so before things got busy.

She sat down on one of the benches and glanced up at the electronic sign jutting out above her head. The first train would be along in five minutes. It felt like five minutes she could better have enjoyed in bed but she fished her papers out of her briefcase and ran through the itinerary of meetings.

She was lost in distracted, sleepy thoughts when, all of a sudden, her mobile buzzed. She pulled the mobile out of her coat pocket and tapped in her passcode. The text message appeared on the screen, a strange mess of what looked like undecipherable smilies. Suddenly, the phone grew hot in her hand and, unable to stop herself, she flung it away. It skimmed across the tiled floor and dropped over the edge of the platform.

'Oh shit,' she sighed, angry at herself. She put her papers back in her briefcase and walked over to the platform edge.

She squatted down, grimacing as her hands touched the dirty floor. Stretching out over the edge, she could see the phone, its shiny black surface glinting in the sooty dirt of the concrete beneath the rails.

She glanced up at the electronic sign. Only one minute until her train was due. Not that she thought she would be stupid enough to climb down and get it. The track was electrified and, as much as she couldn't bear the thought of admitting she'd been so clumsy as to hurl her phone under the tracks, it would be better to be embarrassed than to be dead. Maybe there was time to ask the guard to help?

Just as she decided it was worth running up the escalator to ask, water began pouring down on her. She jumped to her feet, startled. Her shoes slipped on the shiny surface of the painted platform edge and, yet more ignominy, she fell on her back, landing painfully on the concrete floor with a yell.

It must be the sprinkler system, she thought, set off by accident. And yet, as she looked up, covering her face with her hands, she could see no sign of any such thing.

Great. Now she was definitely going to be late. There was no way she could go in to work wet and dirty. She'd have to run back home and change.

'Hey!' she shouted, meaning to call the attention of someone. 'There's something wrong with the ...'

There was a woman stood on the tracks a short distance away. She was dressed all in white, her hair was long, black and straight, hanging over her face as the water rained down on her.

'Get up from there!' Sonia shouted. 'The track is electrified!'

But that seemed the least of the woman's problems as a blast of cool air pushed along the platform ahead of the distant sound of the approaching train.

'Quickly!' Sonia shouted, not caring for the state of her clothes any more, moving along the platform, and holding her hand out to the woman. 'The train's coming, you've got to move.'

It briefly occurred to her that if the woman took her hand and touched the electrified rail, they could both be killed. She pushed the thought away – she couldn't think about that, not if there was a chance she could get this girl to safety.

Absurdly, she thought of her son, impressed by Mummy's real super heroics when she tells him about this later. To hell with being invisible, she thought, I'm Underground Girl and I'm the best hero in the business.

The woman in white looked up at her extended hand. Her movements were slow. Was she drugged?

The sound of the train filled the platform, only seconds away.

'Quickly!' Sonia shouted again, shaking her proffered hand. 'Grab hold.'

The woman in white just stared. Watching as Sonia, overbalanced, fell forwards. As the first Northern Line train to High Barnet exploded out of the tunnel, Sonia found herself slapped across the front of it. Later she will be discussed in angry tones by commuters irritated at the brief delay caused to their journey.

CHAPTER THREE: THE MEETING

a) Offices of Belgrade Entertainments, Soho, London

'What you must remember, Mr Fisher,' announced Belgrade, the renowned psychic, media darling and bullshitter, stroking at a waxed moustache, the only point of interest on a chubby face that looked to have been sculpted from butter, 'is that I can only establish communication with the other side with your help. I need constant affirmation from you, I need to hear your voice, I need to feel you're part of the conversation I am trying to establish and conduct. Does that make sense?'

'Certainly,' replied the man who was calling himself Mr Fisher. He unbuttoned his jacket, shifted forward in his seat and gave the psychic his undivided attention.

This was difficult in a room so filled with distraction. Belgrade (real name: Martin Lumpkin, a surname ill-suited to theatrical posters and onscreen captions) surrounded himself with the treasure of his profession. His office was every bit the equal of any theatrical stage he had performed on. Shelves were filled with copies of his books (in several languages, though the lies remained the same), stacked alongside other works of a suitably esoteric nature. 'Mr Fisher' had no doubt that Belgrade had read none of these other books, though it was clear that he had spent some considerable time making it appear as if he had done so, creasing their spines and filling their pages with bookmarks and Post-it notes.

At the end of every shelf, sculptures and busts held the books in place. From a phrenology head with false craquelure finish to a bust of Edgar Cayce, the effect was that of being watched by countless dead eyes, which certainly chimed with Belgrade's reputation.

Aside from the bookshelves, there was a selection of theatrical posters, all featuring an air-brushed, bottle-tanned version of the man sat in front of 'Mr Fisher', and an enviable host of framed photographs of celebrity clients. Belgrade communed with more stars than your average tabloid astrologer (a role he had also performed in his time until more lucrative gigs came his way).

'I just hope you can establish a connection with my darling Elisabeth,' said 'Mr Fisher'. 'She always promised that if there was any way of getting in touch with me from the other side she would make the effort. I've been to several mediums, though not on a one-to-one basis, and have yet to receive a message.'

'Ah.' Belgrade's face crumpled as if he had just been informed of the death of a favourite pet. 'There are so many charlatans working today. Plus, of course, in a theatre it is hard to pass on a message for everyone. I see my live shows as a valuable way of spreading the positive belief that there is life after death. Sometimes that is just as important as delivering a specific message. Reassuring those who are left behind that their loved ones are somewhere beautiful, that they are happy, that they have found peace. I find them tiring but I think spreading the word is a duty, a responsibility that one such as myself needs to live up to.'

'Mr Fisher' imagined the sizeable chunk of box-office revenue didn't hurt either.

'If you will give me your hand?'

'Mr Fisher' did so, noting the perfectly manicured nails of the psychic. This was a man who took to luxury with an admirable fastidiousness.

'The physical contact is not always necessary but I find it can be a valuable extra focus.'

'It's no problem.'

'Mr Fisher' noted Belgrade looking at his ring finger. There was, unsurprisingly, no recent sign of him having worn a wedding band.

'Poor Elisabeth left you some time ago didn't she?' asked Belgrade in that manner of presenting a question as fact. 'Mr Fisher' was quite aware that there could be no truly incorrect response to Belgrade's query, 'some time ago' being a rather subjective phrase.

'It's been four years,' he replied, having plucked the number out of thin air.

'Four long years,' repeated Belgrade, as if the information had come from him in the first place. 'Four difficult years.' The more he said it, 'Mr Fisher' knew, the more a susceptible client might be inclined to misremember the order of events. Later, when telling a friend about the consultation, many would have ended up giving Belgrade credit for the number.

'You can never truly be prepared for such a loss,' said Belgrade, hedging his bets as to whether the fictional Elisabeth

44

died suddenly or from a long-term illness.

'Indeed not,' agreed 'Mr Fisher', aware that the psychic would have hoped for more information than that but willing to play dirty.

'We all know that there will come a time when we are to be separated from the ones we love,' Belgrade continued, happy to take another stab at the technique, 'especially if our partners are struck by a serious illness.' A statement that could later be claimed as psychic awareness or simply a general comment. 'Mr Fisher' decided to help Belgrade out a little.

'It was cancer,' he said. 'She suffered for such a long time.'

'I know,' Belgrade replied, rather cheekily. 'I can sense the relief, the end of suffering endured.'

'Mr Fisher' had already made his decision as to Belgrade's abilities but he had little else to do that morning so decided to play along further. Then his mobile phone rang in his jacket, a digital reproduction of James Bernard's theme from *Dracula*.

'Do forgive me,' he said, 'I was sure I had turned it off.' He kept hold of Belgrade's hand, pulling the mobile from his pocket, noted the number with interest and then sent the call to voicemail. The call had changed his plans, though – returning it was a far more interesting use of his time than continuing this charade.

'I'm afraid I dislike such distractions,' said Belgrade, scowling. 'They damage my concentration.'

'We wouldn't want that,' agreed 'Mr Fisher'.

'Indeed not.' Belgrade suddenly flinched, having decided to reclaim his client's attention with some more aggressive theatre. 'Oh ...'

'Are you all right?' asked 'Mr Fisher'.

Belgrade held up his free hand and waved it in the air as if the question was akin to the troublesome attentions of a mosquito. 'I am making contact. Elisabeth? Is that you?'

'Mr Fisher' took the opportunity, while Belgrade's eyes were closed, to retrieve a small syringe from his jacket pocket.

'Yes!' Belgrade shouted. 'I can hear you my dear! But only just ... You must come closer ...'

'Mr Fisher' popped the cap from the syringe, turned the psychic's hand upwards and inserted the needle into Belgrade's wrist.

'What the fuck was that!' Belgrade shouted, betraying a touch of the Liverpudlian in his accent.

'Nothing life-threatening,' 'Mr Fisher' assured him, replacing the cap on the syringe and popping it back in his pocket. 'Just a little chemical inducement to speed this along.'

'What ... are ... you ...?' Belgrade sat quite still, his face taking on a vacant air as he slumped back in his chair. He looked as if he was gazing at the wall behind his client's shoulder, entranced no doubt, by the autographed photo of a forgotten pop star that hung there.

'Mr Fisher' reached for the ornate desk lamp that Belgrade kept on his desk, switched it on and turned the light on the medium. 'It has come to our attention,' 'Mr Fisher' said, 'that you have been claiming to have gleaned secret information from some of your more "influential" governmental clients. You have claimed this in order to sell falsified information to other, less friendly, governments. A brave and creative move on your part. Also a stupid one. I had little doubt that you were a fake but you will understand that, in such situations, it is my job to investigate. While the notion of a "celebrity psychic" as a serious security leak is somewhat absurd, it pays to dot one's "i"s and cross one's "t"s.

'An awareness of your rather obvious attempts at cold reading and a predictable reliance on Barnum statements was proof enough. Your willingness to pass on a message from my dead wife was a fun addition.' 'Mr Fisher' smiled. 'It was a miraculous task that failed to take into account the fact that I have never had a wife, nor indeed am ever likely to.'

'Mr Fisher' leaned forward. 'You can thank your lucky stars,' he chuckled, 'the next time you consult them, that I acted before your potential buyers did. I can assure you they would not have been so tolerant. A slap on the wrist from me is much easier than a bullet in the forehead.

'The drug I have injected you with is a simple affair, making you extremely susceptible to influence. A state you will be familiar with in your line of work, I'm sure. It will wear off in a few minutes after which you will have no memory of our conversation. You will, however, be left with a mental suggestion that you will find impossible to break. The suggestion I am going to leave you with is a simple one: if you ever claim to possess an ability in mediumship, or indeed, any form of psychic power, you will find yourself faced with an irresistible urge to strip naked.' 'Mr Fisher' paused for a moment. 'No, it's childish but I simply cannot resist, you will then go on to attempt an act of copulation with the closest piece of furniture.'

'Mr Fisher' got to his feet. 'I wish you all the best for your next theatre tour.'

He removed his phone from his pocket as he left Belgrade's office, redialling the missed call.

'Detective Sahni,' he said. 'It's Charles.' August Shining had

47

so many cover names. 'Sorry to have missed your call. I do hope you have something interesting for me?'

b) Section 37, Wood Green, London

In the Section 37 office, bored from a morning of scouring internet forums and other, assorted web traffic, Toby Greene was spread out on the sofa in front of the window trying very much not to think about the woman who lived upstairs. This was not unusual.

Tamar had become an obsession ever since the conclusion of his first mission as a member of the section. In an operation so convoluted and fantastical that his brain still hurt to think about it, he had been forced to use a device that allowed one to view history. It also, as Toby had proven, allowed one to interfere with it. The risks had been high but the alternative worse. Toby had acted. All had been well. At least until it had become clear that Tamar, an Armenian woman that August Shining had rescued from the Russian Bratva many years earlier and who frequently assisted them on missions as an ad hoc agent, was no longer living in the flat above. It hadn't taken them long to discover that the woman still existed, she had just never met Shining and was therefore still stuck in the hateful life he had once rescued her from. After that, Toby had felt he had no choice: how could he not do everything possible to restore the freedom she had lost?

Shining had agreed, despite the fact that the operation would have to be run off the books – there was no way the British government would have signed off blowing a chunk out of one of the most prestigious hotels in Russia just to rescue a single woman who had no strategic asset.

The mission had been successful. Tamar was back where she should be, living in the small flat above the office. But she wasn't the same woman Toby had met on his first day in the department. How could she be? With several more years of abuse and a drug addiction that she was only just showing signs of recovering from, she was a troubled soul.

On that first night onboard the cruise ship they had used to leave Russia, she had offered herself to Toby. He had woken up to find her hand in his boxer shorts and a look of fatalistic acceptance on her face as she proposed sex. She had simply expected it would be the price for her rescue. He couldn't recall ever feeling so miserable.

He had put her back to bed and then held her during the long hours until morning. He had hoped she might cry, show some kind of release, some kind of emotion. In fact, she had simply stared at the wall of the cabin. Until, that was, the morning, by which time she was so desperate for a fix she was almost uncontrollable.

It had been a difficult few months.

And he felt responsible for all of it.

He listened as she paced up and down on the floor above, a woman still at odds with her environment, unable to fit into her new life. Toby didn't know what to do.

When the door opened downstairs and he heard Shining's feet making his way up to the office, he was struck with a desperate hope that his superior might bring some news that would distract him from standard duties. Section 37 was in a slump and it wasn't helping Toby's mood. He needed something to take his mind off the real world. It seemed a reasonable hope given the special directive of the department.

The door to the office opened and Shining breezed in, his usual dapper self. Today offered a black three-piece suit and a violently pink shirt. As always, the old man made Toby look at his own grey suit and wonder what he was doing wrong. He had gone through a phase of trying to live up to his section chief's sartorial ambitions but had stopped after Shining had pulled him to one side, taken a forgiving look at the green frock coat he had been wearing and suggested he pop home and change. Some people had it, Toby had decided, while others were forced to just watch.

'Afternoon, Toby,' said Shining, settling in behind his desk, 'and how are things here at the very hub of the world?'

Toby looked out of the window at the bored hustle and bustle of Wood Green High Road and sighed. 'Boring. How was the medium?'

'He shall trouble the spirits no more. Never mind him, though. I have something far more exciting to occupy us!'

Toby perked up. 'Last time you said that it turned out you had tickets to see Jethro Tull in concert. I do hope this is better news.'

'No prog-rock flautists for us today, my eager young spy. I've had a fascinating phone call from Detective Sahni. You remember her, of course?'

'Of course.'

'She has been investigating some particularly unusual deaths and, unless I am very much mistaken, we shall soon find ourselves in the almost unheard of position of being called upon by our superiors.'

'You think they want their office back?'

'I think, Toby, that life is about to get more interesting!'

c) Cornwell's Club, Mayfair, London

Shining was proved right in a matter of minutes, a call coming through that requested their presence for a briefing of 'utmost importance'.

Within an hour, they found themselves ensconced in a private room at the Cornwell's Club on Mayfair.

'I'm not sure people like me are allowed in here,' said Toby, shifting awkwardly in his seat and trying to keep his hands off the highly polished meeting table.

'Think yourself lucky,' Shining replied. 'The place is poison, a hell of bigotry, tweed and ironed newspapers.'

The door opened and three men entered. One was a young, professional-looking man. An intelligence officer, Toby decided. The others were a pair of civil servants. They were of a type, the sort of men who spent their weekends pointing shotguns at wildlife. One of them was particularly familiar.

'Sir Robin,' said Shining extending his hand to the most corpulent and familiar of the trio. Looking at him in his suit, Toby was reminded of the way a plastic bag filled with water strains and wobbles into unexpected shapes. 'How delightful to see you.'

Sir Robin ignored the extended hand, as Shining had known he would. He kept it there for a brief moment then popped it back into his pocket where it played contentedly with some loose change.

'This meeting is not my idea, Shining,' Sir Robin said. 'My attitude towards your department is well known.'

'It is indeed,' Shining said with a smile as if Sir Robin had offered a compliment.

'The meeting was called by me,' said one of the other men. Toby recognised him as Clive King, the assistant Business Secretary, a man who occasionally languished on *Newsnight* when the day's current affairs had been minimal. 'I had no idea such a department existed, I must say, but if the night's events are anything to go by then we will have good reason to be grateful it does.'

'We'll see about that,' muttered Sir Robin, sitting down at the head of the table. 'You know Fratfield?'

Toby was thinking of a small town in Gloucestershire when he realised that Sir Robin was gesturing to the third member of the party. 'SIS.'

Fratfield, looking almost as uncomfortable as Toby to be in such pompous company, reached out and shook their hands. 'Bill Fratfield, Section K, I'm here to keep an eye on the foreign aspects of the matter.'

'And what matter might that be?' asked Shining, offering a look of utter innocence that Toby knew was as false as the majority of Sir Robin's hair. 'Perhaps the death of Sir James Lassiter?'

Bill Fratfield smiled while Sir Robin and King exchanged uncomfortable glances. 'You've heard?' asked King.

'I would hardly be worth my budget had I not,' said Shining, grateful of the hour or so head start that had been offered to him by Sahni, the chief investigating officer on the case. 'He was found dead on his kitchen floor this morning. The evidence suggests he slipped on the wet tile floor, hitting his head on the sideboard. Of course, the real mystery is why the floor – as well as the carpet throughout his hallway – was so wet in the first place. "Saturated" was, I believe, the word used by the chief

CSO. There was no sign of a water leak, no natural explanation found for its presence.'

'Indeed not,' agreed King. 'It is most curious.'

'But hardly due cause to go running to Section 37,' said Sir Robin, back-pedalling slightly when he saw the look on King's face, 'with all due respect.'

'But then,' continued Shining, 'there is also the matter of Sir James's personal assistant. Dead under the wheels of the 5.12 Northern Line train to High Barnet. I believe the platform was also unaccountably wet?'

Toby smiled. He enjoyed watching his superior dance his little dance, so polite, so charming, so completely ahead of the game.

'The video footage shows something even more strange,' said Fratfield, reaching into his briefcase to pull out a data tablet.

'All in good time,' said King staring at Shining. 'I really must ask how you came by this information so quickly.'

'With respect, sir, we intelligence officers must be allowed to keep the sources of our information secret. If it helps, that's all I know. I was meaning to investigate further when my colleague and I were called here.'

'Then at least you haven't heard about Leonard Holley,' said King. 'He died last night, too. Run over by his own car.'

'Clumsy,' said Shining. 'Where have I heard that name before?'

'He was part of the trade delegation run by Sir James,' explained King, 'working to improve business ties with South Korea.'

'Ah,' replied Shining, 'that must be it.' He looked to Toby who was always more well informed on matters of current politics. Toby was quick to jump in and prove his credentials.

'Of course,' he said, 'the much-vaunted new deals after President Geun-hye's visit. I believe the plan is to double both foreign trade and direct investment between the UK and South Korea by 2020?'

'It is,' King agreed. 'The UK will take all the business opportunities it can get right now and our South Korean friends are only too happy to establish stronger ties.'

'Lovely people,' said Shining. 'Such a shame about their neighbours.'

Fratfield smiled. 'Exactly. I confess that's why I'm here. We have no evidence linking North Korea to any of this but, well ... it would seem that someone's trying to damage the negotiations and ...'

'Occam's Razor,' agreed Shining. 'The North are the most likely candidates.'

'At this stage,' said King, 'the who is not so much the question as the how, that's why I asked to meet with you. From what I can tell you have considerable experience with matters that fall outside the ... ah ... conventional.'

'Indeed we do,' Shining agreed. 'When it comes to the impossible, we're the department to call.'

Sir Robin made a scoffing sound. 'Improbable more like.'

'I'm afraid,' continued Shining, 'this has marked us out for a quantity of cynicism amongst the more traditional offices of Whitehall.'

'To say the very least,' Sir Robin said, 'the man's a bloody menace.'

'A menace that is sitting right next to you, Sir Robin,' said Fratfield and Toby found himself warming to the man. He had no doubt the SIS officer had his own doubts about Section 37 but at least he had the sense of departmental honour not to express them to their faces.

'With respect, Sir Robin,' said King, 'the decision isn't yours. It is clear to the Secretary of State, and indeed myself, that the circumstances surrounding these deaths fall under Section 37's purview and they will be added to the ongoing investigation. They will also advise on security moving forward. The new head of the delegation is quite insistent on that fact.'

'And who would that be?' Shining asked.

'Me,' King replied with a somewhat self-conscious smile. He looked to Fratfield. 'Would you like to take over explaining the details?'

'By all means.' Fratfield pulled a pocket-projector out of his briefcase, connected it to his data tablet and drew the curtains. 'I've included all the relevant information on here,' he skimmed a USB drive across the table which Shining snatched up and dropped into his waistcoat pocket, 'but it's worth mentioning a few especially curious factors. As I mentioned earlier, there are some unsettling details to be found on the security camera footage from the Tube station.'

He swiped his fingers across the screen of his tablet and a grainy shot of the platform at South Wimbledon appeared on the far wall. 'Can everyone see that clearly?' he asked, tinkering with the focus on the projector.

'Oh, do get on with it,' sighed Sir Robin.

'Right,' said Fratfield, clearly irritated.

He started the footage and they watched as Sonia Finnegan took her seat on the platform, waiting for her train. She pulled her mobile phone from her pocket and then flung it away before looking around in embarrassment and moving over to the platform edge in an attempt to retrieve it. Then she flinched, stood up and fell over. Fratfield paused the footage.

'It's hard to tell as the quality isn't all that good, but this is the point when, well, the water appeared.'

'Sprinkler system?' Toby asked.

'You would have thought so, but the fire alarm wasn't engaged and all evidence points to the system having remained inactive.'

'So where did the water come from?' asked Shining.

'If we knew that we would hardly be talking to you,' said Sir Robin.

'It gets stranger still,' said Fratfield, resuming the footage.

They watched as Sonia shouted at what appeared to be an empty platform. Then she moved further along and reached out towards thin air. As if trying to grab something that was suspended above the rails.

'There's nothing there,' said King.

'Nothing captured on film at least,' qualified Shining. 'That's not necessarily the same thing.'

Suddenly the train appeared. The whole room winced as Sonia Finnegan tumbled forwards, her body hitting the train.

'Play that again,' said Shining.

'Do we have to?' asked Sir Robin.

'Just the moment when she's leaning out over the tracks.'

Fratfield did so, pausing the footage just before the collision.

'She's reaching out to somebody,' said Shining. 'It's what overbalances her.'

'Here we go,' sighed Sir Robin.

Fratfield played it again. 'I see what you mean. But surely there's nobody there?'

Shining shrugged. 'As I said before, nobody we can see. She certainly seems to believe there is. What about the mobile phone?'

'Yes,' said Fratfield with a smile. 'Curious, eh? Even more so when I tell you that a damaged mobile was found at the scene of the other deaths too. In all cases the phones were completely fried. Not a working circuit left in the things.'

'Anything interesting on the call records?' asked Toby.

'In each case, there's no record of any received calls or texts at the time of death, first thing I checked.'

'And yet, Sonia clearly received one,' said Shining. 'She wasn't just reaching in her pocket to check something, surely?'

Fratfield rewound that portion of the footage. 'Hard to tell for sure. She certainly acts like someone responding to an alert.'

'You say Holley was run over by his own car?' asked Toby.

Fratfield nodded. 'Sounds absurd I know. He and his wife had been in New York for two days, flew in last night. Rather than stay in a hotel, they were driving from Gatwick to their home in Weedon, little place just outside Aylesbury. Presumably, Holley had things he wanted to do at home before travelling back into London the following morning.

'Unfortunately, his wife has yet to regain consciousness otherwise we would know considerably more than we do. She was in the car when it apparently lost control at the top of a hill.'

Fratfield projected a couple of colour stills of the crash site on the wall.

'For some reason, Holley had exited the car and started to walk down the hill.'

'Probably a bloody argument,' said Sir Robin. 'The pair of them were always taking potshots at one another.'

'I doubt he would have got so cross he decided to walk home,' commented Fratfield. 'They were still thirty miles away.

'Holley leaves the car,' he continued, 'and walks down the hill, at which point the car's brakes fail and it rolls after him. Holley is lying on the road by the time the car hits him otherwise he might have survived.'

'He was lying down?' asked Shining.

'Best guess is that he turned to see the car, lost his footing in the wet—'

'Ah ... the *wet* ...'

'Indeed, and then the car ran over him. It eventually collided with a tree, hence Mrs Holley is still in intensive care. She was thrown from the vehicle on impact and has suffered severe cranial injury.'

'Do we know for a fact that the brakes failed?' asked Toby. 'Is it possible she did it on purpose?'

'That had occurred to the investigation team, though given the effect the accident had on her they're inclined to dismiss her involvement. There is no actual evidence of damage to the brakes.'

'Just because she was hurt doesn't mean she wasn't the instigator,' said Shining. 'She may have taken what seemed a golden opportunity to dispose of her husband, not realising the trap she was springing would close on them both.'

Fratfield shrugged. 'It's a possibility, certainly. But the damaged mobile and the rain would suggest it's linked to the other two deaths rather than just a spontaneous act of murder.'

'Ah yes,' said Shining, 'the rain. You said the ground was wet.'

'Absolutely. Obviously, it's harder to be so precise given the accident happened in the open but there was no rain reported in the area last night. That specific area appears … what was the word you used?' He looked to Shining. '"Saturated", exactly that.'

'It's all most bizarre,' said King.

Sir Robin remained silent.

Shining looked at the photo for a few seconds longer then nodded. 'Bizarre indeed. So what's the plan moving forward?'

'I'm taking over from Sir James,' said King. 'Though talks have been delayed for today, the Secretary of State is determined to get back on schedule. We are due to meet with the South Korean contingent tomorrow. In an attempt to increase security, both delegations have agreed to relocate discussions to a place called Lufford Hall, a stately pile in Warwickshire that we like to fall back on occasionally. The hope is that, with all of us under the same roof, security can be more easily handled.'

Shining nodded. 'Though an expression involving eggs and baskets also springs to mind.'

'If that's the case,' said Fratfield, 'then we'll be jumping into the basket too. As well as the trade delegation, there will be a number of security officers in attendance. Details are on the memory stick.'

Shining patted at his pocket. 'I shall review them with interest. The first obvious suggestion would be to ban all mobile phones.'

'Naturally,' said King, 'though I can't tell you how much GCHQ kicked up a fuss at that.'

'Of course they did,' said Fratfield. 'They'll have been gleefully bugging them all.'

'Other than that,' said Shining, 'I'd have to look into it a little more before offering any suggestions.'

'There's a surprise,' said Sir Robin. 'Told you it would be a waste of time.'

'Tell me, Sir Robin,' asked Shining with an innocent smile, 'will you be attending the summit at Lufford Hall?'

'Of course not,' Sir Robin replied. 'I have more than enough to contend with.'

'What a shame,' Shining continued. 'Still,' he looked at King, 'at least you can be assured that I will be doing all I can to ensure the safety of those who are.'

CHAPTER FOUR: THE AUDITION

a) Regent Street, London

The briefing dragged on for another half an hour or so, as things descended into laborious agreements over departmental minutiae. It often seemed to Toby that the biggest enemy in Intelligence was organisation, the constant battle between sections as to who held responsibility for what. Unsurprisingly, nobody was quite ready for Section 37 to be anything more than an adjunct to the whole affair. He and Shining were to be advisers, allowed to pursue their own line of investigation and offer suggestions as to security matters at Lufford Hall. It was clear, however, that King, reserved the right to dismiss whatever suggestions they might offer.

Toby found it hard not to be a little insulted, but Shining didn't care.

'Just knowing that I brought Sir Robin's ulcers one step closer to erupting is joy enough,' he said as they walked along Regent Street.

'That certainly helped,' Toby admitted.

'You know what they're like,' said Shining, pausing to look at a shirt in the window of Hawes and Curtis, 'it's a wonder they wanted to talk to us at all. Anyway, we're not in this to further our egos, we're here to save lives.'

'I know,' Toby agreed, 'but a little pandering to the ego wouldn't hurt.'

Shining smiled. 'You don't need their validation, to hell with them, look at how far you've come in less than a year. Remember what you were like when you first appeared on my doorstep?'

Toby nodded, he had been at his lowest ebb at that point. Crippled by PTSD and panic attacks, uncertain of his place in the world, let alone the service. He had been sent to Section 37 as a punishment, a way of killing his career stone dead. In actuality, it had been the making of him.

As he thought about that first day, arriving on the doorstep of the Section 37 office, he thought of Tamar, who had originally opened the door to him and that soured his mood even further.

'She'll get there,' said Shining. 'Just give her time.'

Toby scowled at his superior. 'Are my thoughts that obvious?'

'Yes!' Shining laughed and they continued their way along the street. 'I can always tell when you're thinking about Tamar.'

'How?'

'You take on a sort of beaten dog look.'

'Lovely.'

'I think it's terribly sweet. Anyway, enough introspection.' They cut past Piccadilly Circus. 'What do you think about the matters in hand?'

'The mobile phone is obviously some form of delivery mechanism, though God knows of what.'

'Yes, the mobiles do seem key, don't they? And the fact that they're all destroyed afterwards is suggestive.'

'Someone covering their tracks?'

'Perhaps. Either that or it gives us an idea of the potency of whatever it is the mobiles are triggering.'

'Some form of signal? Perhaps with a hallucinatory effect?'

'I have no doubt that's the line Fratfield is taking, the police too. Doesn't explain the rain, though, does it?'

'No. But then, what does?'

'Brilliant isn't it? About time we had something exciting to sink our teeth into.'

They entered Leicester Square, Toby tutting as he had to circumnavigate a group of tourists distracted by the questionable wonders of the M&M's store. 'Where are we going?' he asked.

'To consult an expert,' Shining replied, 'though I'm afraid we've come at a rather awkward time.' He gestured towards Leicester Place. 'She's performing at the Leicester Square Theatre.'

'She's an actress?'

'She wants to be,' Shining sighed. 'She's appearing in an acting showcase. One of those awful things where a bunch of actors strut around performing little set pieces in front of audiences of agents and casting directors. I was invited but I was determined to be far too busy to attend. As we need her help, however, it might be politic to show our support.' He looked at his watch. 'We've got an hour or so before it starts. Hopefully she's here already.'

He pulled out his phone and made a call.

'Cassandra, darling ... Yes ... Of course I am, in fact I ... Yes

... Well, I was wondering ... Right ... Of course ... Yes ... So is there any chance? ... Right ... Yes ... Fine ...' He hung up.

'She seems a quiet woman,' said Toby with a smile.

'Impossible. I'm no wiser as to her whereabouts now than I was when I started. Apparently, she had to go and do some breathing exercises.'

'She does do it then?'

'I'm sorry?'

'Breathe.'

'Very occasionally. That's when someone else gets the chance to say part of a sentence.'

'So, we have to wait an hour, do we?'

'Afraid so. It should be worth it, though. For all her eccentricities, Cassandra Grace is an undoubted expert on the subject in hand.'

'Which is?'

'Curses.'

b) Leicester Square Theatre, Leicester Square, London

In a manner so lazy as to seem positively treasonous to Toby, the two officers pottered around the bookshops on Charing Cross Road while they waited for the show to begin.

While they were making no forward steps on the operation in hand, Shining did find a pile of cheap Modesty Blaise novels so he, at least, was happy.

They returned to the theatre and Shining announced himself to the woman behind the box-office window as Christopher Barclay.

'And this is my colleague, Terry Nevill,' Shining said. 'I'm afraid he's not on the guest list but I only heard he was flying over from Los Angeles this morning. He's here to look into casting for the latest Cruise picture.'

'Cruise?' the woman asked, her eyes lighting up. 'Tom Cruise?'

'Tom-Tom,' said Toby in a passable West Coast accent. 'What a guy.'

'I'm sure it'll be fine if you go in,' the woman said, reaching for her mobile phone and Twitter feed. 'Do help yourself to drinks and canapés.'

'Cool,' said Toby. 'I haven't had a damn thing since a bagel at LAX.'

'Do try to remember it's the actors that are auditioning for a role,' said Shining to Toby as they descended the stairs towards the basement theatre, 'not you.'

'You're just jealous of my considerable talents,' Toby replied.

The drink and canapés turned out to be lukewarm Cava in plastic cups and egg sandwiches. They helped themselves to both and sat down on the back row of the little theatre space.

'If I could just give you the information sheets about today's performers,' said a woman who was wandering about the place in a state of panic. 'Did you give your contact information to the box office?'

'They know who we are,' Shining assured her with a smile, taking the proffered sheets. 'So good of you to invite us.'

'Not at all,' she replied, her eyes wandering towards the backstage entrance where a loud voice was explaining to anyone in Central London with functioning ears that she had lost her 'cardboard mandibles'. 'If you'll just excuse me for a moment?' she said and ran off looking tearful.

'What's this, then?' Toby asked, flicking through the sheets. It contained the casting photos of the afternoon's performers and space for the audience to make notes.

'No need to worry about it,' said Shining. 'Nobody else will be.'

'No, the important thing about maintaining cover is sticking to the details. If I'm supposed to be a casting agent, I intend to act like one.'

'If we were doing that, we wouldn't have turned up in the first place,' said Shining.

A handful of other people trickled in. They all looked as if they didn't really belong, eating their egg sandwiches with a guilty air.

'When you organise these things,' said Shining, 'you end up with a room full of family and friends, all pretending to be someone terribly important as it's supposed to be open to industry professionals only. And backstage, every actor looks at another actor's mum and wonders if she's going to give them their big break. It's a bit miserable really.'

'Well,' said Toby, loudly, in his West Coast accent, 'I think some of them show real promise. Look at the eyebrows on this kid, he's got the makings of a star, I tell you.'

'You've just made every male actor behind that curtain wet themselves, you awful bastard,' said Shining with a grin.

Eventually the show started and they were treated to a procession of couples performing three-minute duologues from various plays. It was, for the most part, awful. Desperate actors hurling their biggest performances against the poky walls of the little room. Lots of standing up and walking purposelessly across the tiny stage in an attempt to look dramatic. There is nothing quite so sad as an actor fighting for your attention.

When Cassandra came onstage, Toby was surprised to see that she appeared to be dressed as a giant insect, pipe-cleaner antennae bobbing as she wrestled with her fellow actor in an apparent attempt to eat him. Ninety seconds later she had walked off proclaiming herself to be Queen of Colony Nineteen. After a few silent moments, her co-star crawled off on his hands and knees.

'What the hell did I just see?' whispered Toby.

Shining looked at his notes. '"A theatrical adaptation of Saul Bass's 1974 film, *Phase IV*, written and directed by Cassandra Grace",' he announced.

'Right.'

Toby stared in silence at the rest of the show.

c) Leicester Square, London

Once the show had finished, Cassandra burst into the auditorium trailing curly blonde hair and scarves.

'We need to go,' she told Shining. 'If I stay in this room any longer, I am likely to kill someone.' With that she stormed back out again, and Toby and Shining were forced to jog after her, pushing their way past disappointed-looking actors who had been hoping to network with the only people in the building that looked like they might actually work in the industry.

'I don't believe it,' one was heard to mutter. 'You see that? They only went chasing after fucking ant girl. I think I'll just retire.'

By the time they got on the street, Cassandra had bought herself a cup of ice cream from the Häagen-Dazs café and was shovelling it into her mouth where it vied for space with insults for her fellow actors.

'They just don't know real creativity!' she was saying. 'I mean ... Ibsen? Chekhov? Do we really need to sit through more amateurs being miserable in Russian? I was engaging with the audience! I was offering something fresh!'

'You certainly were, darling,' Shining assured her. 'It was a revelation.'

'I'm wasted,' she said.

'On what?' Toby muttered.

'Oh,' said Cassandra, suddenly stopping and pointing at him with her little plastic spoon, 'I don't even know you.'

'This is my colleague, Terry,' said Shining. 'He started working with me about eight months ago.'

'I see,' said Cassandra, screwing up her eyes as if this would help her see right into Toby's soul.

He tried to see beyond the frizzy hair and glasses, the layers of curiously mismatched clothes and the ice cream. He guessed she was in her late teens, early twenties. She seemed to be the sort of person who had yet to settle on the personality she was after so was going to try on all of them to see what might stick.

'I like him,' she said. 'He's nice. Terry's a stupid name, though. What's his real one?'

'Don't start,' Shining told her. 'You know how this works.'

'Oh yes!' Cassandra laughed, spinning around the square like a ballet dancer. 'Spies and their silly games.' She swooped in on Toby, put her arm in his and kissed him on the cheek. 'Doesn't matter,' she said. 'My name's not Cassandra either.' She looked at him. 'You'll probably fall in love with me in a minute, just give in to it, you're only human.'

She turned to Shining. 'Are we going for a drink then?'

d) The Moon and Sixpence, Wardour Street, Soho

They settled down in the Moon and Sixpence, Cassandra attacking a large Diet Coke with gusto. 'I don't like alcohol,' she said to Toby, 'it makes me all squiffy. So what are you working on at the moment, then?'

'It's a weird one,' said Shining. 'You'll like it.' He gave her a vague rundown of the details, avoiding names but listing the pertinent facts in the deaths of Sir James, Leonard Holley and Sonia Finnegan. 'It seems to me,' he concluded, 'to bear all the hallmarks of a curse.'

'Could be,' Cassandra admitted, surprising herself with a burp after drinking her Coke too quickly. She laughed and then suddenly looked deadly serious again. She looked at Toby. 'How much do you know about curses?'

'Not much.'

'Didn't think so, you looked too vanilla for that sort of thing. The principle behind a curse, or hex, or execration is simple enough: you wish someone ill and so you put that illness on them. In practical terms, it's obviously not that simple. Human beings can't go around wishing the world into the shape they want. Otherwise,' she scowled, 'I'd already be at the RSC.

'Theoretically, it is possible to alter the physical through conjuration but the effects are usually limited and the skill needed to achieve such a thing are beyond most of us. Beating physics up with words is like trying to knock a brick over by blowing on it. For curses to work they have to tap into something else.

'For example, you can't blow a building up by talking at it and yet an army captain can speak a few commands into his walkie-talkie, order up a missile and achieve the same thing.'

'But the missile is doing all the hard work,' said Toby.

Cassandra smiled. 'Is it? The command, the desire, is coming from the army captain. If he hadn't ordered it then the building would still be standing. The missile is just a tool, a means to an end. In magical terms (and philosophical ones for that matter), the power lies in the command not the method of execution.

'Another important distinction: a curse is not a prayer. When casting a curse, it's all about retention of dominance, you're asking something to intercede, to act out your wishes, but you don't want to concede power to it.

'That said, to fall back on my terribly clever example, the missile can develop a mind of its own if the army captain isn't careful. It's a dangerous and complex business.' She turned back to Shining. 'From what you've told me, this could be a curse, yes. Or a more basic summoning.'

'A summoning?' asked Toby.

'For that you'd need to talk to a demonologist,' Cassandra said, grabbing at a menu. 'Are we eating? I'm famished.'

'I'm sure we can order something,' Shining replied.

'Just some nachos. Or garlic bread. Or maybe burgers. They do nice burgers. Or scampi. I like scampi. Funny little things, scampi. Have you ever seen one in the wild? I haven't. I wonder if you can keep them as pets.'

'What's the difference between a summoning and a curse?' asked Toby, trying to get things back on track.

'Oh, well, they're easy. A summoning is just calling on something. Invoking a force that then acts according to its own

70

natural behaviour. It's all about control again. In a summoning, the person calling on that force has no real control over what that force does, they just know that it will act in a certain fashion dependent on its usual habits. For example, if you unleash a lion in a field of sheep you can be fairly sure it's going to end up with a belly full of lamb. If you put a lion in a fish tank you're just going to end up with a lot of splashing and an angry lion. It's all about knowing what you're summoning. In fact,' she smiled, 'it's all about choosing correctly from your menu.' She handed the menu to Shining. 'A double burger with bacon and brie with extra onion rings, southern-fried chips and plenty of barbecue sauce.'

She turned back to Toby. 'But summonings are sloppy. And dangerous. To be avoided if possible. A curse retains the control. The person doing the cursing calls the shots.'

'So how can we tell which this is?'

'By asking an expert like me,' she said, before throwing her hand to her forehead. 'If only I could think clearly. I'm so terribly hungry. I think I may faint.'

'I'll order,' said Shining, smiling. He looked at Toby. 'Want anything?'

'Of course he does,' said Cassandra. 'I'm not eating on my own. He'll have a burger as well.'

'Will he?' asked Toby.

'Of course you will,' she replied. 'Who doesn't like burgers? Or scampi … or maybe a pie …' She slowly reached for the menu again but Shining snatched it away.

'I'll order three burgers,' he said, retreating to the bar.

Suddenly Cassandra grabbed Toby's thigh. 'You in love with me yet?'

'Not quite yet,' he admitted, backing away.

'You're only lying to yourself,' she said, letting go of his leg. 'It's sad, really.' She grinned and stared at him. 'To live under such denial.'

'No doubt I'll succumb any moment,' he said.

She inclined her head, thought for a moment, then shook it. 'No. You love someone else. Oh Lord ...' She fell back in her chair. 'I'm always the bridesmaid. Poor girl. It was a tragedy, that foolish little thing she called life.'

Rather than get involved in a discussion as to whether he loved anyone else, Toby decided to keep the talk on subject. 'So how did you become an expert on curses?'

'At school,' she said. 'Everybody hates me because I'm weird.' She said it without expecting sympathy, to her it was a simple expression of fact and Toby suddenly felt sad for her. 'I'm used to it now and, you know, to hell with them, but when I was at school it used to really hurt. I just wanted people to be nice. And when I gave up on that I just wanted them to feel as badly as I did. I'm not much cop in a fight so I looked into alternatives. I found one!' She grinned. 'You haven't known real pleasure until you've seen an entire netball team sprout facial hair.' She gazed into the distance, a dreamy look on her face. 'I think Clarissa Hedges still needs to shave twice a week.'

Shining returned from ordering the food. 'Done,' he informed them. He looked to Cassandra. 'So, what do you think?'

She sighed. 'For it to be a curse there are certain obvious signs. Firstly a delivery method. Curses aren't just spoken, you need to mark the victim out, plant a target on them. Usually this is by a written form of the incantation.'

'The mobile phones?' Toby suggested.

'It would seem likely,' Shining agreed.

Cassandra shrugged. 'If someone has found a way of digitising hexes then they're a better magician than I am. Curses don't like being written down, they're too powerful. It takes a strict methodology and control to even set pen to paper.'

'The phones were destroyed.'

'True,' she nodded. 'It does seem the most likely. It just worries me.'

'The whole thing is worrying,' said Toby.

'Yes,' she agreed, 'but brilliant experts like me don't like things to contradict their view of their subject. Digitised curses? That's just freaky. I'll be panicking about email attachments for months.'

'So what are the other obvious signs?' Toby asked.

'Method of death. In a summoning you never know what you're going to get. Demons are a weird bunch and terribly creative. I once heard of a man eaten by toads. I mean, that's just sick ... imagine!' She began miming a toad eating people. It was like a sequel to her earlier performance, Toby thought, and just as disconcerting.

'It must have taken ages too,' she said, finishing her mime abruptly. 'In a curse,' she continued, 'despite the fact that a third presence is becoming involved – the power that enacts the curse – the cause of death is usually something natural. There are exceptions but a hex spirit doesn't usually kill directly, it encourages an external state where death becomes likely. It makes the world around the cursed person excessively hostile.'

'That fits. All three deaths could appear accidental.'

'Perhaps it's simplest to look on the forces that fulfil the curse as agents of death,' Cassandra continued. 'Once invoked, they follow the victim around, affecting their environment wherever they go. They don't do the killing themselves, they just create an environment in which it's likely to happen.'

'Right, anything else?'

'There are limitations. In magic there always are. Firstly, the person who cast the curse has to be close by. Nobody's sure why, it's just part of the recipe. One of the factors that has to happen for the curse to trigger. Victim plus attacker plus external magical force equals *boom*. It's the rules. Also, the curse can be reversed, but the victim has to stay alive long enough to do it. It's like a game of Black Queen.'

Toby shrugged. 'I'm not that up on card games.'

'No? Brilliant! We should play strip poker! I bet you have really funny pants.' She screwed her eyes up and stared at him again. 'Do they have cartoon characters on them?'

'No,' Toby replied.

'Don't believe you!' Cassandra laughed.

'Black Queen,' she said, 'is a game where you take cards off one another, trying to make up pairs and stuff but the real object is not to get stuck with the Queen of Spades. If you're left with that as your only card you're dead! Well, not dead, not unless you play *really* competitively. That's how you lose, though. Curses are the same. It's dealt to the victim and they're stuck with it unless they manage to hand it to someone else, preferably, unless you're just horrid, the person that gave it to you in the first place.'

'And how do you do that?'

'Well, that's where the idea of a digital curse is even more freaky. Traditionally, the curse is written on a piece of paper. That piece of paper is then given to the victim. It can't just be slipped into their pocket or something, they have to actually accept it. You can be cunning about it, obviously. Say you sent it to someone by registered post so they have to sign for it, they open the envelope, the curse is inside it, you know? There are ways of sneaking it onto people, but the rules are strict – there has to be some kind of acceptance from the victim.'

'Pressing the button on your mobile that opens the text message for example,' said Shining.

'Yeah, I guess that's close enough. There is at least an act of acceptance. Then, once you have it, the only way to escape it is to pass it back in the same manner. So you have to get the person who sent it to you to accept it back.'

'Which they're unlikely to do,' said Toby.

'Well, no, you'd have to be really, really clever about it. Again, it's all about acceptance. Say you dropped the piece of paper and someone else picked it up. That doesn't count. It wasn't an active act of exchange, yes? The person casting the curse usually takes a few safety measures too, tries to build in a self-destruct, you know? So, the piece of paper is likely to get caught by wind, or fall in the fire.'

'It has a life of its own?'

'No, but it's the same as the world changing around the victim, becoming an environment where something horrible is likely to happen. The world around the curse is likely to get hostile too, accidents will happen.'

'But if the curse is being sent by SMS,' said Shining, 'and the phone destroys itself on receipt of the message ...'

'Then you couldn't text it back,' Cassandra agreed, 'you're stuck with it. Dead man walking.'

CHAPTER FIVE: THE HIGHER POWER

a) Piccadilly Line, Northbound, London

They ate their food and said their goodbyes to Cassandra, who did her best to ignore them.

'There's no need to go rushing off,' she said. 'I'm free as a bird. Why not go and have some more fun? We could go on a boat trip? Or the aquarium! Or the London Eye! I've never been on that!'

'Nor should you,' said August, 'unless you want to end up in an alternate dimension. It's nothing but a portal to other worlds built by the Illuminati.'

Cassandra skipped on the spot in ecstasy. 'I knew it! Brilliant! Let's go and blow it up.'

'Another day, perhaps. We really must go.'

Eventually accepting that she wasn't going to get her own way, she agreed to look into the curse in more detail and strolled off in a sulk.

'She's a handful,' said Toby as they joined the Piccadilly Line at Leicester Square to head back to the office.

'Isn't she?' agreed Shining. 'Knows her stuff, though. We'll see if she comes up with anything we can use.'

'It all seems a bit grim,' said Toby. 'Death by remote control. An assassin's dream.'

'It certainly is, though usually the casting of curses comes with a weighty risk. It's generally accepted that the more you interact with such forces the more aware of you they become. The more aware of you they are, the higher the price you might one day pay.'

'Like a radiologist developing a tumour.'

'There are powers and forces out there that are potent and dangerous. I hesitate to call them demons or anything so loaded with religious significance because I'm not sure that's relevant. Just because ancient cultures defined them in such terms doesn't mean we should. They couldn't help but convey the divine on something powerful, it was in their nature. You know my attitude, magic is simply science we don't understand yet. These forces are no different. For centuries, mankind has believed in the presence of "higher beings", they certainly exist. Some are little more than forces of nature, like so many of the powers that Cassandra described, forces that enact the wishes of someone casting a curse. These seem rigid in their thinking, single-minded, narrow-visioned, they force their nature onto our world.'

'"Agents of death", she called them.'

'Exactly. They are animalistic, impossible to reason with, though dealing with them is controlled by strict rules which can be an advantage.'

'As long as you know the rules.'

'Precisely, which, hopefully, will be where Cassandra proves useful.

'Then there are the others,' Shining continued, 'forces that are more sentient, forces that negotiate, forces that have desires of their own.'

'And these are the sort of forces you would use in a summoning?'

'Sometimes, though in my experience they are best avoided altogether. Think of them as enemy agents, sometimes a deal with them can seem advantageous but you always know that there will be a long-term cost. And that cost may be more than you can bear to pay.'

'Sounds like you're talking from experience.'

Shining gave a rather sad smile. 'In this business, we've all made deals that stick in our craw. Though if I had negotiated with one of the higher powers, and I'm not saying I have, I couldn't tell you. That's one of the rules.'

Toby sighed. 'Just when I think I'm beginning to get a handle on this weird world of yours I lose my grip.'

'Of course,' Shining laughed. 'And don't think it gets better with age, I'm surprised by the world every day. That's life. Ultimately, though,' he continued, 'it's all familiar enough. Deals and danger, destructive power that might be more than you can handle, decisions and doubt. That's a life in espionage. It's only the terminology that's different.'

Toby thought about that for a moment then something else occurred to him.

'Is the London Eye really a portal to other dimensions?'

'Of course not, but I didn't think she'd believe me if I told her what it really was.'

b) Section 37, Wood Green, London

Back at the office, Shining inserted the memory stick that Fratfield had given him into his computer.

'Let's look at who we're dealing with,' he said, opening the various files.

At which point, the door crashed open and April Shining, August's sister, came in. She was the sort of person that couldn't help but change a room by entering it, like a poison gas or an explosive device.

'Hello my darlings,' she said, crash-landing on one of the sofas as if shot by a nearby sniper. 'I trust you missed me terribly?'

'Have you been somewhere?' Toby asked, heading through to the kitchen to put the kettle on.

'You must have noticed your lives had been dreary for the last seven days?' she asked, unburdening herself of a selection of woollen garments and flinging them around the place. By the time she had finished the office looked like a market stall in Camden. 'I've been to Switzerland with the President of Lithuania.'

'Of course you have,' said Shining. 'When is war to be expected?'

'You're so awful,' his sister complained. 'It is a constant wonder to me that I love you. It was just a girl's weekend, you know, skiing and shopping.'

'Since when could you ski?' Shining asked.

'I can do lots of physical things I don't discuss with you, brother dearest,' she replied offering him a coquettish look from behind a sofa cushion.

'Given the things you do tell me, I dread to think.'

'Oh!' She clapped her hands. 'Is that Clive?' She was looking at the computer screen where Shining had just opened Clive King's dossier. 'That brings back memories. The banks of the Avon will forever be marked by our young love.'

'Like industrial pollution,' Shining muttered. 'Is there anyone in the Cabinet you don't claim to have had dalliances with?'

'I'm not one to kiss and tell,' she replied, moving over to stand behind him.

'Of course not, darling sister.'

'So what's the current beef, old thing? Had time to look into that business with the gremlins at Westfield?'

'Having your credit card refused at Debenhams is not proof of occult activity.'

'It was Anne Summers, actually.'

'Then we can only assume it was divine intervention.'

Toby came in with a cafetière and three cups.

'Come and be nice to me, darling,' said April, patting the sofa next to her. 'The old man's being beastly.'

'Work calls, I'm afraid,' Toby replied, trying to restrain a look of fear.

'Work, pish and tish, you're just mooning about the girl upstairs again.'

'Why does everyone ...' Toby sighed and tried to swallow his exasperation. 'I am not mooning over anyone.'

'Nonsense,' April replied with a devilish grin, looking to her brother. 'He loves her, August darling, isn't it delightful? Her knight in shining armour!'

'I was there too, you know,' Shining replied.

'A mere chauffeur. Toby did all the hard work, like the brilliant man he is. You're so lucky to have him. As is she. I fair melt just looking at him. I swear I approached orgasm the minute he walked into the room. Mark my words, she won't be able to resist, he'll be wallowing in her knickers before the year is out.'

'I have no intention of "wallowing" in Tamar's knickers!' Toby shouted, embarrassed.

'This is good,' said Tamar, walking in. 'They would be too small for you, I think.'

April burst into hysterics and hid behind her cushion. Toby sat at his desk and considered the viability of suicide by stapler.

'The water is off again,' said Tamar. 'I have call landlord but he pretend he not understand. He is liar. My English is good. Why you not let me talk to him face-to-face, I do not know.'

'Because you'd probably end up killing him,' said Shining, 'and that would cause all sorts of complications.'

'I'll call him,' said Toby, reaching for his phone, glad of something constructive to do.

'See?' said April. 'What a gentleman. Always happy to assist with a woman's plumbing.'

'April!' Shining glared at her. 'Do leave the poor boy alone.'

'Jesus,' sighed Toby, wandering out of the office, his mobile to his ear, 'it's like having a pair of dysfunctional parents fighting over me.'

'Mummy knows best!' April laughed.

'You say too far,' said Tamar, sneering at her. 'You make him embarrassed.'

'So cheer him up, then,' said April with a smile. 'I'm sure you know how.'

Tamar clicked her tongue in irritation and walked out after Toby.

Shining shook his head. 'April, I love you but you are a pain.'

'Nonsense, if I didn't bring the subject up he'd just keep ignoring it. He may be embarrassed but at least she knows how he thinks about her.' She winked. 'There is some method in this old girl's madness, you know.'

'No doubt.' Shining returned to looking at his computer screen, deciding to change the subject. 'Lufford Hall, know it?'

'Lord, yes, dusty old pile of bricks in Warwickshire, they use it for conferences and what have you. I once spent a draughty weekend there avoiding the attentions of the Chief Whip's whip. Why?'

Shining explained about the talks with the delegates from South Korea.

'How frightful!' said April. 'Sir James was a lovely old stick, he backed me when I had that fuss with the Chechens.'

Shining had no idea what 'fuss' she was referring to; his sister's career in politics and espionage was a complex rug he had never quite been able to unravel.

'And his poor PA, she seemed a lovely girl. Leonard Holley was a pest but still, I wouldn't wish a car on top of him. I don't understand, though – if someone's got an axe to grind with the Koreans, why are they having a pop at our lot?'

'I imagine they think we're more likely to be scared off from the talks. Of course, given the current financial mess it would take a lot more than this to have the government pull out. We need the money too badly.'

'How tiresome it is to be poor.'

'If, as seems likely, the mobile phones were the trigger, the attackers probably also wanted to avoid GCHQ flagging anything up.'

'Because they'll be all over the South Koreans like a rash.'

'Standard practice these days, I'm afraid. The Korean delegates will be wired for sound.'

'Never let it be said we don't know how to extend the trusting hand of friendship.'

'Oh, GCHQ worries about its budget too much to let an opportunity like this pass it by, they'll be crossing their fingers that they've got a productive source of intel for years to come via key-logging.'

'I hope nobody's planted anything on my laptop.'

'So do I. They'd see things no mortal man should be expected to witness.'

She clipped him on his arm. 'So they actually called you in?'

'Sir Robin was on the verge of tears.'

'Wonderful! About time they treated you with a bit of respect.'

'I wouldn't quite go that far. We're very much the silent partner in the operation. Most of the security is going to be down to Box.' He clicked open another dossier. 'They've put Mark Rowlands on it.' 'Box' was a colloquial term for the Security Service and the dossier showed its seal watermarked across it. 'He seems a decent chap, though I've never worked with him.'

'Too young for me, too,' April said, scanning the man's file. 'I was long gone by the time this lad was a gleam in his talent spotter's eye. Where did they find him?'

'Police background, Serious Organised Crime Thingie, or whatever they're calling it this year.'

'He looks nice,' said April. 'Sexy eyes.'

'If it were down to you, the entire intelligence service would be nothing but a parade of calendar models.'

'Nonsense, I'd hate to put you out of your job. Who else?'

'We'll meet Rowlands' team tomorrow at Lufford. I haven't been briefed on them. Fratfield is on hand from SIS.'

'Him I do know, though he was after my time. My dear pal George says the nicest things about him. Apparently, he recruited him out of some ghastly polytechnic in the north.'

'You consider anywhere that isn't Oxford or Cambridge a "polytechnic", you terrible snob. They don't have them any more, you know.'

'Quite right too. Ghastly places.'

Shining sighed and shook his head. 'He seems a good man. Obviously there's Clive King running the show. Add to him a chap with the quite awful name of Lemuel Spang.'

'Please tell me you're joking.'

'Afraid not, his parents must have been even more psychotic than ours. He's there from the Bank of England so he'll be minding our pounds, shillings and pence.'

She looked at his photo. 'He looks like an advert for a particularly cheap brand of electric razor,' she said. 'I bet he wears a lot of pinstripe and drives an Audi.'

'Not that you're in the least bit judgemental.'

'He's called Spang, he deserves whatever I care to throw at him.'

'The Diplomats have sent Ranesh Varma. I hear good things about him.' Shining opened another file. 'He's sharp, a good egg.'

'You're so bloody English. "Good egg", honestly ... You'll be talking about cricket with him next.'

'He's from Pakistan, we'll only end up in a fight.'

'Bless you, you're pretending to know things about sport, how sweet. If he's a diplomat he'll probably just smile at you.'

'I imagine he has a team of his own, too. HMDS don't like to skimp.'

'Well,' said April, sitting back down, 'one of them had better be a woman, it's a terribly sexist bunch of buggers otherwise.' She picked up her coffee and took a sip. 'I know!' she said. 'Give me a couple of tics.' She ferreted for her phone in her handbag. 'Vince owes me a favour after I helped him practise his bloody foxtrot.'

'I have no idea what you're talking about,' said Shining. 'As usual.'

She waved at him and wandered off into the kitchen with a trill of hearty hellos into the phone.

Shining quietly clicked through a few more files, bringing up the plans for Lufford Hall and vaguely familiarising himself with its layout. By the time she came back in, he was reading up on the South Korean delegates.

'All sorted,' she announced with a happy sigh. 'I shall be coming with you.'

Shining stared at her. 'Don't be so ridiculous.'

'I am not being ridiculous, I think you forget what a terribly important person I am within Whitehall.'

'You're a menace. An old ghost who persists in rattling around its corridors.'

'Dangsin-ui eongdeong-i wilo.'

'Are you having a stroke?'

'I'm speaking Korean, another distinct advantage I have over you.'

'Since when did you learn Korean?'

'Since I dated a restaurant owner in Brighton, hunting for the perfect gejang. I shall be there as an attachment to Her

Majesty's Diplomatic Service. And you're bloody lucky to have me.'

Shining sighed and stared at his coffee in misery. 'Now I have to contend with two threats to international relations, wonderful.'

c) Section 37, Wood Green, London

Toby was doing his level best not to scream down the phone at their landlord.

'I don't care what the problem is,' he said for what must have been the fifth time. 'You're breaking the law and need to get the water back on.'

There was another round of complaints from the landlord, involving his brother's forthcoming gastric bypass operation and the currently poor exchange rate for Australian dollars. Toby had no idea how either was relevant.

'Look, it's perfectly simple, either the water is back on by this evening or we'll be taking legal action.' He cut the call.

Turning round he noticed Tamar had followed him out into the stairwell. 'Oh,' he said, feeling immediately awkward, 'hello. Should be back on in a bit.'

'Is good,' she said, 'but next time I speak to him. I do not need you fighting my battles.'

'I know,' Toby replied, feeling even more awkward now that what he had intended as a kindness had been construed as patronising. 'It's just that we're the tenants, really, so it's better if one of us deals with him.'

She shrugged. 'I do not like this,' she said. 'You are very kind but it is like I am still owned.'

Toby didn't really know how to respond to that. 'Of course it isn't ... I mean, we're just subletting to you, that's all.'

'For subletting you would need a payment of rent.'

'You do pay. You help out with section business and we keep a roof over your head. Purely business.'

'That is what the Russians say.'

It was partly embarrassment and partly pride that had Toby finally lose a temper that had been fragile from the moment April Shining had entered the building. 'For Christ's sake, Tamar! That's not fair! I risked my bloody life getting you away from the Bratva. To say that you're just as badly off now ...'

'I do not say that. I just say that I am still owned. I do not want to be owned. Either by them and their threat or you and your kindness. I not ask for rescue.'

'Oh, so you'd rather I'd left you there, then?'

'Don't be stupid. But it is a debt. And one I do not know how to make gone.'

'You don't owe me anything.'

'You say that, and I think you mean it, but inside I think you believe something else. You do this thing for me, yes. But you do it for yourself too. You do it to make you feel strong. And to make me feel owned.'

'No.' Toby shook his head and wondered how to get out of this conversation that was tying him in knots.

'She's a remarkably perceptive one, isn't she?'

Toby felt a chill settle over him as he stared at Tamar. The voice had come from her but he knew it wasn't hers.

'It's been a while,' she said, her face taking on a gleeful air that made it seem like it was the face of someone else entirely. 'When did we last have one of our little chats? Oh yes, of

GUY ADAMS

course, just after your blundering in the Krishnin matter ended up costing this poor girl several years of her life. We talked of consequences, did we not?'

Toby had first met this person, this *presence*, on his first day after being transferred to Section 37. He had no idea how to define it, though his recent conversation with Shining now came to mind – could it be that this was one of those 'higher powers' he had talked about? Toby had a feeling it could.

It had tried to put him off joining the section – as if he'd had any choice. When it first talked to him, it had met him outside Euston station, using the body of a woman and then, much to his confusion, it found him again not a stone's throw from the office. That second time it had occupied the body of an old man. Whoever – whatever – this was, it seemed to have no body of its own, it preferred to borrow others. That it now chose to borrow Tamar's, a woman who had suffered enough at having herself ill-used by others, made his fists clench. It was pointless though: the only person he could hit was the victim.

'I seem to remember,' the voice continued, 'that I promised you a bleak future. That you would see the full fruits of your interference in the fullness of time. Don't worry, that time has not yet come. Not quite.' 'Tamar' sat down on the stairs, leaning against the wall and crossing her legs, the very epitome of nonchalance. 'Good for you, though! Rescuing this silly thing from the life you sent her back to. I'm proud of you. I do love a man who refuses to yield.' She smiled. 'They're a challenge.'

Toby moved towards the door to the office, deciding that the only thing to do was to drag Shining out here. He had told him before about this intruder. It was about time they 'met'.

'Don't do that,' it said. 'If you bring the old man out here, I'll just vanish and where's the advantage in that? Remember your training. Knowledge is everything. The more you talk to me, the closer you'll be to understanding what I am. And then ... well, then we may be able to play a different game.'

'I know who you are,' Toby said. 'You're a "higher power", a force that wants to manipulate us.'

'A "higher power"?' she laughed. 'Is that what the old man calls us? He never did like to use the old words. Demons. Gods. The words scare him so he hides them behind meaningless rationalisation. It would be sweet were it not so insulting. Has he told you about me, then? I'm surprised. That's against the rules ...'

'He didn't tell me about you specifically,' said Toby, suddenly worried he might have caused trouble for Shining. 'We talked about your kind in general.'

'Oh, I see. And the little spy put two and two together, did he? You're so sharp. You've taken to all this terribly quickly. To think how you questioned everything when you first arrived. How quickly you dropped your scepticism.'

'Scepticism is different from naivety. I believe what I experience. To do otherwise would be stupid. You exist. You are. Why waste time arguing the obvious?'

'Ah yes, *time*, such a precious commodity to you people. I forget how you run around, trying to fill your days. I could help with that, you know? All you have to do is ask. The powers I have ... Are you familiar with the Doppelgänger Contract? I could make copies of you, utterly alike in body and mind. Just think of the things you could achieve then! That was a terribly popular request in the old days; I once had a man split into a whole army. Of course there's a price, isn't there always? For every day your double lives, you lose one against your natural lifespan. Still, what's a natural lifespan to you? You'll probably be dead from an assassin's bullet in a couple of years, or blown into pieces on a foreign field. You can afford to gamble the odd day here or there.'

'No thank you.'

'How about something even simpler? I could make the girl love you? Would that be nice?' She laughed again. 'Of course it would! Walk in the park for me, that, just a little nudge here and there and she'd be yours. Any interest?'

'No.'

'Liar. You're tempted and I know it.' She stood up and moved over to him, putting her arms around him. 'How about a quick fumble on the stairs, just to try her out?'

Toby pushed her back. 'Get the fuck out of her!' he shouted. 'Right this minute.'

'Or what? Empty threats, boy, nothing but empty threats. I come and go as I please.' She sat back down. 'And if you anger me, I'll make you regret it. It wouldn't take much.' She held up her hand and reached for her little finger. 'I could just start snapping these dainty little things one at a time and there's nothing you could do to stop me.'

'Fine, you've proven your point. So what do you want?'

'Ah ... I thought that would bring out a little contrition. You want to be careful. It's no good for a man in your position to have such an obvious weakness. It puts both of you in danger.'

'I asked you what you wanted.'

'For now? Nothing, just thought it would be nice to catch up. To remind you that I'm still here. One day, though – and, oh, how I look forward to it – you will need me. And then we will come to an arrangement. One day. Ta-ta for now.'

Tamar slumped on the stairs, her head falling against her chest. Toby ran over to her, taking her hands, only to have them snatched away.

'What you doing?' Tamar asked, staring at him in suspicion. She got to her feet. 'What happen?'

Toby didn't know how to answer that question truthfully so he decided not to. 'I think you fainted.'

She scowled at him. 'Never fainted in my whole life. Not starting now. You keep away.' She stormed off up the stairs leaving Toby feeling beaten and alone.

CHAPTER SIX: THE SPIRIT

a) Flat 3, Palmer Court, Euston

There was always something miserable about waking in darkness, Toby decided, shuffling around his flat and trying to wake up. It was as if humans still possessed a race memory that insisted you were doing it all wrong. The sun isn't up, so why are you?

The clock on his oven said it was half past four. A ridiculous, unhelpful time that he tried to ignore by putting on some coffee. August would pick him up in forty-five minutes, by which time he would be doing his level best to at least feign consciousness.

While the kettle boiled, Toby showered and tried to stop thinking about the business with Tamar the day before. The thought of it had kept him awake and returned the minute his eyes had opened.

He'd told Shining about it, of course – waiting until after April had left, he couldn't quite bring himself to discuss it in front of her. As before, when he had passed on previous meetings with the enigmatic presence that so liked to hop between hosts, his superior did his best to brush the matter away.

'Think of it as an enemy agent,' he had said in the end, 'from a foreign power that is more foreign than most. It wants to unsettle. It wants to erode. Working in the field we do, we're bound to attract the attention of certain forces, there's nothing they'd like more than to disrupt our work. I know it's difficult but you just have to ignore it.'

Which was easily said. Toby trusted Shining. Still, he knew there was more to this business than he was letting on. One day he would find out what it was. Until then, he supposed he didn't have a choice but to follow the old man's advice. He should concentrate on the operation in hand. And stop thinking about Tamar. And about how she had looked at him before storming off up the stairs. And how much she clearly hated him.

He realised he was just stood under the shower, being rained on, his mind so occupied he had stopped moving.

He scrubbed at himself in irritation and tried to think about other things.

He felt the shower water pouring on his head and tried to imagine what it might be that had claimed the lives of three people. Something that brought rain and death. A spirit of the curse. An agent of death. Given the right mission, he thought, aren't we all?

He got out of the shower and slowly drank coffee while putting a few clothes in a small suitcase. He stared at the food cupboards for a couple of minutes and then gave up on them; eating seemed like too much effort for that time of the day.

By the time August rang the doorbell, Toby was ready to go.

And still thinking about Tamar.

b) M40, Northbound, Beaconsfield

April had spent most of the journey out of London sleeping on the back seat. Her fellow passengers were left in little doubt of this due to her snoring and occasional, unconscious utterances.

'There's no earthly point putting it there!' she had assured them at one point. 'It's tantamount to treason.'

Toby dreaded to think what went through her dreaming head.

'Are you quite sure we can't dump her off at a service station and do a runner?' he asked. 'I'm not sure South Korea is quite ready for your sister.'

'Tempting,' Shining admitted. 'I am, once again, agog at her ability to worm her way into any situation.'

'She's a force of nature,' Toby agreed.

'So is a tsunami. You don't want to share a country house with one.'

Just outside High Wycombe, Shining pulled off the motorway. 'We can at least find breakfast,' he suggested, 'with a bit of luck, she'll get confused in the shop and we can make a break for it.'

'Whose confused?' asked April from the back seat, her sleepy mind coming around at the promise of a fry-up.

They parked up and made their way inside, queuing for food with a selection of bleary-eyed travellers and sullen, commercial drivers.

'You take me to the nicest places, boys,' said April poking at an overcooked egg with a knife Toby was fairly sure would snap were you to try and stab anything with it.

'I take it you've not heard from Cassandra?' Toby asked, trying to butter some burned toast without it shattering into crumbs.

'Not yet,' Shining said, 'and without my phone she couldn't get in touch now even if she wanted to. I'll check in with her later. She's a little high maintenance but always pulls through in the end.'

'You just described all the best women,' said his sister.

Toby gave up on his toast. 'Back in a sec,' he said, getting up and wandering off towards the toilets.

As a kid he had loved service stations, welcome islands on the long road of boredom. Now they just seemed like irritating, enclosed worlds of tile and glass filled with bleeping vending machines and arcade games. Everyone you saw looked miserable and lost, stuck between home and the place they had to be.

The toilets were empty, a cavernous hall of chipboard cubicles, piped music and the overpowering smell of bleach.

'These facilities were last cleaned by ...' assured a sign on the wall with a list of scribbled names following after. 'If they fail to meet your expectations then please contact BriteWite Hygiene with full details.' There then followed a phone number and email address. Toby imagined an empty office at the receiving end of both. Immaculately clean but for the skeleton sat at the desk still waiting for someone who cared so much about a public toilet they felt they should get in touch.

'They meet my expectations entirely,' he said, looking at a vending machine of 'chewable toothbrushes' and another for condoms.

He urinated, glazing over at the sound of a twenty-year-old pop tune being piped in through the speakers, then went to the long row of sinks to wash his hands.

He was trying to make the automatic sensor for the tap

engage, his cupped hands filled with bubbling foam soap, when the music stopped. It took him a moment to realise what was wrong. The sound had been aural wallpaper, almost beneath his notice; it was only once it was gone that he became aware that something was amiss.

The lights flickered.

'Don't make me call BriteWite,' he muttered, staring up at the concealed neon lamps boxed away beneath clear Perspex ceiling tiles.

They flickered again and, just for a second, Toby thought he caught a glimpse of someone stood behind him.

He shook the soap from his hands, grabbing a couple of paper towels and rubbing his palms dry. Then he walked along the row of toilet cubicles.

He couldn't have said what it was that had triggered his nerves, all he knew was that he was on edge and, in his line of work, that was a feeling it was best not to ignore.

There was a crackle from the speakers. A burst of static.

He stepped from one toilet cubicle to the next, checking each one was empty.

The speakers crackled again. Then offered a new noise: the sound of rain. It was distant, gentle, an autumnal sound, water hitting leaves.

Then the whispering began.

The lights flickered once more and then turned off entirely.

The room was now completely dark. Toby reached into his trouser pockets for his house keys. He kept a small pencil torch on the key ring, useful for when the light was on the fritz at the outside gate to his flat building. He turned it on, the bluish-white light of the halogen bulb washing across the open doors of the toilet cubicles and reflecting back at him from the mirrored wall behind the sinks.

The whispering continued through the speakers, the sound so quiet he couldn't pick out any words. It was like the distant sound of prayer, promises to God being uttered under a penitent's breath.

He continued to move along the row of cubicles, pushing each door open wide.

Part of him knew he should leave, but that would reveal nothing and information is what an intelligence officer is for.

Something moved out of the corner of his eye and he turned around, sweeping the light across the room but seeing only his own reflection staring back at him.

Then his reflection began to change. In the mirror, rain began to fall. Even in the low light of his torch he could see it pour down on the head of the Toby Greene that lived behind the glass. The shoulder pads of his suit darkened as they soaked it up. It poured in rivulets across his static, empty face.

Involuntarily, the real Toby put a hand to his cheek, feeling it dry against the tips of his fingers. The Toby in the reflection didn't move.

The real Toby watched, keeping the torch at an angle so the reflection of its light didn't whiteout the image in the mirror.

The rain continued to fall and, slowly, behind the Mirror Toby, the door of one of the cubicles began to open.

Toby glanced over his shoulder, reassuring himself that the corresponding door on his side of the mirror remained still.

Then he looked back. From within the shadows of the cubicle in the mirror, a woman appeared. She was dressed entirely in white, a plain, silk dress that hung over a body that was too thin and angular to possess much in the way of flesh. Her face was hidden by her hair, long and black, plastered flat by the falling rain. He squinted at it, trying to catch a sense of it between the long, wet strands, but there was nothing.

The woman moved out of the cubicle. There was no sign of her feet, the white dress reaching the floor and dragging across the wet tiles.

She came closer and closer to the Mirror Toby who continued to stare ahead, oblivious it would seem, to what was creeping up behind him.

The whispering through the speakers became louder but still Toby couldn't break the noise down into words. They were as hidden and unintelligible as the woman beneath the hair and dress.

She slowly reached forward, the sleeve of her dress falling back to finally offer a glimpse of what lay beneath. It was nothing but corruption, and the fingers, if they could even be called that any more, left a little of themselves behind as they touched the Mirror Toby's cheek.

Then the room was flooded with light and his reflection was once more his own, dry, confused, and staring at nothing but himself.

c) Beaconsfield Services, M40

Of all the responses Toby's experience could have enlisted from Shining, glee was the least expected.

'Wonderful!' shouted the old man, clapping his hands in barely restrained enthusiasm.

'So glad you think so,' Toby replied, taking a sip of his coffee and wishing it contained alcohol.

'Honestly,' said Shining, 'we couldn't hope for better. I remember a loathsome mission in Poland during the 1970s ...'

'Oh dear Lord,' sighed April. 'Mr Nostalgia's off ...'

'It was miserable,' Shining continued, ignoring her. 'I knew there was a double in their local section but nobody would believe me. I ended up being chased through Warsaw by a rabid bear.'

'Sounds charming,' said Toby, entirely uncertain as to his superior's point.

'It was an interesting evening,' Shining admitted, 'I ended up killing the poor thing in Saxon Garden, using a cyanide pill and a noose made from my braces. The point, though, was that the powers that be couldn't accuse me of seeing shadows any longer. If someone was willing to kill me, I must be on to something. I exposed the double in the end. Ran him over with a tram, actually ...'

'Stop now,' said April, 'you're spoiling my breakfast. We get the point.'

'I'm glad to be able to prove that we're involved in something life-threatening,' said Toby, 'though I would hope that the three dead bodies we've already had to contend with went some way towards that.'

'True,' agreed Shining, 'but at least we know that we have the culprit worried.'

'Them and me both,' Toby replied.

'And,' Shining continued, 'we also have a bit more to go on. You saw the curse spirit!' He pulled out a small notebook and began hunting through it. 'You should call Cassandra and give her the extra details.'

'Oh God, do I have to?'

'Shush now, she's a lovely girl.' Shining handed the notebook over, tapping at a phone number. 'Remember you're Terry.'

'How could I forget?' Toby sighed and looked around for the nearest payphone. Being without their mobiles was already proving irritating.

'Do you have plenty of change, darling?' April asked, ferreting in her handbag. 'I can lend you some, if you like. As long as you'll sign a chit for it, I need the fifty pees for the meter.'

'You must be the last person in London who still keeps the lights on by shoving coins at the situation,' her brother sighed. 'I thought they were phasing them out?'

'I hold the line.'

She dropped a stack of coins on the table and Toby grabbed a couple of them. 'Can I leave you to handle the paperwork?' he asked Shining, strolling off in search of a phone.

d) Flat 4, Thompson Lane, Ealing Common

When the phone rang, Cassandra Grace was occupied in an attempt to master what her Tai Chi instructor assured her was 'White Crane Spreads Wings'. In her experience, the crane's wings were somewhat ill-balanced and she was extricating herself from the cushions of the sofa as the call came through.

'Cassandra Grace,' she said, still trying to circumnavigate a set of pernicious scatter cushions, 'theatrical wunderkind and future Hollywood star?'

'Hi Cassandra,' said Toby. 'It's Terry.'

'Terry? Do I know a Terry? I don't think I do, I'm sure I would remember a Terry.'

'We met yesterday, I was with Christopher.'

'Christopher?'

'We had lunch,' Toby sighed. 'You were looking into a curse for us.'

'Oh yes!' Cassandra replied. 'That Terry. Are you asking me out for dinner? I bet you lay awake all night thinking about me, didn't you. Well, I say "thinking", I really mean—'

'No,' Toby interrupted, desperate to stop the flow of the conversation. 'I was calling to give you a little more information about it. I've seen something. A woman.'

'The bitch, you're mine!'

'Please, Cassandra ...'

'Oh, all right.' She sat down on the sofa, immediately finding it a hard and uncomfortable place now she had scattered the cushions all over the flat. 'Tell me all about it.'

Toby did so.

'It sounds brilliant!' Cassandra replied, once he'd finished describing what the woman had looked like. 'Well, brilliant in that way that you really wouldn't want it to happen to you but it's great when it happens to someone else.'

'Glad you enjoyed it. Might it help?'

'Bound to. Though I'm terribly worried about you now. Are you sure you don't need me to come up there and stay with you? Just in case?'

'Would it help?'

'It would take your mind off things.'

'You're fine, thank you.'

'Are you sure you haven't been cursed?'

There was silence for a moment. 'Well, I'm not dead.'

'Yes, there is that. Given the others, you would have probably been found half-flushed down a toilet. Or with your mouth stuck around the vent of a hot-air dryer. Or drowned in a sink.'

'I'm going now, my change is running out. We'll have to call you later, we haven't got our phones.'

'Shame, I could have sexted you all day!'

'Bye now.'

He hung up and Cassandra went for a run around the flat to work off a little of her excitement.

e) Beaconsfield Services, M40

Toby found Shining and April in the shop. Shining was looking impatiently at his watch while April rifled her way through the newspapers.

'Look!' she announced, holding up the front page of a tabloid, 'that lovely medium-chappie has got in trouble for shagging an occasional table in front of Cheryl Cole.'

'The things people get up to these days,' her brother replied, glancing at the photo where a shamed Belgrade tried to hide his face from the snapping cameras of the gutter press. 'If you don't mind, we need to be going.'

'All right, all right,' she snapped. 'Shame, though. I liked him. He had wonderfully amusing hair. Sticking up all over the place. Perhaps it was haunted.'

She dumped the newspaper back on the rack.

'Any luck?' Shining asked Toby as they walked back out to the parked car.

'She was as excited as you were. But then, as far as I can tell she always is excited. She's looking into it some more. I said we'd call her later.'

'Excellent. I'm sure you've helped narrow it down.'

'Glad to be of service,' Toby scratched at his cheek, recalling the sight of those dead fingers touching him there.

CHAPTER SEVEN: THE HOUSE

a) Lufford Hall, Alcester, Warwickshire

After leaving the motorway, they circumnavigated Stratford-upon-Avon and the small village of Alcester, driving out onto quiet, open roads surrounded by winter fields.

'I'm breathing so much fresh air,' April commented, 'I suspect I shall get the bends.'

'Just work through it, dear,' said Shining, 'it'll add years to your life.'

'A wonderful thought,' said Toby, ducking as she reached forward from the back seat and tried to punch him.

The gatehouse of Lufford Hall appeared on their right and Shining pulled in. 'Do try and act like grown-ups,' he said. 'It would be awfully embarrassing to be refused entry.'

'There isn't a building in the land that would dare keep me out,' muttered his sister.

To the left of the large, wrought-iron gate, was a small office. Toby could see the flicker of several TV screens, monitoring security cameras, he assumed.

Either side of the gatehouse, a high, pale, stone wall surrounded the grounds of the Hall. At the top, Toby noted a thin wire framework that was no doubt alarmed.

Two cameras looked down on them from either side of the gate, one fixed, one moving, panning up and down the road.

'It looks secure enough,' he said.

'I've yet to meet a curse spirit that gives two hoots about barbed wire,' said Shining.

The door to the gatehouse opened and a young man walked over to the car. He was wearing a dark blue uniform, a privately contracted security firm, Toby reckoned. They always farmed the grunt-work out to the private sector these days.

Shining unwound his window. 'August Shining,' he said, 'Toby Greene and April Shining.'

'Hello, dear,' said his sister, giving the guard a wave from the back seat.

He ignored her. 'Have you been issued with passes yet, sir?' he asked Shining.

'Obviously not,' said April, 'otherwise we'd be showing them to you, wouldn't we?'

He glanced at her, an unfriendly look in his eyes. Private security firms were always inflexible when it came to dealing with people, Toby thought. Too many slapped wrists and public dressing-downs. They could have had the Prime Minister in the back and this lad would still be wanting to see paperwork. Irritating but reassuring all the same.

'I'll have to talk to the house, sir,' he said. 'Please stay in the vehicle.'

He returned to the guardhouse, leaving April to mutter angrily to herself in the back. 'Why do jobsworths always say "vehicle" when they mean car?' she wondered.

'He's just doing his job,' Shining replied. 'I'd rather he was officious than negligent, wouldn't you?'

She chose not to reply to that, just settled back in the seat for a sulk.

After a few minutes, the young man returned.

'Sorry to keep you, sir,' he said. 'Just be a couple of minutes more, someone's coming down to meet you.'

'Should have brought a tent,' April muttered.

Eventually, a black car drew to a halt on the other side of the gate. The passenger door opened and Bill Fratfield climbed out. He peered through the gate at Shining and Toby, gave them a distracted wave then leaned back into the car. He spoke to the driver, shut the door and moved over to the guardhouse, the car returning up the drive without him. He reappeared, exiting through the guardhouse and walking up to their car.

'Sorry about this,' he said. 'Someone screwed up with the passes. Pain in the arse.'

Toby wondered if Section 37 had been forgotten. He wouldn't have been surprised.

'No problem,' said Shining. 'As we were just saying, better a delay than lax security.'

'Quite,' Fratfield agreed. 'I'll ride up to the house with you, if that's OK. I'll give you the guided tour.' He glanced at April in the back seat. 'You must be Mrs Shining.'

'"Miss", dear, still sexually available, unencumbered by any current husbands.' She opened the door and scooted over to give him space. 'Hop in.'

'Thank you,' Fratfield replied, looking, Toby thought, like a man who was about to walk in front of a firing squad.

'I confess,' he said as he brushed discarded boiled sweet wrappers away from the safety-belt socket so he could strap himself in, 'I was surprised when we were told you would be joining the party. Not your sort of thing, I would imagine.'

'Oh shush now, darling, I'm not just tagging along for the free dinners, you know.'

Toby smiled. He had certainly assumed that had been her main motivation.

'I don't want you thinking I'm my brother's keeper,' she continued. 'This isn't a family outing.' She patted Fratfield on the thigh. 'People always get confused when I turn up. I imagine they forget I'm influential enough to have you all shot let alone fired.' She grinned at him. 'But don't let me intimidate you, my lovely little secret service man, you were going to give us the private tour, I believe?'

August gritted his teeth, pulled the car through the opening gate and onto the drive.

'Yes,' said Fratfield, 'well, I'm sure you'll be a great asset.'

The drive ascended upwards before cresting and dropping back down, presenting them with a wide view of the house and grounds beyond. It was a large, two-storeyed building split into three sections. The central section was slightly receded, a triangular roof-piece topping off an impressive four-columned portico. From there, steps divided off to either side and descended to the large gravel forecourt. In front of the Hall, the garden was laid to lawn with a central fountain.

'Lufford Hall,' said Fratfield. 'Jacobean, though the inside is so baroque it makes your hair stand on end. Like most of these old piles, it's spent a good number of years as an albatross around the neck of the fading aristocrats saddled with it. Military hospital during the Second World War, government property thereafter.'

He reached between the front seats and pointed to the left of the main building. 'Extensive stables to the one side, mainly office space now, though they keep a few horses to entertain the foreign dignitaries. You know what these places are like once we get hold of them, half office block, half bauble to dangle in front of diplomatic visitors.

'The gardens are mainly landscaped lawns, though there's a rather ragged box maze to the right and a sculpture park, of all bloody things, to the rear. I think they let tourists potter around it in the summer.'

'Got to pay its keep,' said Shining.

'Madness, isn't it? But nobody can keep the fires burning in a barn like this without a good chunk of funding. I think we get something from the arts council for letting the local college use some of the facilities. Though, obviously, that's off for the next few days. No visitors allowed.

'Behind the house, the grounds rise up towards woodland. That's the most vulnerable area, frankly, we've got the rest well eyeballed. Still, even if someone did get over the wall and through the trees, they'd have to cross an open rear terrace that we have tabs on. The wall's wired too.'

'I noticed that,' admitted Toby. 'Movement sensors?'

'Dotted around the perimeter,' Fratfield replied with a nod. 'Recent additions. We decided to take advantage of the extra day afforded us by Sir James's death to throw some extra bells and whistles around the place. Hopefully we've got the place tight now.'

Shining pulled up in front of the Hall.

'You can park at the stables,' said Fratfield pointing towards the left. We're trying to keep the main entrance clear.'

'No problem,' said Shining, driving the car around and parking next to an army jeep. He nodded towards it. 'We've got uniforms on top of the private boys?' he asked.

'Actually, that belongs to one of the kitchen staff. King decided it would look better without a load of khaki about the place.'

'I don't imagine they would have been very useful anyway,' said Shining as he climbed out. 'If the threat is as supernatural as it seems, a rifle bullet isn't going to slow it down much.'

'Yes,' Fratfield laughed. 'Well, we have to take all things into account.'

'I sense the awkward sound of a cynic,' said April, getting out of the car after Fratfield.

'Well,' he admitted, 'I don't know anything about the subject. It all seems a bit bizarre to me but, and this is the important thing, your files tell a different story. I can keep an open mind.'

'Then you'll never get anywhere in the Service,' she said, 'but good for you anyway.'

'Leave your bags,' Fratfield said. 'We'll have them sent up to your room shortly.'

'Once you've had security give them a once-over?' asked Toby.

'Naturally.' Fratfield shrugged. 'I'm afraid it's all belt and braces here for the foreseeable. I take it you haven't got any phones on you?'

'No,' Shining assured him, 'or laptops, tablets, anything along those lines. We're positive Luddites.'

'Good job. Come inside and I'll introduce you to whoever's about.'

b) *Lufford Hall, Alcester, Warwickshire*

The entrance hall was big enough to play sport in, thought Toby as they stepped inside, though doing so was bound to result in the destruction of something cripplingly expensive. The floor was laid in large black and white tiles running at a diagonal across the room. Entering was like walking across a mammoth chessboard. The ceiling and walls were, as Fratfield had promised, covered in baroque plastering, the details picked out by concealed lighting. A twin set of staircases held the room as if in a pincer, running up either side of the hall and meeting in the middle. Looking up, Toby felt almost dizzy as his focus was lost amongst the glittering shards of a giant chandelier.

'Homely,' he said. 'I could fit my whole apartment in here.'

'Wait until you see the conference room,' said Fratfield, leading them up to a door on the right, beneath the stairs. He gestured inside the pink-walled room. It looked like the belly of a whale, a whale that had swallowed a massive mahogany meeting table. 'I run every morning, trying to keep in trim, if it rains one day I could just do a couple of circuits in here. Damn room needs three fireplaces to keep it warm.'

'It would take a lot of your fifty pees to keep the place going,' Toby whispered to April.

She tutted and nodded. 'Never own a dining room you can get lost in,' she said. 'They're more trouble than they're worth.'

Fratfield led them back out into the entrance hall and across to the other side. They were in a corridor winding its way around more function rooms and living areas. Each took on a bold colour, leavened by stark white cornicing.

'We've hired in a fully vetted catering team,' he said, gesturing vaguely towards another set of stairs leading down from the corridor. 'Kitchens and staff quarters are down there. There's also a second stairwell servicing the other wing. This place is a rabbit warren, built in the times when servants walked a different route to guests. I'll be shocked if you don't get lost during your first day. I'll happily admit to a frustrating twenty minutes I spent yesterday wandering around the cellar.'

'Cellar?' asked Toby, conscious of security.

Fratfield smiled. 'What isn't taken up by the kitchens and staff quarters is just storage space. You can't move down there for relics and dusty paintings. There's no external access and it's been thoroughly swept for possible threats. Very thoroughly, given that I couldn't find my way back out again. Whole place is sealed up. Not my job, really, but Rowlands' boys appreciated the helping hand. You've seen the size of the place.'

They had reached the rear of the building, the corridor opening out into a large conservatory filled with potted plants, extensive seating and a bubbling water feature. The sudden rush of light through the glass walls and ceiling made them realise how dark the rest of the building had been by comparison.

'Talk of the devil,' said Fratfield, nodding towards a man sat at a small table in the corner who was working his way through a stack of paperwork. 'Morning, Mark.'

Mark Rowlands looked up as they approached and Toby was all too aware of an appreciative sigh from April.

'Ah,' he said, with an affable smile, getting to his feet, 'the spooks have arrived.' He shook Shining's hand and then turned to Toby. 'Good to meet you, we have a mutual acquaintance, actually, Jeffrey Dean?'

'Oh,' said Toby, feeling immediately uncomfortable. 'Yes, Jeffrey.'

'Took over from you handling the music chap.'

'Yoosuf.'

'That's the one. Gave you quite a beating, I heard?'

'Not really, just got the jump on me.'

'Bust of Beethoven wasn't it?'

'Yes.'

'All better now?'

'Much.'

Yoosuf had been his last assignment before being sent to Section 37, an asset he had let slip, a mistake for which his previous Section Chief had struggled to forgive him.

Toby wondered if he could make his awkwardness any plainer to Rowlands.

'Your loss,' said Shining, trying to turn the conversation around, 'was definitely our gain. Toby's a real asset to the department.'

'I'm sure,' said Rowlands, giving Toby one last appraising look before turning back to Shining, 'and what a department! I was very surprised when Bill told me just now that Clive King had brought you onboard. I've only just finished looking at your files. Still, I'm sure he knows best.'

'Hello,' said April, pushing her way through, her initial impression of Rowlands fractured by his attitude towards Toby and her brother. 'I'm April Shining. On attachment to HMDS.'

'Yes,' said Rowlands, distractedly, 'another late addition.' He glanced at the paperwork on the table. 'I don't seem to have a dossier for you.'

'Never mind,' she said, 'all you need to know is that I'm here and there's nothing you can do about it. Now, if you've quite finished swinging your dick around and being patronising?' She turned to Fratfield. 'Any more to see?'

'No need to be rude,' said Rowlands, sneering at her. 'For a diplomat, that's a remarkably big mouth you have.'

She smiled. 'All the better to eat you up and spit you out, my dear.' She walked back into the house. 'Come on then, some of us have work to do.'

c) Lufford Hall, Alcester, Warwickshire

'Well,' said Fratfield, as he led them back towards the main entrance hall, 'so glad there won't be any squabbling between sections.'

'There won't be a problem,' Shining assured him. 'My sister does tend to get easily riled.'

'Something of a character flaw in her line of work, I'd have thought.'

'You don't have to worry about me,' she said. 'I just can't stand jumped-up office boys, that's all.'

'In fairness,' said Toby, 'as security's his show, you can't blame him for being put out when three extra people get dropped into the mix. As far as he's concerned, we're extra complications.'

'Ah yes,' said Fratfield, stopping in front of a large oil painting of red-jacketed huntsmen being beastly to a stag, 'on the subject of which … obviously your role is clear, Miss Shining, but the Korean contingent have been told Section 37 are here as independent security consultants. We didn't really want to get into the whole, erm ...'

'Preternatural is a good word,' said Shining, 'it sounds more scientific than some of the alternatives.'

'Fine,' Fratfield nodded, 'yes, we didn't want to go into the whole preternatural angle. King felt it was best to be vague about that side of things. Not just because ...' he struggled to think of diplomatic phrasing.

'Nobody believes in it?' suggested Toby.

'It's not that,' said Fratfield. 'As I said, your record stands for itself. It's just not a discussion King thought would be helpful. Better all round if we're seen to be adopting a wide-ranging response to security matters.'

'Just not *too* wide-ranging?' Toby asked.

'Hell,' Fratfield sighed, exasperated, 'you're here, aren't you? I'm sorry, I'm not dismissing your work, just asking you to be discreet.'

'I can't see that being a problem,' said April, staring at him, an open challenge in her eyes, 'can you?'

'Absolutely not,' he replied. 'Anyway,' he smiled, eager to change the subject, 'I should introduce you to the rest of the diplomatic gang.'

He looked to Shining and Toby. 'Can I leave you to it?'

'Of course,' said Shining, giving him a friendly wave.

Fratfield began to lead April away when a last thought occurred to Shining. 'Oh!' he said, 'one other thing before we get stuck in. Our bedrooms?'

'Ah ... yes.' Fratfield looked awkward again. 'Bit of a snafu with that, actually. They've put you downstairs.'

'Downstairs?' asked Toby. 'As in the basement?'

'Servants' quarters. Sorry, I'll try and have a word and see if we can't get it shifted to the guest rooms. No idea what they were thinking.'

With that, he made a break for it, April complaining in no uncertain terms as she followed on behind.

'Bloody servants' quarters,' Toby muttered. 'Nice.'

'Doesn't matter,' said Shining, 'in fact we might be better off down there.'

'Really?'

'Well, if someone is determined to bump off the delegates, I'm happy to be sleeping a couple of floors away,' he grinned. 'Let's go and take a look, shall we?'

d) Lufford Hall, Alcester, Warwickshire

'Well, yes,' said Shining, stuffed into the corner of a room that felt like a prison cell. 'All it really lacks is a window.'

'And a bathroom,' added Toby, sat on a bed whose springs were slowly but surely giving out beneath him, inclining him towards a piece of graffiti that had been chipped into the plaster of the wall. 'Sven fucks Janice,' it warned, though whether that was an ongoing situation or an ungrammatical yell of pride, nobody could tell. 'And a wardrobe,' he added, 'and more than one pillow, and an absence of mildew.'

'Well, it's bound to be a bit damp down here,' said Shining. 'We're planted in the Warwickshire earth like a potato.'

'A sad and uncomfortable potato.'

'We could list its deficiencies all day,' Shining admitted, 'though we've probably got more important things to do.'

'Like pop out to the car for a kip on the back seat so we don't suffer from a lack of it in here tonight?'

'Oh, cheer up, mine's just as bad.'

'That doesn't make me feel any better. You're like my mother, trying to put a smile on my face by discussing the starving in Africa. I never quite got the logic of being cheered by the fact that others were worse off than me.'

'It's the sort of logic that has kept the secret service happy for years. Comparative misery.'

'Then I should be the happiest spy in active service. Let's leave now before I start laughing and just can't stop.'

They got up to leave as another private security guard appeared with their bags. He dumped Toby's suitcase inside the door and held up a battered leather holdall. 'This yours?' he asked Shining.

'Yes, is there a problem?'

'Depends what this is,' the guard asked, holding up a ceramic jar of dense paste.

'Gentlemen's relish.'

'I beg your pardon?' the guard asked, in the manner of some-one who can't even begin to process the words he's just heard.

'It's not as pornographic as it sounds,' Shining sighed, 'and it harms nothing but anchovies.'

'I think we'll have to confiscate it,' the guard said, holding it out from his body as if worried it might bite him. 'Until we've done some tests.'

'Might I suggest you use toast rather than test tubes?' Shining said. 'I'd hate to think it was completely wasted.'

They left the man to his confusion at archaic spreads and climbed back up to the main body of the house.

'So what's the plan?' asked Toby. 'We're clearly not going to find ourselves troubled by any official duties.'

'Which, as I said before, is the solid advantage to our somewhat lacklustre reception. At least, by being ignored, we can get on with the important stuff. To hell with them, Toby, you really do need to stop worrying about what others think. People are terribly silly, by and large. Their opinions shouldn't be sought.'

Toby smiled. 'Fair enough. I'll still give Rowlands a slap if the opportunity presents itself though.'

'I'll hold your coat.'

They stepped out of the front door, looking out across the wide expanse of lawn.

'Do you have any of that protection stuff you can do?' Toby asked.

Shining raised a solitary eyebrow. '"Protection stuff"?'

'You know, muttering in ancient languages and drawing funny things in chalk.'

The old man nodded. 'I do. I'm not entirely sure how effective it will be but at least a bracing stroll around the perimeter will give us a good idea of the lay of the land.'

'And keep us away from people I might end up arguing with.'

'A stroll it is.'

They cut across the front lawn towards the driveway and the guardhouse beyond. The lawn split up into ornamental flowerbeds, at the centre of which was a giant urn, bubbling away as a water feature spurted up through its centre. The rush of the water seemed to build in volume before resolving itself into a different noise, the air above them filled with the roar of rotor blades. Looking up, they saw a helicopter curve down towards the edge of the lawn directly in front of the house.

'And to think,' said Toby, 'we had to drive.'

The helicopter dropped gracefully onto the grass and Shining and Toby watched as Clive King walked up to it, flanked by a man they had yet to meet but could guess was Ranesh Varma, the man from the Diplomatic Service.

The helicopter's rear door opened and four people climbed out.

'The Korean contingent,' said Shining. 'I wonder if they have the first idea of the mess they're stepping into?'

'They will soon enough,' said Toby. 'Come on, let's leave them to it.'

They continued on their way towards the edge of the property. Having cleared the front garden, the land rose and then fell, an open stretch of lawn leading towards the external wall.

'It's like a medieval castle,' said Shining, 'the house itself recessed into lower ground so you can't see it from outside.'

'All well and good if the enemy attacks using bows and arrows.'

'It's still useful. As Fratfield said, it's hard to get in here unobserved.'

'I don't believe for one moment you haven't known someone in your time that could have managed it. What about that bloke you worked with in the sixties? The one who could remain unnoticed?'

'Cyril? He'd have had a job on. It's not as if he were invisible, after all, people were just inclined not to pay attention to him in the first place. A set-up like this is different. We have a whole stack of folk whose job it is to be alert at all times, Cyril couldn't have snuck past them. Besides, there's the electronic security systems, too.'

'Security systems can be overcome, we know that.'

'True. In fact it is often our job to do exactly that. Still, short of holding the conference in an underground bunker, we're as secure as we could hope to be.'

They'd reached the perimeter wall now and Shining had taken a small metal case from his pocket. Opening it, he took out a piece of chalk and began to draw on the old stone. Toby glanced towards the guardhouse, where the man who had reluctantly let them in earlier was keeping an eye on them.

'I give it five minutes before he's over here with a bucket of hot water and a jay cloth,' said Toby.

'He can do what he likes,' said Shining, holding up the chalk. 'This is somewhat specialist. Good for outdoor work. Once the sigils are drawn, they're indelible. The act of drawing them makes them permanent. Even if he wiped away the outward signs of them, their effect would cling to the stone.'

'A graffiti artist's dream. So what do they do?'

'They're the magical equivalent of the security system. If someone comes over the wall I'll know about it.'

'They linked to a walkie-talkie in your room?' Toby grinned.

'Something like that. In modern terms, think of them as an open circuit. When someone crosses them, they close that circuit and energy flows through them. That energy will trigger an alarm in my delightfully cosy room. A candle I picked up in Peking in the eighties; its flame turns blue when the line is crossed.'

'Of course it does.'

'It's the same as the bursts of coloured light you'd see when exposing different chemical elements to heat.'

'Magic as the lost branch of physics again?'

'Precisely. Though the candle is extremely sensitive to work at such a long distance, of course.'

'I shall, as always, just nod wisely and trust you.'

'Much the best way. I usually know what I'm talking about.'

'So what else should we do?'

'Well ...' Shining led Toby further along the wall, stopping after about twenty feet and drawing again. 'Like so much of our work, magic will only take us so far. We'll need to fall back on our more traditional skills too.'

'Eyes and ears open.'

'And expect the worst, yes. We may be superfluous given the security staff involved, but they'll miss the sort of things we're looking for. If nobody believes the assassin is using magical methods, they'll discount clues that may be all-important to us.'

'If they even strike again.'

'Oh, I'm sure that's a given. Anyone willing to kill three times doesn't just give up. They'll see this through until the bitter end.'

CHAPTER EIGHT: THE TRANSLATOR

a) Lufford Hall, Alcester, Warwickshire

Fratfield led April to a small drawing room that lay just off the main conference room then did his best to get out alive.

'And you've diplomatic experience, you say,' asked Ranesh Varma, after Fratfield had briefly introduced them before running off in a strafe run of insults from April.

'Oh,' she said, 'just ten years or so, a while ago now. He made me cross, that's all.'

'It is to be hoped our Korean friends don't do the same.'

'It is, I do so hate being cross.' She smiled and shook his hand. 'Don't worry, I can be a fiery old hag but I'm not such a liability as to bring the conference down in flames.'

She gave Ranesh a quick once-over: early forties, public school, terribly sweet. His eyes, always a fair measure of a man, she believed, sat gentle but inquisitive behind the lenses of a pair of wire-framed spectacles. She made an instant judgement: Ranesh Varma was, indeed, to quote her brother, 'a good egg'.

'I hope you won't think me rude ...' he said.

'Uh-oh, that's never a good start to a sentence.'

Ranesh smiled. 'I know, it's like when someone prefixes a statement with "No offence, but ..." I was just going to admit that we were surprised to have you sprung on us at the last minute.'

'Entirely my fault, and I won't tread on anyone's toes. Probably. Or if I do, feel free to stamp on mine in return. I just felt I might be useful.'

'And I'm sure you will,' Ranesh replied, proving, if nothing else, that he was good at his job. 'Do you speak Korean at all?'

'Like a native.'

'That is good. I don't, I'm afraid, though I have Lucy with me who does.'

'Lucy?'

'Baxter. You'll meet her just now, she should be down any minute.'

'Now it's my turn to be rude,' said April, taking his arm in the hope that a bit of a cuddle might move things along, 'but what on earth were they thinking sending someone from HDMS who didn't speak the lingo?'

'A good question,' he admitted. 'In truth, I think I just pissed off the right person.'

April laughed. 'Well, I'm glad you're looking forward to your time here.'

'I was, until people started dying.'

'Oh, don't worry about that, it just adds a bit of spice.'

'I am used to spice, Miss Shining, but this feels a little too hot even for me.' He smiled and glanced at his watch. 'And Lucy too, perhaps. Where is she? They'll be here in a minute.'

'Happy to take a look if you point me in the right direction,' April suggested. 'See? I'm being useful already.'

Ranesh sighed and glanced at his watch again. 'I should go.'

'But then, if the Koreans arrive, you won't be here to greet them. Much more embarrassing. Just point me in the direction of her room and I'll rustle her up.'

'Very well. Are you in the East Wing?'

'Let's not go into that just now, or I'll start swearing again. I can find it.'

'Hers is the Ophelia room. They are all named after Shakespeare characters.'

'Of course they are.'

'You enter the East Wing, walk along the corridor and it's ...' he had to think for a moment, 'third on the left.'

'Perfect,' she began to stride back towards the entrance hall. 'I'll be back in a jiffy.'

By the time she entered the East Wing, she was still complimenting herself on how terribly charming she could be when she wanted. She was only too aware that her brother and Toby considered her a liability while at Lufford Hall but there was life in the old dog yet and, while she may have slipped into the habits of increased age, giving not a brace of hoots about what she said or did on a day-to-day basis, she wasn't quite so far gone that she couldn't be politic when needed.

She walked along the long corridor, taking a moment to study the grumpy old restoration gentlemen in the oil paintings that lined the walls. 'All wigs and flatulence,' she decided, then reminded herself she was supposed to be being quick. She looked at the nameplates on the doors. Rosalind, Juliet and ... third on the left, Ophelia.

She knocked on the door. 'Lucy?' she called. 'Ranesh is wearing out the carpet with worry.'

There was no answer. She knocked again. 'Miss Baxter? Lucy?'

Probably overslept, April decided, then, thinking of the reason August and Toby were here, her thoughts grew darker.

She tried the door. It was unlocked.

The room beyond was dark, the heavy curtains blocking any light from the windows. 'Lucy?' she called, 'are you all right?'

She ran her hand across the wall on the inside of the door, searching for a light switch, but not finding it.

'Save me from old houses with weird wiring,' she muttered, rooting around in her handbag for her cigarette lighter.

It was a battered old Zippo with a picture of James Dean on it and she'd owned it for longer than she could remember. Hadn't an old boyfriend bought it for her? Probably. One's memory of such things began to blur.

She ignited the Zippo and made her way inside. 'Lucy? Sorry to intrude, dear. If you're even in here ...' It suddenly occurred to her that the girl could be walking around the grounds or downstairs having breakfast. No doubt she'd be over the moon to discover a stranger was poking around her room.

Then again, she thought of the three people who had already lost their lives to whoever was preying on members of the delegation and decided now was not the time for pussyfooting around people's privacy.

She made her way over to the main curtained window and pulled the heavy drapes back, letting the light in.

The room was beautiful. The walls an eggshell blue, the furniture even older than her. The floor was thickly carpeted in cream, a nightmare for stains, she thought, of which there were many.

She followed the dark brown patches – *blood*, she thought, *it's blood* – into the en-suite bathroom. Which is where she finally found Lucy. She was lying back in the bathtub, fully clothed, her legs sticking up in the air. One shoe hung off a cold set of toes, the other foot was bare. There were further bloodstains on the bathroom floor but it was behind the poor girl's head that most of it had pooled. It seemed that she had slipped, fallen backwards into the bath, hitting her head on the jutting-out soap tray as she'd done so.

One arm was folded beneath her but the other was lying across her chest. There was a deep cut on her thumb, a further bloodstain having spread out from that to bloom across the belly of the bright white shirt she had been wearing.

'Oh, Lucy,' April sighed.

April glanced back into the bedroom. It looked like the girl had cut her thumb somehow, bad enough to bleed on the carpet as she made her way into the bathroom, no doubt hoping to wash and dress it. Then she had slipped on something and fallen back into the bath.

An accident. Or at least, that would have been the obvious conclusion were it not for ...

April moved back through into the bedroom and placed her hand on the carpet. It was wet.

b) Lufford Hall, Alcester, Warwickshire

April closed the door behind her. She would have preferred to report the girl's death to her brother before anyone else, but as neither he nor Toby had their mobile phones she didn't know how best to find him.

As she began to head back down the corridor she became aware of the sound of a helicopter approaching the building.

'Oh Lord,' she said, 'here they bloody come.'

As she descended into the entrance hall, she could see Clive King and Ranesh walking out across the gravel forecourt to greet the helicopter.

A suitably grim selection of security agents hung back by the door. She spotted Rowlands, barking commands and sending a couple of them back into the building, no doubt to check all was well in the conference room.

What to do?

Ah hell ... She didn't have much choice but to play by the rules.

She walked through the main door, noting the barely disguised sneer on Rowlands' face as she approached him.

'Now isn't a good time, Miss Shining,' he said, '*obviously.*'

'I'm fully aware of that, you stuck-up arse,' she whispered, looking towards Ranesh who was greeting the Koreans and looking back over his shoulder in slight panic, 'but I thought I ought to mention you have a translator lying dead in her room upstairs. It's the Ophelia suite. If you would be so good as to inform my brother, I shall go over there and do my job.'

'What are you talking about?' Rowlands was, unsurprisingly, thrown by this news.

'Job? No, I suppose that isn't a concept that you would immediately understand. It's the thing some of us do while you're being an insufferable turd.'

She descended the steps and walked quickly towards the

helicopter, fixed smile in place. The look of relief on Ranesh's face was extreme. She was quite sure that the Koreans probably spoke English but Ranesh would be ashamed not to be able to greet them in their own tongue. She felt a welcome boost of pleasure to note the look of absolute terror on Clive King's face as he recognised her. Was he married now? She imagined he probably was. Had he been, back when they had first met? Oh, probably ... the buggers usually had been despite their promises otherwise.

'Good morning,' she shouted in Korean. 'My name is April Shining. It is with extreme pleasure that we welcome you to Lufford Hall.'

She winked at Ranesh.

The Korean party was three men and a woman. The woman walked in front, clearly in charge. April guessed she was in her late fifties, dressed in an extremely well-tailored light brown suit, precise in her manner and dress, April decided. She smiled graciously at April's greeting and replied, in English.

'I am Son Tae-young. It is good to finally be with you. Apparently turbulence delayed our arrival.'

Yours and mine both, thought April.

'Which makes my own delay even more inexcusable,' said April, keeping her tone as deferential as she could.

'Nonsense,' the woman replied, this time in Korean. 'I'm amazed all these officious men let you out of the house.' She grinned and looked at King and Ranesh who simply smiled in ignorance. 'God save me from more of the old-school tie and the slightly patronising nodding, it is all I have been exposed to since I came to this country.'

April laughed. 'Tae-young,' she said, 'I can see you and I are going to get on famously! Shall we put them out of their misery and get inside?'

'If only so they can stop grinning like children at me,' Tae-young agreed.

'Lead the way, Clive,' said April, gesturing for him to walk in front. Ever the professional, the look of fearful recognition had now vanished and he was charm itself as they moved away from the helicopter.

'Where is Lucy?' Ranesh asked, once they were far enough away from the whirring blades for her to hear him without his shouting.

She patted his arm. 'I'm afraid there's been an accident. She's dead. I think it best we keep quiet about it for now, don't you?'

She looked at him and the sheer weight of sorrow that appeared in his eyes made her realise that he and Lucy had not been simply colleagues. 'Oh God,' she said. 'I'm so sorry ... I didn't realise.'

He shook his head. 'Not now.'

'Don't be ridiculous, I can handle our visitors, off you go.'

After a moment he nodded and peeled away from the party.

It was only once they were inside that Clive King turned around and noticed. He stared at April, clearly torn between whether he should draw attention to Ranesh disappearing by asking about it or simply acting as if nothing had happened. April took pity on him and addressed Tae-young once more.

'That's better,' she said, in Korean. 'I'm afraid my boss had to dash off for a moment. I didn't think you'd mind.'

'Not at all. Can you get rid of the other one too?'

April laughed. After a moment King joined in, not wanting to appear left out.

'What did you say?' he whispered to her as Tae-young turned and looked appreciatively at the decorative plasterwork.

'That I used to be able to make you come just by breathing on you, darling,' she replied, keeping her sweet smile in place as he had a brief choking fit.

'I hope you are all right, Mr King?' asked Tae-young, speaking in English.

'Forgive me,' he replied, wheezing slightly, 'just a ... something tickling my throat.'

'We've all felt that in our time,' said April, continuing to smile innocently.

'Allow me to introduce my colleagues,' said Tae-young. 'Kim Man-dae,' she gestured to a young man who nodded somewhat nervously at them all. 'He is here representing his father Kim Sang-min, one of the largest of our potential private investors.'

She turned towards an older man, his greying hair jutting out at the back in a manner that put April in mind of a seabird. 'Bong Jae-sung, from the Ministry of Strategy and Finance.'

'Excellent to be here,' he said in accentless English.

'And finally, from our Ministry of Foreign Affairs, Ryu Chun-hee.' This last member of the party tried to smile from behind the rather austere lines of a thin goatee black beard. April found the effect more terrifying than charming.

'Ms Tae-young,' said Rowlands, having joined them, a slight redness to his cheeks showing he had been running. 'I'm Mark Rowlands, handling security here at Lufford Hall.'

'Tae-young is Ms Son's given name, Mr Rowlands,' said April. 'In Korea, the family name comes first.' Read up on your bloody subject, she might have added, but remembered she was supposed to be being a diplomat.

'Forgive me,' Rowlands said, embarrassed but too stressed by what he and his men had seen upstairs to let it faze him. 'I was just going to ask if everyone would like to go straight through to the conference room for coffee?'

'I was rather hoping to unpack first,' Tae-young replied, 'gather my papers.'

'Just a slight delay with the rooms, I'm afraid,' he said. 'Security, you understand. On the subject of which. Has it been explained that you must leave all electronic devices with us?'

Tae-young sighed. 'It was said, but certainly not explained. I am not used to handing my phone and laptop over to strangers.'

'I know it's a pain,' said April, in Korean once more, 'but we do have good reasons, I'm afraid.'

Tae-young looked at her for a moment then nodded. 'Very well,' she replied in English, 'though it's extremely inconvenient.'

'Let's go and have some coffee and biscuits while the boys run around playing soldiers, shall we?' suggested April, speaking to them all. 'Once they've played their games, they'll be all tired out and much less likely to trouble us.'

Tae-young laughed, stepped close to April and spoke in Korean, 'I can't believe the way you talk about your employers.'

'Well,' said April, equally confidentially, 'I'm the only one that can speak Korean. What are they going to do? Fire me?'

They filed into the conference room, where two of Rowlands' men were standing in the far corner like intimidating statues. They weren't the only people in the room. A man wearing a suit that cost more than April's apartment and a tie that made her wish for blindness was bounding towards them.

'Love your faces, great for all eyes!' he said in Korean, performing a deep bow before adopting a pose that suggested he was expecting a round of applause.

'Dear God,' said Tae-young in Korean, 'what am I supposed to say to that?' She looked to the rest of the group who were naturally as baffled as she was and only too happy to take a back seat while she dealt with the conversation.

'Sorry,' said the man who could only be the ludicrously titled Lemuel Spang. 'I'm afraid I only learned how to say hello. I may have sounded fluent,' he winked, 'but really it's just Google-Fu.'

'You acquitted yourself wonderfully,' said Tae-young, giving a warning glance to the rest of her party. April noticed that Chun-hee in particular seemed about to say something. He turned away and gazed out of the window as if distracted by something much more interesting.

'I'm the banker,' said Spang. April briefly imagined she'd misheard. 'Try not to hold it against me!'

'We all need banks,' Tae-young replied, 'Mr ...?'

'Sorry, I didn't say. Spang, Lemuel Spang. Weird name over here, what happens when you have Eastern-European parents and a father who loved Jonathan Swift. I don't suppose it sounds weird to you, I mean ... being from somewhere different.'

April wondered if she might be fulfilling her duties better were she to hit him over the head with a chair.

'Well,' said King, having obviously decided the conversation needed rescuing, 'why don't we all take a seat until the coffee arrives?' He looked to Rowlands who nodded and vanished. So nice to see him demoted to a waiter, April thought.

They sat down, Tae-young careful to ensure April sat next to her. 'In case I need rescuing,' she explained.

'Where did you learn your Korean, Miss Shining?' asked Jae-sung. 'It's excellent.'

'Not as excellent as your English, I'm sure,' she replied, deciding, now that the man had smiled a little, that while he still reminded her of a seabird it was a kindly one, perhaps a puffin.

'I attended university here,' he explained. 'Manchester Polytechnic.'

'Metropolitan University now,' said Spang.

Jae-sung inclined his head, accepting the correction. April did her best to smile, remembering August's comments with regards her snobbery towards academic establishments. 'How lovely,' she said.

'I had fun,' he admitted. 'Lots.'

I'll just bet you did, she thought, noticing the twinkle in his eye and correcting her judgement of him: a *naughty* puffin.

'I was in a relationship with a man from Gangwon-do province,' she explained, 'many years ago. I've always been quick to pick things up.'

'My father has an office in Chuncheon,' said Man-dae. He shrugged. 'But then he has offices everywhere.'

'I once spent a strange holiday there during the puppet festival,' April admitted.

'You like puppets?' he asked.

'As a woman in government I've often been one,' she replied. Tae-young laughed and patted her hand.

King was obviously feeling left out, having spent a minute or so staring at the door and wishing it would produce some refreshments. He tried his hand at joining in the conversation. 'You know what they say,' he announced, 'you'll never keep a good man down. Or, you know, woman.'

'We do like to come up for air occasionally,' April agreed. 'Ah! Biscuits!'

One of the catering staff had appeared in the doorway, wheeling in a fully stocked trolley.

She loaded herself up with as many chocolate digestives as seemed polite – or, at least, not excessively rude – and settled down for a long day of discussion.

She could only hope that August and Toby had been informed about the fate of poor Lucy.

CHAPTER NINE: THE PRINT

a) Lufford Hall, Alcester, Warwickshire

August and Toby returned to Lufford Hall an hour or so after they had left it, completely unaware of what had happened to one of the delegates. This state of ignorance continued for some time, as nobody saw fit to tell them about the death of Lucy Baxter. It was only after they had decided to explore the stable block that they saw her wrapped-up body being loaded into the back of a van.

'What's happened?' asked Shining, walking up to Mark Rowlands, who was supervising.

'Translator working with HMDS,' he said, 'managed to fall over in the bathroom and brain herself.'

'You're obviously cut up about it,' said Toby.

'Damn right. This whole conference is a big enough mess without this sort of thing. Now I'm having to run around tidying up after the clumsy.'

Shining turned on Rowlands and Toby took a step back. His employer was unquestionably one of the gentlest men he had ever met, which is not to say that a special kind of idiot didn't bring something ferocious to the man's surface on occasion.

'A woman is dead and all you can do is whinge like an infant? What sort of pathetic man are you?'

'I beg your pardon?' Rowlands almost choked with shock.

'Not only pathetic but idiotic. We have three deaths that could seem like accidents, and now a fourth. How stupid do you have to be to ignore that?'

'The whole thing was so obvious we may as well have caught it on camera,' Rowlands shouted. 'She cuts her thumb on a pair of nail scissors, runs to the bathroom, bleeding like a stuck pig, slips, falls into the bathtub, hits her head going down. Only someone stupid would try and turn it into something it clearly isn't. Stupid or mad.'

'Mad? I'm beginning to think I must be … Did you not read the reports on the other deaths? Have you not twigged the fact that they all appeared natural?'

'Yes, they did. And in my opinion obviously were …'

'Then you're so mentally deficient you shouldn't even be here!' Shining shouted. Toby noted a couple of Rowlands' men smirked at that. 'What's the bloody point of you?' He did his best to calm down. 'Why did nobody think to come to us with this?'

'You're here under sufferance—'

'Oh I know, and so far it's everyone but you who is suffering. Which was her room?'

'We've been all over it—'

'I doubt that. Was it wet?'

Rowlands paused and that was enough for Shining.

'It was! And that wasn't enough for you to twig there might be more to this than met the eye?'

'Look ...' but Rowlands was on the back foot now and Shining knew it. He moved over to the body bag, unzipped it and made a cursory examination.

'Medical expert now, are you?' Rowlands asked.

Shining ignored the comment. 'What room?' he asked again.

'Ophelia,' said one of the other men. 'East Wing.'

'Thank you!' Shining replied spinning around and walking back towards the house.

'Impossible man,' said Rowlands.

'Oh, piss off,' said Toby, unable to help himself, before following on after his Section Chief.

b) Lufford Hall, Alcester, Warwickshire

By the time Toby caught up with Shining, the man was working out his anger by bounding up the stairs two at a time. It never ceased to amaze Toby how much energy the older man possessed.

'I've spent the whole morning telling you not to get cross, haven't I?' Shining asked, finally pausing at the entrance to the East Wing.

'Yes, but I don't hold it against you. He had it coming.'

'He did.' Shining agreed and pushed the door open.

They walked along the corridor, checking the names on the doors. They found the Ophelia suite and made their way inside.

The security officers had done their best to tidy up after themselves, acting with the sort of automatic arrogance that only really comes from inflated authority. There would be no police investigation here, just an investigative report signed off and rubber-stamped by offices nobody could even begin to argue with. Eventually, a family would be left to wonder exactly what had happened to their daughter and why they seemed to have been told so little about it.

The curtains had been drawn, the brightness belying the eerie patter of bloodstains leading towards the bathroom. Those stains were now part of an extensive network of markings, the wet carpet having taken an impression of the muddy shoes of those who had come in after. Looking around, Shining could partially recreate the work of the security officers as they had moved around the room, searching for sensitive material and indications of foul play.

'Clod-hopping lot,' he said, standing up straight and moving through to the bathroom. Here the officers had made more of an attempt to clear up, the bath had been showered down in a rush, the corner of the soap dish still bore a smudge and a couple of hairs. 'To hell with the truth, just make it go away, that's the Security Service way.'

'The bed's soaked, too,' said Toby, still in the bedroom. 'I can't understand how they could just ignore the fact.'

'Because sometimes that's easier,' Shining replied, appearing in the bathroom doorway. 'Rowlands can't believe in the real solution so he ignores the evidence that makes it undeniable. He isn't the first, won't be the last.'

'But it's stupid.'

'It's human nature. Minds are born open and then are slowly closed shut from that point on.' Shining tapped at his chin. 'I wonder how the curse was sent. Not digitally, unless she had snuck a phone or something in.'

'There's no sign of anything,' said Toby, 'unless Rowlands has it.'

'I doubt he'd see it as significant. After all, he doesn't believe in the curse as a method of assassination. I suppose it's not altogether important. "How" is neither here nor there. A note would do it. "Who" is what we need to know.'

Toby nodded. 'Another thing: if the curtains were closed then it happened overnight,' said Toby, 'before you put the marks on the wall.'

'Yes. Though that leaves one other small detail we need to know.'

'The light?' Toby moved over to the light switch but paused before flicking it on.

'Precisely. She was fully clothed. It's safe to assume she hadn't gone to bed. So she can't have been sat here in the dark cutting her nails.'

'She was sat by the dresser,' Toby pointed towards the initial sign of blood on the carpet. 'The curse spirit appears, she's shocked, cuts herself ...'

'Backs away,' continued Shining, edging back into the bathroom, 'hits the edge of the bath ...'

'Or just slips, we know this thing increases the chances for an accident.'

'Absolutely. Into the bath she goes.'

'So we need to know if the light was still on when Rowlands found her.'

'Yes, chances are the killer is the one who turned it off when they checked up on their work but we need to know for sure. Won't it be fun to ask? Maybe we should try and make friends with one of his subordinates.'

'Could be easier. I'll do that, you get a print off the switch and finish off whatever needs to be done with the chalk and the candle.'

Shining nodded. 'Yes, boss. Meet you by the front entrance in half an hour.'

c) Lufford Hall, Alcester, Warwickshire

Toby intended to avoid Rowlands as the only thing he was likely to share with him was punches.

Stepping out onto the balcony over the main entrance hall, he saw the small team of security officers gathered at the centre of the chessboard floor. Rowlands was whispering instructions to them, pointing for two of them to stay by the conference room while the other three accompanied him towards the rear of the house.

Whatever you're up to, Toby thought, I hope you stay out of my way while you're doing it.

He descended the stairs and moved over towards the conference room where the two remaining security officers stood.

'Nobody else died since we last met?' he asked with what he hoped was a suitably friendly smile.

'We're taking bets on your boss being the next in line,' said one of them, a black guy who clearly worked out so hard Toby was surprised the floor tiles didn't crack underneath him as he walked.

'Yeah, well, he's normally a mild-mannered old thing.'

'Rowlands isn't,' the man admitted.

'Why don't you shut up?' the other officer suggested. 'He doesn't want us talking to either of the spooks.'

'Just being friendly,' the black guy replied. 'I'm Arnold and this grumpy sod is Bateman.'

'Toby.' He shook Arnold's hand. 'Bateman your first name?' he asked the other.

'Piss off.'

'Some parents have no shame.'

Arnold smirked slightly at that. Bateman was obviously not all that popular. 'How did you end up working for Shining, then?' he asked.

'Fucked up,' said Bateman.

'True enough,' admitted Toby. 'It's not worked out badly, though.'

'You hear stories,' said Arnold. 'The old guy's been in the Service for years.'

'Which speaks for itself,' said Toby. 'Our caseload is unusual but the man's a genius.'

'Not if he picks fights with Rowlands, he isn't,' said Bateman. 'Rowlands is going places.'

'Oh,' said Toby, 'like that, is it? I remember when some of us looked at this job as a vocation as well as a career.'

'Eh?' said Bateman.

'Doesn't matter.' Toby turned back to Arnold. 'Who found the body upstairs?'

Arnold grinned. 'Shining's sister. You should have heard her … That whole family's on Rowlands' shit list this morning.'

'I can imagine. She can be—'

'Called him an "insufferable turd".'

'— Outspoken,' Toby finished. 'Do you know where she is?'

'In there.' Arnold inclined his head towards the conference room. 'She's being diplomatic.'

'Great. Don't suppose you know when they might be taking a break?'

'Rowlands rushed them in there while we sorted the upstairs out but they're not due to start formal discussions just yet so they'll be back out soon enough. We've cleared the Koreans' rooms and luggage.'

'Fair enough.' Toby looked at his watch. 'I'll pop back in about twenty minutes. If you see her before then, could you ask her to hang about?'

'I can try,' Arnold replied. 'But she strikes me as the sort of person who doesn't take kindly to being asked to do anything.'

'You're not wrong there,' Toby admitted. 'If she kicks up a fuss,' he nodded at Bateman, 'get him to shoot her.'

d) Lufford Hall, Alcester, Warwickshire

Toby spent the spare time taking another quick walk around the building. He thought he ought to familiarise himself with it as much as possible.

He found himself in the building's library, its walls piled high with old books. In the centre was a large, revolving globe, no doubt labelled with countries that hadn't existed for years.

Climbing up a small stepladder to reach an upper shelf was Fratfield.

'Short of night-time reading?' Toby asked.

Fratfield jumped slightly, having not heard Toby come in. He visibly relaxed once he realised who it was. 'Now if I'd fallen off and broken my neck ...'

'I could have just pretended you were the latest victim.'

Fratfield nodded. 'Lucy Baxter? Mark is determined to write it off as an accident.'

'Do you agree with him?'

Fratfield climbed down, an old book in his hand. He turned the cover towards Toby. 'Don't laugh.' It read *Ancient Superstitions and the Occult*.

'That'll keep you up all night.'

Fratfield appeared deeply uncomfortable. 'I just ... Well, it doesn't seem like it could have been anything but an accident, but after what happened before ...'

'You thought you'd think outside the box a little.'

'Yeah, which probably seems silly.'

'Not to me, obviously, though Rowlands would hate you for it.'

'He's not so bad you know. He's just determined to keep this conference safe and when faced with something he doesn't understand ...'

'He ignores it.'

'No, he just tries to find an alternative that does fit. That's no bad thing.'

'It is if focusing on the alternative makes you ignore what's really going on.'

'Yeah, maybe.' Fratfield held up the book. 'Which brings me back to this.' He looked around, trying to pick his words carefully. 'When you first joined Section 37,' he said, 'did you believe in this sort of thing?'

'Not a word of it. I thought I'd been transferred into the care of the biggest lunatic in the Service.'

'Which is saying something!'

They both laughed.

'I say that,' Toby continued, 'but it's not quite true. I didn't believe in the supernatural, no, or preternatural as Shining calls it, but I didn't think he was a lunatic. From the first moment

I met him he was too ...' he tried to think of a suitable word, *'together* for that. That was the really confusing thing. I couldn't believe what he was telling me but I also couldn't write him off. He's not mad.'

'No,' Fratfield admitted, 'and his record is amazing. Accepting the fact that every report he files gets junked, anyway ... People don't want to talk about him, but when they do they're like you, they can't say anything but good things.'

'I became a believer,' Toby said, 'that's the important thing. In a matter of days.'

'What convinced you?'

'My own experience. That's the only thing that can, really. Being told about things that you think are impossible is never enough, however convincing the person is who's telling you. You have to experience it. You have to see it. You have to feel it. You have to hold the impossible in your hands, accept it as real and then move on. There's no point in denying something just because you're uncomfortable with it, that's just sticking your head in the sand. I saw so much during those first couple of days in the section, experienced so much ... Denying it would have been idiotic. In fact it would probably have killed me.'

'I'm surprisingly envious,' Fratfield admitted.

'I wouldn't go that far. To be honest it was more comforting to not believe a word of it. The world is a bigger and scarier place for it.'

'Doesn't look like it's knocked you back, though.'

'No,' Toby admitted, only too aware that Fratfield had probably read all about him. His record was not exactly glowing. 'If anything, it's made me stronger.'

'Well, then,' said Fratfield, holding up the book, 'I'd better get reading.'

e) Lufford Hall, Alcester, Warwickshire

Toby and Shining were lucky in their timing. No sooner had they met at the front entrance and Toby had explained who had discovered the body, than the conference room doors opened and the gathered delegates began to file out.

'How does she do it?' Shining wondered, looking at his sister, who was now arm in arm with Tae-young. 'There's just no middle ground with her. She's either your worst enemy or your best friend.'

'Darlings!' April waved. 'Come and meet the loveliest woman in all of South Korea.'

Tae-young laughed in embarrassment and waved the compliment away. Behind her, Chun-hee scowled slightly, clearly uncomfortable at the familiarity being shown by his superior. A little further back and the same look could be seen on Clive King's face. Toby smiled, he couldn't help but love the effect April had on her environment, she was like an adorable atomic device.

'You are April's brother?' Tae-young asked, taking August's hand. 'You are a very lucky man.'

'I am,' August admitted.

'He doesn't usually say that,' April chipped in.

'As long as he thinks it,' said Tae-young, turning her attention to Toby. 'And this is your son, perhaps?'

Toby found himself robbed of words at the thought. As always, April had no such problem. 'Lord, no,' she said. 'I'm far too young.'

Toby raised an eyebrow but said nothing. He went to introduce himself and suddenly realised he wasn't used to giving his real name. 'Toby Greene,' he said, feeling utterly exposed. 'I work with Mr Shining.'

'The only one who does,' said April, 'except me, and our upstairs tenant and ... oh, lots of people, I suppose, but he's the only one who gets paid a salary.'

'Thank you for putting it so well.' Toby shook Tae-young's hand.

Clive King was now in a panic that Section 37 had introduced itself to the head of the visiting delegation and buzzed around them desperate to butt in.

'If you'd like to go to your room now?' he asked the Koreans.

'Like naughty children?' Tae-young laughed.

'Oh, I'm sorry, I didn't mean it like that. To check that you are happy with your accommodation, I mean.'

'Dear Clive always likes to make sure a woman is happy in her bedroom, don't you Clive?'

'Obviously, I want you all to be happy with the rooms we've laid on for you.' He glared at April. 'You're all in the West Wing, if you'd like to follow me?'

'I like her,' said April once they had been led away. 'She's terribly nice.'

'I see you've made yourself quite at home,' said Shining.

'Well, I didn't have a great deal of choice did I? After that poor Lucy girl—'

'Which is exactly what we'd like to talk to you about,' said Shining, taking her arm. 'A walk in the fresh air, perhaps?'

The three of them stepped outside with April scrabbling in her handbag for her cigarettes. 'I'm gasping,' she admitted.

'Never have I talked for so long without the aid of minty death.' She put a menthol cigarette in her mouth and began hunting for a lighter. 'I'm glad they fetched you,' she said. 'I rather feared they wouldn't.'

'Fetched us?'

'Oh, the buggers,' she said, having lit her cigarette. 'I would have kept schtum until I could have told you myself, but I had to leap into the breach and thought it was a bit off to just leave her up there. Ranesh sent me to fetch her, you see – have either of you seen poor Ranesh? He was terribly cut up about it.'

'No,' Toby said. 'I'm sure he's around somewhere.'

'I do hope he's all right ... Anyway, she was late so he sent me to find her. I went up to her room and, well, you know.'

'Was the light on when you went in?' asked Shining.

'No, pitch black, I nearly went base over apex trying to get the curtains open. Why?'

Shining looked at Toby.

'Oh, boys,' said April, puffing away on her cigarette, 'now you're being annoying. What's so important about the light that has you throwing chilly looks around the place like a knackered ice-maker?'

'The light must have been on when she died,' said Toby. 'She was fully dressed, sat up in her room. So, if it had been an accident ...'

'Which none of us thinks it was for one moment,' she added.

'You'd think not,' said her brother, 'but Box aren't quite so convinced.'

'Box are stupid, then.'

'More to the point,' continued Toby, 'for the light to have been turned off between Lucy Baxter dying and you discovering her, then either she was discovered by somebody else earlier—'

'Who turned off the light but chose not to mention it,' she said.

'Or, more likely, the killer turned it off once they had checked all was well.'

'A clue!' April giggled. 'How wonderfully Agatha Christie!'

'I managed to get a reasonable print off the switch, though I've no way of checking it without internet access,' said Shining. 'I could get it scanned and send it to one of our friends at the Met.'

'I might actually be able to help there,' said Toby. 'I know someone with quick access to IDENT1.'

'Toby's got an agent!' April clapped. 'He'll be a real spy yet! Shame he works at an opticians.'

'I've got plenty of contacts, thank you, they're just not flaky loons who specialise in potions.'

'If Herbert, my chief potion specialist, ever heard you call him a loon, he'd be livid,' said Shining. 'In fact, he'd probably poison you.'

'Anyway,' Toby continued, 'IDENT1 is the central database for biometric information. As well you know.'

'Oh, if it was set up after '89, darling,' said April, 'it's all news to me. I get lost with the new departments.'

'It's not a department, it's a ...' He sighed. 'Never mind. Give me the print and I'll take the car into town. See what I can do.'

'Perfect.' Shining handed over a piece of card. 'It's terribly old school, I'm afraid,' he said. 'Graphite dust and sellotape.'

'Old school is what we do best!' said April, grinding her cigarette out in the gravel.

Shining handed Toby the keys to the car and the young officer descended the steps and walked around the house towards the stables.

'You seem to be getting on well in your diplomatic duties,' Shining said to his sister.

'But of course I am,' she smiled. 'Actually, Tae-young is lovely. She's got her head screwed on.'

'How envious you must be.'

'Hush your face, you horrid man.'

They climbed back up the steps and walked into the entrance hall. There was nobody else there now, and it was with some relief that they settled down into an armchair each and stared up at the decorative plastering.

'Poor Lucy,' April said, 'bumped off just because she pulled the wrong shift.'

'Story of our lives,' said Shining. 'How many people have we seen die just because they happened to be in the wrong place at the worst possible time?'

'True, I never did get used to it, though. Dying for a principle is one thing, being a random statistic …'

'Which is all we are at the end of the day.'

'Speak for yourself. I intend to go out in a blaze of glory.'

For a few minutes they just stared at the plasterwork, moving from one detail to the next. It made Shining think of his career, weird, baroque and ancient.

'I do hope you have a bit of a plan,' said April eventually. 'I've rather become a target, haven't I?'

'Aren't we all? As for a plan … That's rather difficult in that the whole situation has us on the back foot. All we can do is take every precaution possible and hope we're clever enough to catch and stop whoever it is that's so good at killing people from a distance.'

'Oh good, I did so want to hear something deeply reassuring.'

Shining shrugged. 'What can I say? We have so little to go on. I've placed some protection on the walls of the place, hopefully that will give us some pre-warning before something else happens.'

'Hopefully.'

'Your basic rule should be never to accept anything from anyone.'

'What a perfect recipe for a boring week.'

'One that you might survive.'

April sighed and nodded. 'I suppose that makes up for it.'

'And when something else happens,' Shining continued, 'as it surely will, we'll just have to hope that it leads us closer to whoever it is that's behind this.'

'How morbid. Now you have us looking forward to something awful.'

'Well, not "looking forward" exactly, but you know what I mean. The more evidence we have ...'

'The closer we'll be to finding them, I know. Fine.'

She got to her feet. 'I'm going to go and find Tae-young, see if she can get me a room upstairs. I'm damned if I'm going in the servants' quarters.'

She nearly fell back into her chair as the sound of an explosion rocked through the building.

Shining was immediately on his feet, running out of the main door.

April came after him, looking around in confusion until they both saw a plume of smoke curling around the corner of the building from the direction of the stable block.

'Toby?' April asked but Shining didn't answer, just ran in the direction of the explosion.

As the parking area by the stable block came into view, the source of the explosion was immediately obvious. It was Shining's car. Now a blackened hulk, its interior filled with flame that roared and flowed from the blown-out windows.

In the driver's seat there was the shape of a man, his entire body consumed by fire.

CHAPTER TEN: THE SHADOW

a) Lufford Hall, Alcester, Warwickshire

Toby was heading towards the stables when he bumped into Fratfield again.

'Popping out?' Fratfield asked.

'Just to town, I need to get online.'

'Stratford's your best bet,' Fratfield said. 'If you don't mind waiting a couple of shakes, I need to head out myself. Or would you rather go alone?'

'Not at all.' Toby liked Fratfield and couldn't see the problem in his tagging along.

'Are you OK with us taking my car? I need to get some petrol.'

'Fine, I've spent too long relying on the Tube, I'm hopeless behind the wheel these days.' This was only partly true, but Toby didn't mind being the passenger.

'I'll be right with you.' Fratfield threw a set of car keys to Toby. 'Saab parked at the front.'

'Righto.'

Toby strolled over to Fratfield's car, opening it with the

electronic key that hung from the man's fob.

He climbed into the passenger seat, guiltily having a poke around while he waited. He tried to tell himself nosiness was his job rather than just an unpleasant character trait. Not that there was a great deal to see: the glove compartment held only the car manual, a pair of gloves and some windscreen de-icer. It was with some disappointment that Toby found nothing in the little storage box between the seats either. Fratfield didn't even own any embarrassing CDs. Or any CDs at all. He was a perfect Secret Service officer – you could have gone over the entire car and not had the first idea about the man who was driving it. Toby was utterly bored by the time Fratfield returned.

'Sorry about keeping you waiting,' said Fratfield. 'I was caught by Mark.'

'No doubt wanting you to shoot me and dump the body in a ditch between here and Stratford.'

'Nah, he would never approve the expenditure of a bullet. I'm to garrotte you instead.'

'Look forward to that.'

Fratfield reversed the car out of its parking space and headed out on the drive towards the guardhouse. He rummaged in his coat pocket for his pass. 'Still haven't sorted one of these for you, have they?' he asked as he held it up towards the security man at the gate.

'No point in wasting government resources if I'm going to be dead within the hour.'

'True, true. I'll see if I can get someone to get a wiggle on, though, just in case you escape. Be nice if you had your own ID before the conference is over.'

'It would make a delightful leaving present.'

They drove away from Lufford Hall.

'Been in service long?' Toby asked.

'Haven't you read my file?' Fratfield smiled.

'Nah, I leave that sort of careful preparation to the old man, I get by on small talk.'

'Always fun in the intelligence service, we do so love to chinwag.'

In Toby's experience, most intelligence officers did when in the company of another. After all, they didn't get to talk much outside the office, at least not about work. And, for an intelligence officer, work tended to be pretty all-consuming. Toby had known a couple of officers who had lost marriages over the fact. People tended to become absent both literally and figuratively and that was something nobody enjoyed living with.

'I was recruited from college,' Fratfield continued. 'This will be my fifteenth year of being a professional liar for Queen and Country.'

'How lovely,' said Toby. 'You must be proud.'

'I am actually,' Fratfield admitted. 'I know it seems unfashionable these days but I do like to think we do some good in the work we do. I'm certainly not in it for the money.'

'Just as well,' Toby laughed, 'or your career would be a disappointment.'

'What about you?'

'Same, I came in as a post-grad, sifting data and wanting to be James Bond.'

'How did that work out for you?' Fratfield smiled.

'I now spend most of my days dealing with subjects that would make Ian Fleming's dead toes curl.'

'Fair enough.'

'As I said before, though, it's good. I actually feel I'm making a difference these days. That alone makes it worthwhile.'

'What about outside the office? You married?'

The fact that Toby didn't wear a wedding ring didn't mean much, he knew; a lot of married intelligence officers didn't.

'No, terminally single.' He paused and then added, 'There's someone but, frankly, I think the feelings are a bit one-sided.'

Fratfield sighed. 'I know all about that. It's hard. You can't really give anything of yourself, can you? Who'd be stupid enough to fall for someone who does our job? What about family?'

'My mother died a few years ago.'

'Ah ... shit, sorry.'

'Don't worry about it. Father's still alive. Unfortunately.'

Fratfield laughed. 'I can tell you're close.'

'Our relationship is a bit complicated. He's a funny old bugger. We don't really get on.'

'Sorry to hear that. He cleared?'

'No, he thinks I work for the Department of Works and Pensions.'

'Oh.'

'Which he finds surprising. He never thought I'd get a job in the first place.'

'Supportive. Nice.'

Toby shrugged. 'He can't help it, really, it's just the way he is.' He didn't like discussing his parents so tried to shift the attention away. 'You?'

'Both retired to Spain. They spend their days playing bowls with pensioners and going on coach trips to old potteries.'

'Thrilling stuff.'

'Absolutely. And they think I work for the DTI.'

'We're just a pair of boring civil servants out for a drive,' said Toby.

'Indeed we are.'

b) Sheep Street, Stratford-upon-Avon, Warwickshire

Fratfield parked the car on a hill leading down to the canal basin. They were surrounded by timber-framed buildings and old shop fronts.

'I need to find an internet café,' said Toby.

'There's a newsagents at the end of the road, they'll put you on the right track. I need to grab a few things, how long do you need?'

'Give me forty-five minutes, that OK?'

'Perfect, meet you back here.'

Fratfield walked off up the street and Toby went into the newsagents to ask for directions. After finally accepting that Toby was unlikely to buy the knocked-off smartphone he kept under the counter, the shopkeeper pointed him in the direction of a small café a few minutes' walk away.

Toby stopped off at a payphone en route and put through a call to Ben Topham, his friend at the South Hampshire Fingerprint Bureau.

Unlike a lot of agents, Ben knew exactly who Toby was (though was at least vague as to what he did). They had gone to school together. On graduation, Ben had gone into forensics and the Met whereas Toby had vanished into the elusive world of the Security Service.

'If it isn't yourself!' came a shouted reply through the handset. 'How long since you last got in touch, eh?'

'Sorry Ben, been a busy old time,' said Toby. 'You know what it's like.'

'Not really. I just sit in the same old office day after day and try not to go out of my mind with the boredom. I stare at people's fingerprints. I am an expert of stains. You know, the highlight of my day is a hot chocolate from the vending machine mid-afternoon? It's good. Thick and creamy and full of the sugary promise of home time. I've got another couple of hours to go before I can even think of walking down the corridor and ordering that bad boy. Never work in an office, it kills the soul.'

'My soul has had its fair share of near-mortal injuries over the years. Listen, I can't really chat.'

'No change there.'

'Literally, I'm in a call box.'

'Don't worry, I'm only pulling your leg. What do you need?'

'If I send a scan of a fingerprint through to you how long will it take for you to run it?'

'A lot less than it should do, because you wouldn't be asking unless you needed it now, right?'

'Right.'

Ben sighed. 'Email it through to me, highest resolution the server can stand, and I'll get right on it. You'll still need to give me an hour or so, though.'

'Done.' Toby was aware that didn't fit with the time he'd said he'd meet Fratfield but he'd have to make the SIS man hang around. 'I'm not in my office at the moment.'

'The glamour! How I hate you!'

'Nowhere too exotic,' Toby admitted, 'but I'm having to use an internet café.'

'Which makes the paranoid in both of us have a conniption.

Should be fine. Use BloodstainBen@Gmail.com. Got that?'

Toby repeated the address back, spelling it out.

'That's the one,' said Ben. 'I'll be looking out for it.'

'Give it ten minutes or so, I'll be as quick as I can.'

'No worries. And, Toby?'

'Yeah.'

'Next time you call it should be to invite me for a pint, yes?'

'You live in Hampshire. Who goes to Hampshire?'

'Screw you.' Ben laughed and hung up.

Toby carried on to the internet café, a small shop with four PC computers and a vending machine. It was, thankfully, empty.

'Help you?' asked the man behind the counter who had the look of a man who had played bass in his school band thirty years ago and never got around to changing his hair.

'Hope so,' said Toby, holding up the fingerprint. 'Bit of a weird request,' he pulled out his wallet and offered ID that alleged he was a DI in the Met, 'but it's official business.'

'Bit off your beat, aren't you?' said the man, staring at the warrant card. 'Detective Stanley Hopkins?' The man laughed. 'I bet you get a lot of flak for that.'

'For what?'

'The name. He was in Sherlock Holmes. You might as well be called Lestrade.'

'Oh. I didn't know.' But now he did he'd certainly give Shining, who was responsible for the false ID, some stick over it.

'That's the problem with modern policing, you don't know the classics.'

'Well, as soon as I'm on the hunt for a supernatural dog knocking off landed gentry I'll be sure to read up.' It occurred to Toby that, in his section, the likelihood of that ever happening was not quite as unlikely as you'd hope.

'Only saying.' The owner was on the back foot now and Toby was angry at himself for getting the man's back up.

'Sorry, don't mean to be rude,' he said, doing his best to relax and appear open and friendly. 'It's just been one of those weeks.'

The owner shrugged. 'Tell me about it. You think it's easy running a place like this these days? Outside the tourist season I'm sat on my arse from nine to five.'

'Then you'll be glad of a bit of excitement,' said Toby, 'though I'll have to ask that you keep it to yourself.'

'Of course,' the man said, more interested. Toby had no doubt this entire encounter, with extra embellishments, would be on several internet forums before the day was out.

'I need you to do a decent, high-resolution scan of this for me,' he placed the fingerprint on the counter, 'and I then need five minutes online to send it to my man in the fingerprint bureau.'

'There's a bureau for fingerprints? Cool.'

'There are lots, most divisions have one.' Add that to your knowledge of Sherlock Bloody Holmes, Toby thought.

'No worries. I can do that.' The man made to snatch the fingerprint.

'Sorry,' said Toby picking it up, 'but make sure you lift it by the corners, would you?'

'I'm not stupid,' the man said, grumpy again.

I'm doing so well today, Toby thought.

The man took the fingerprint out the back and Toby was forced to pace up and down for a couple of minutes while listening to the distant sound of whirring and clunking as the scanner did its work.

Eventually, the man returned and pointed at the computer closest to the door. 'I've sent it to that one. Folder on the desktop marked "Shared".'

'Brilliant,' said Toby, holding his hand out for the fingerprint. The man grunted, went back into his office and fetched it.

Toby put it back into his pocket and sat down at the computer, waggling the mouse to get rid of the screensaver of a spiralling cat. He clicked open the folder and opened the image to check it. It was a bit smudged but not half bad. Certainly good enough to work with. 'That's perfect,' he said. 'You're a star.'

'Yeah,' the owner replied. 'I know.' He went back behind the counter and Toby wondered whether he was already telling people about the weird policeman he was dealing with. This whole thing was a security nightmare. The grumpy sod was bound to have kept a copy of the fingerprint, too. If need be, he could have a word with some people in tech support and see if something horribly viral could be sent over to the shop's computer network.

He opened a web browser, logged on to his email and sent the file to Ben.

That done, he cleared the browser history, just to pay some lip service to security, and went back to the counter.

'All done,' he said.

'Fair enough,' the man said, returning from his back room. 'Murderer or something, is it?' he asked.

'Nothing so exciting, just a man who's sleeping with my wife,' Toby replied. 'How much do I owe you?'

c) Sheep Street, Stratford-upon-Avon, Warwickshire

Toby met Fratfield back by the car.

'Listen,' he said, 'sorry to be a pain but I need to hang around for a little longer. Half an hour at the most. Can I buy you a coffee or something?'

Fratfield shrugged. 'I guess we're both a bit superfluous for now back at the Hall anyway. Why not?'

They walked a little way up the road and into a coffee shop filled with faux-aged prints of Royal Shakespeare Company posters.

'Apparently, this place has something to do with Shakespeare,' Fratfield joked. 'There was a giant teddy bear down the road dressed in doublet and hose.'

Toby looked at the menu and smiled. 'You ain't seen nothing yet.' He looked up at the waiter who had arrived at their table. 'I'll have a black coffee please.'

'And a cappuccino,' said Fratfield. 'It's all Shakespeare themed,' he said looking at the menu. 'Dear God, the hamburgers ...'

'The Full Pound of Flesh.'

'With extra cheese.'

'Or the Merchant of Venison?'

'Bit obvious, that one. I dread to think what might be in the Titus Andronicus pie. And what about the ice creams? Oh, Christ ... the chocolate is called an Othello Sundae.'

They both laughed and continued to work their way through the most choice items while they drank their coffees.

After a while, Toby checked his watch. Ben had had fifty minutes, give or take, that would have to do. He was probably only drinking hot chocolate anyway.

'Don't suppose you have a payphone, do you?' he asked the waiter.

'My friend has to make a quick Corialanus,' Fratfield said, his face utterly straight.

'You just wait Lear,' Toby replied, following the waiter past the bar to a phone near the toilets.

He called Ben.

'Sorry, mate,' he said, 'I know it hasn't been a full hour.'

'That's not the only thing you need to apologise for,' Ben replied, clearly stressed. 'That bloody print lit up the system like it was Christmas. I'll probably have GCHQ kicking down my door come the morning. I'll be found dead from isotopes. Knocked off as a bloody security risk.'

'What do you mean?'

'It was one of your lot, that's what I mean,' said Ben.

Toby ignored the fact that Ben shouldn't really know what 'his lot' were. 'Who?' he asked.

'Bloke by the name of Rowlands. Mark Rowlands. Know him?'

'Shit, yes,' Toby tried to keep his voice calm. 'It must just be a mistake. Can you skip entering a log for it?'

'Already did. Obviously. I don't want people thinking I'm a bloody terrorist, do I?'

'Nobody's going to think you're a terrorist just because you look up someone's fingerprint, Ben, you know that.'

'That's what you say. I'll have MI5 kicking down my door tonight.'

'Never happen.'

'Promise?'

'Promise. Because they're not really called MI5, they're the Security Service. Bye.'

He hung up and took a minute by the phone to try and process what Ben had told him. It must just be a mistake. Rowlands must have checked the light when he went in the room. Obliterating any other print. Yes, that was the logical explanation.

He went back to their table.

'All's Well That Ends Well?' Fratfield asked.

'It was Much Ado About Nothing,' Toby admitted.

d) B49, Alcester, Warwickshire

Toby and Fratfield spent a good deal of the drive back to Lufford Hall chatting and joking about their time in service. Toby had felt relaxed around Fratfield from the first time he'd met him but the jolly half an hour in the coffee shop had sealed the deal. He enjoyed being able to be completely open with his fellow officer. Fratfield, in turn, seemed genuinely interested and amused about the work Toby performed in Section 37. As much as Toby knew Shining was quite right to insist that the approval of others didn't matter, it felt good to be able to discuss his work with someone that didn't immediately dismiss it. That was not to say that Fratfield was completely convinced, Toby would have been surprised if he were, but he didn't laugh it off.

As they pulled off the main road from Stratford and onto the quieter road that led to the Hall, Toby found he was extremely relieved to feel that at least there was someone else in the building that was on their side. That was a rarity for Section 37.

'It's remarkable,' Fratfield was saying. 'You've almost got me considering a transfer.'

'You'd never get one. There were enough people angry that I

was put on the books; they're certainly not going to stand by and let an officer of your reputation join up.'

'I've got a reputation?'

'Certainly better than I had. Though that's not hard.'

'We all make mistakes.'

'I know. It was the number of them that was the problem.' Toby shrugged. 'Doesn't matter. That's all behind me. Now I don't have even half a career to worry about!'

'Oh, you'll be taking over Section 37 one day. Shining can't go on for ever.'

'Don't you believe it. Anyway, once he goes they'll probably close it down. He's the only thing that keeps it running. Some edict that says the section will operate as long as he's alive to run it. If it wasn't for that, they'd have closed us down years ago, for sure.'

'More fool them.'

'As I said before, whatever reports we file, nobody can ever really believe the things we've seen without experiencing it for themselves.'

'I'm not sure I'd want to. Hey – what time is it?' Fratfield glanced at the clock on the dash. 'Don't you think it's getting a bit dark for three o'clock?'

Toby leaned forward and peered out through the windscreen. 'The light's fading really quick.'

'Jesus!' Fratfield shouted as something collided with the left-hand side of the car, making it veer towards the verge. Fratfield wrestled with the steering wheel, trying to pull the car back on track. 'What the hell was that?'

Toby had spun in his seat, trying to look behind them but the fading light was making it difficult. As far as he could tell there was nothing behind them. He had a feeling that Fratfield was about to experience the world of Section 37 whether he liked it or not. 'Just keep your eye on the road,' he said. 'Something's not right here.'

'You're telling me.' Fratfield turned on the headlights, trying to pierce the darkness that had fallen all around them. 'Night doesn't fall this quickly.'

The car was buffeted again, this time by something on the right. There was a crunch of metal as whatever it was punched a dent into the chassis.

Toby shifted in his seat.

'You armed?' Fratfield asked.

'No,' Toby admitted. 'I don't tend to requisition a fire arm when I go shopping. Not that it would probably do much good if I was. Whatever this is, it's more my field than yours and a lot of what we face doesn't care much about being shot at.'

The car veered again and Fratfield gave an angry shout as it left the road, mounting the verge. He hit the brakes – better to be a sitting target who was still alive than a crash victim. 'What now?' he asked. 'You're the expert.'

A position Toby in no way felt he could live up to.

He stared out of the window. It was now completely dark outside, they could see nothing beyond the glass.

'Well,' said Toby, 'we haven't got a lot of choice, have we? We can't just sit here.'

'You want to go outside?' Fratfield was shocked. 'Without knowing what's out there?'

The car rocked as something jumped on the roof. Above them, the roof bowed beneath its weight. Then the rear windscreen imploded and they were showered with glass.

'You think we're any safer in here?' Toby asked, opening the door. He pointed with his hand. 'The road was there, hopefully it still is. We make a break for it, move as fast as we can.' He climbed out and ran in the direction he'd pointed. Behind him he heard Fratfield following.

They could see no more out here than they had from inside the car. It was like running through a void. Except, thought Toby, they knew it wasn't quite empty, didn't they? It contained something strong enough to punch its way into a car.

He looked over his shoulder. Fratfield was catching up. 'Come on!' Toby shouted, 'before whatever it was that was attacking us catches—'

He felt something hit his side and he was suddenly spinning through the air.

Behind him, Fratfield was shouting and there came the sound of gunfire. It seemed that Fratfield was a man who was only too happy to take a gun on a shopping trip.

Toby rolled along the grass verge, trying to keep his body loose, fall like a drunk, it was the best way to avoid breaking bones.

He could get no sense of the size or shape of what it was that was attacking him. It just felt like a pressure, a weight, beating at him as he tried to bring his arms up to defend himself.

'Toby?' he heard Fratfield shout.

'Just run!' Toby replied. Whatever this thing was, he had no doubt there was little Fratfield could do about it. At least if there was only one of them, the other man might be able to break for freedom while it was concentrating on Toby.

'Yeah right,' he heard Fratfield say, much closer now. 'I can't even see it? Where is it?'

Right on top of me you silly bastard, Toby thought as the thing bore down once more and slowly suffocated him.

e) Who knows?

Toby awoke. In itself this was not entirely expected and he took a couple of seconds to appreciate the fact.

He suffered no illusion that he had found himself in the afterlife – as open-minded as he now was, he was quite sure Heaven wasn't a place of splitting headaches and bruised palms. It also helped that, after a few moments of confusion, he recognised exactly where he was. It had been just over a year since he had last been here but he would never forget this cold, marble floor. It helped that the last time he'd seen it was in similar circumstances, lifting himself up from it after a considerable trauma. He looked up and noted the oil-paintings of classical composers, the bookshelves filled with sheet music and the empty plinth where, once upon a time, had stood a . . .

He was suddenly aware of the sound of someone creeping up on him. Just a soft brush of shoe on tile. No, he thought, not this time.

He turned, just avoiding the bust of Beethoven that, until recently had been sat on that empty plinth, as it was brought crashing down towards his head. It collided off his shoulder, exploding on the floor in a shower of fragments of porcelain sculpted to look like curly hair.

Toby spun round, his shoulder throbbing with the blow but its owner blessedly more conscious than the last time this scene had played out.

He put up his hands, his attacker barrelling into him with a cry of frustration. Yoosuf, Toby thought, intelligence asset, collector of sheet music and the man who had been instrumental in his career ending up on the rocks. Well, no, perhaps that was a little unfair, it was Toby's mishandling of him that had done that. Still, braining him with a statue of a dead composer meant Toby still bore a bit of a grudge.

They rolled on the floor, Toby getting the upper hand, only to find the man he was wrestling was not Yoosuf after all. He wore Yoosuf's clothes but the face that peered out at him from a nest of brightly coloured scarves was the scrawny, salt and pepper bearded, face of his father.

'What are you doing?' his father asked. 'You silly bugger, you could have done me a mischief.'

At which point Toby gave up on the evidence of his senses altogether.

'Right,' he said, getting to his feet. 'The car's attacked, I'm knocked out cold and now I seem to be at the mercy of a psychoanalyst's wet dream.'

'What are you talking about?' his father asked, getting up and brushing himself down. 'You never make any sense. Head in the clouds, that's your problem. You're a dreamer.'

'That sounds about right,' Toby admitted, looking around. The room was exactly as he remembered it. The shelves and paintings, the scattered china, the short run of steps leading up to the exit and the street outside.

'Pay attention to me when I'm talking to you,' his father said. 'God know where we went wrong with you.' The old man sighed. 'We tried our best but you were always a disappointment. When your poor mother died the last thing she said was—'

'Oh shut up,' said Toby punching the old man as hard as he could in the face.

His father's head cracked like the bust of Beethoven, the remains of which they were crushing into powder beneath their feet. Half of it fell away to reveal a hollow shell of oyster pink.

'Now look what you've done,' his father said, the voice echoing around that empty skull so it sounded like an old gramophone record played through a trumpet. 'Could you make more of a mess?'

'Probably,' Toby admitted, picking up a large binder of sheet music from one of the shelves and bringing it down on the remains of his father's head.

The body toppled to the floor and Toby ran up the steps towards the front door, pulled it open and found himself looking out on a warehouse in Shad Thames.

This was familiar too ... Of course, it was where he had first met what remained of Russian spy Olag Krishnin. His first case for Section 37. It had also been where August Shining had been ...

A gunshot rang out and he saw the old man fall backwards, two bullet wounds to the chest. He hit the dusty ground of the warehouse, its insubstantial boards quivering and creaking.

Looking around, he saw Krishnin. The gun was in Krishnin's hand, still smoking. The last time Toby had been in this situation he had been astral travelling, his body insubstantial. Not so this time. He wrestled the gun from Krishnin, turned it towards the man and fired.

Whatever this was, whatever imaginary world or mind-scape he had tumbled into, he really didn't have the time or inclination to play its games.

Krishnin's head exploded much as his father's had done, this time, a thick, black liquid poured over the little that remained of it, a jagged cup made from the man's lower lip and chin.

Toby gave one last, sad glance towards Krishnin and then ran towards the opposite side of the warehouse where a wide-open hatch led to the outside world.

Toby jumped through it, not altogether caring where it might lead him.

He fell through the brightness of sunshine, a world of light that contained no distinguishable shapes. For a moment there was utter peace.

Then he hit the ground, back in the black emptiness he and Fratfield had found themselves in after the car had been attacked. He rolled along what felt like grass, coming to rest at Tamar's feet.

'You keep away,' she said, folding her arms and giving him a look that, a day ago, had chilled him.

'Shan't,' he replied, kissing the illusion on its sneering lips and running on into the dark.

'Fratfield?' he shouted, looking around – pointlessly, he knew but he couldn't help it – for the thing that had attacked him earlier.

There was a groaning noise a short way ahead and he saw the SIS officer lying on the ground. No doubt he was imagining similar nightmarish images.

He grabbed him and, with a struggle, got the man into a fireman's lift.

He stumbled on, Fratfield draped over his shoulder. Ahead the darkness seemed to fade, the black turning to grey.

Behind him there was a loud crashing sound. The car, he decided, breathing its last.

He could now make out the road in front of him. If he could just get there ahead of whatever thing this was that swooped around them in the shadows, he sensed they would be safe. Back in the real world, back on firm ground.

He sensed, rather than heard, that something was gaining on him. Perhaps it was just fear, paranoia, but he was certain that the presence was chasing after him, desperate to catch them both before they left its domain.

It was so hard to run with Fratfield on his shoulder. If he dropped him there was no doubt he could make it out, one last sprint and he would have the sky above him once more, the tarmac of the road beneath his feet. But he wouldn't leave the man behind. He wouldn't add to his memory of regrets.

He kept his eyes ahead. Pushing on, even as he was sure the presence that pursued them was almost touching.

Just a few steps more.

He could feel a chill on his neck, something reaching out.

Then a cold wind, and a late-winter afternoon sky, beginning to grow dim.

He shuffled to the verge, carefully dropped Fratfield onto the grass and turned back to see the car, only a few feet away. It looked like it had been in a major collision, smashed on both sides with the roof compressed almost flat.

Fratfield groaned, his hands going to his face as he came around. 'What happened?' he asked.

'What do you remember?'

Fratfield sat up and stared at the smashed car. 'I remember running from that while something tried to kill us. I remember thinking that you could keep your Section 37. You still can. I like an enemy that, when all else fails, I can shoot in the head.'

'No more transfer for you, then?' Toby smiled. He had thought for one moment that Fratfield was going to say that he remembered none of it. That Toby would have been left trying to explain something the SIS officer was unlikely to believe.

'No,' Fratfield replied. Toby helped him to his feet.

'How did I get out?'

'By almost dislocating my shoulder,' Toby told him.

'You carried me? Thanks.' Fratfield seemed slightly uncomfortable at the thought.

'It's fine, I won't remind you how I saved your life every day. Just once a week or so.'

'That's good. Because, unlike whatever that thing was, you *can* be shot in the head.'

'Such gratitude. Come on, we've got a short walk ahead of us.'

As they walked up the road towards Lufford Hall, Toby looked around them, trying to catch sign of anyone else out here. If what they had experienced was some kind of curse then Cassandra's advice was lodged in his memory. The person who was doing the casting had to be nearby. Of course, quantifying 'nearby' would have been useful. Did that mean in the same postcode or stood next to you? Toby couldn't see anyone, especially not in this fading light. There were countless places someone could have been hiding, what was the use?

f) Lufford Hall, Alcester, Warwickshire

It took them about twenty minutes to reach the main gate of the

Hall. The security guard on duty was the same man who had let them out earlier. He gave them a distinctly suspicious look as they approached.

Toby's face was smeared with mud and Fratfield's suit was torn.

'Could I see your passes?' he asked.

'Piss off,' said Fratfield, 'and get someone to sort out the wreck of my car that's parked about a mile down the road. If you're that bothered about my paperwork, you might want to take a look in the pocket of my coat. It's on the back seat. You'll have to climb in through the window, I suspect. It's all in there.'

The security guard looked as if he intended to argue but clearly changed his mind and waved at the guardhouse to let them through.

They walked up the drive towards the Hall. On the gravel forecourt they found April Shining, smoking a cigarette and staring at them as if she were a disapproving mother.

'And where do you think you've been?' she asked. 'You've had this place in chaos.'

Fratfield and Toby looked at one another. 'Which of us are you talking to?' Toby asked.

'You, you daft sod, we thought you were dead. Well, for all of five minutes anyway. What's that on your face? Have you been playing silly buggers in the garden?'

'Not quite. Our car was attacked.'

'So was August's. You know, the one you were supposed to be in. And when I say "attacked", I mean blown to kingdom come with someone in it.'

Toby took a moment to process this. 'Who?'

'Poor Ranesh, my boss for all of five minutes.'

Fratfield was already moving around the side of the house, wanting to see the wreckage.

'There's nothing to see,' April told him. 'Once we could actually get the fire out, what was left was moved into the stable block.' She returned her attention to Toby. 'We thought Ranesh was you until I noticed the glasses melted onto his face.'

'You think it was meant to be?'

'Seems likely, don't you think?'

'But what was he doing in our car?'

'How am I supposed to know?' She sighed, then grabbed him in a big hug. 'I'm glad you're not dead. Stupid boy. Now if you'll excuse me, as the last remaining member of the diplomatic service, it's my job to go and try and convince our Korean friends not to leave.'

CHAPTER ELEVEN: THE DINNER

a) Lufford Hall, Alcester, Warwickshire

Tae-young was sat in her room, wishing she could dispel the smell of burning flesh from her nostrils.

There was a knock on the door. It took Tae-young a moment to respond, to pull herself back from the mental image of a man turning crisp in artificially stoked flames.

'Come,' she said, lapsing into Korean. She didn't have the concentration to talk in English.

April entered, came over to the window where Tae-young was sitting and settled down into the armchair facing her.

'You are hoping to convince me to stay,' said Tae-young.

'I'm sure I probably don't have to,' April replied. 'Let's be honest, both the UK and South Korea need these plans to be successful.'

'But can they be in the current circumstances? Don't misunderstand me. You know enough about my country to know that its history is no stranger to violence. We are no strangers to assassination.' She continued to gaze out of the window.

'My mother was there when Park Chung-hee was shot,' she continued, 'when his own chief of security put a bullet in his head and his chest.'

'Kim Jae-kyu, director of the KCIA.'

April chose not to mention that, during the time Kim had been head of the Korean Central Intelligence Agency, she in turn had been working with SIS and had, for a time, been tasked with monitoring the growing dissent over Park's rule amongst Kim and others.

Park's reign had become a dictatorship and both the UK and their American allies had been very enthusiastic about the idea of the man being replaced by someone they could be seen to have more fruitful relations with. Of course, people had talked about the acts of repression committed under Park's regime, and his threats to increase his domination over the populace. They had talked in terms of morality. Ultimately, though, governments were not overly concerned with such intangible concepts. They just wanted to monitor the troublemakers and ensure the flow of money remained constant.

Park had been shot during a private dinner party, the conversation and increased threats of retaliation against political dissenters allegedly driving Kim to take his leave, fetch a gun and then return with murder on his mind. The argument as to whether it had been a political act, a murder bred of jealousy (Kim's career was on a downward turn thanks to the influence of Park's chief bodyguard) or even an act of espionage instigated by the CIA, was still ongoing over thirty years. Well, thought April, ongoing amongst those who didn't know as much as she did.

Tae-young nodded. 'She was part of the waiting staff. She

wasn't in the room at the time, though she often used to wonder what would have happened had she been.'

'That's life in this business,' April admitted. 'It's all a matter of luck.'

'Today has not been lucky. Two of your people are dead.'

'Yes.' Tae-young had been informed of Lucy Baxter's death and any attempt to write it off as an accident had floundered given what had happened to Ranesh.

'And before them,' Tae-young continued, 'three others.'

'But that can't stop us.'

'Why? Because that would mean the assassin had succeeded?'

'Partly.'

Tae-young nodded. 'I can understand that. And yet, if we stay, who will be next?'

'So far there is no indication that the assassin has any interest in attacking your party.'

Tae-young looked angry. 'I am not only thinking of the lives of my people, I would not be so selfish. My point is that, as long as this conference continues, people's lives are in jeopardy.'

'Forgive me, I didn't mean to suggest you were being selfish. And yes, there is no guarantee that Ranesh will be the last. But these talks must be resolved, and will be one way or another, through us or someone else. They will happen here and now or somewhere else later, where the same risk will apply until we catch whoever is behind this. All we can do is trust in those who are doing their best to keep us alive and hope that they find the killer before they can strike again. That's their job.'

'And are they any good at it?'

April struggled to answer that one. 'Do you believe in the supernatural?'

'What has that got to do with anything?'

April knew that she wasn't supposed to explain the work of Section 37 or the reasoning behind their presence here but, to hell with it, the only way she could keep Tae-young onside was to be open with her. 'You'll understand when I explain. Do you?'

Tae-young sighed. 'It's not only violence my country understands, we have as long a history of myth and legend as you do. I can't say it's something I think much about. My grandfather used to claim he could speak to spirits. As a child I found the idea fascinating and terrifying but now ... If you are a woman in politics you become ...'

'Single-minded. I know.'

April took a deep breath and then explained the background of the three deaths that had brought both her and her brother to Lufford Hall in the first place. It occurred to her as she was explaining that GCHQ had likely put listening devices in the room and that, even now, her name was being dragged through the dirt.

'But that's ...' Tae-young struggled to find the words.

'Unbelievable, yes. In that, both you and my government superiors agree. Nonetheless, the unbelievable is what my brother deals with every day. Has done so through his entire interminable career. The point is: even Clive King couldn't dismiss the possibility and that is why August is here. And, in my experience, which is almost as long as his, he will be the only man who can put a stop to this. That opinion certainly isn't shared by the likes of Mark Rowlands or his team and, rest assured, they are doing their best to address this in a more conventional manner.' April didn't believe a word of that but couldn't see any mileage in badmouthing Rowlands to Tae-young – all that would do was increase her concerns.

'I don't know if I can believe it,' Tae-young admitted.

'You don't have to, I suppose,' said April. 'All you have to do is know that you are surrounded by people who are working to bring this to an end. That is their business and this, talking, is ours. The sooner we get on and finish the conversation, the sooner we shall all be safe.'

Tae-young nodded. 'Very well, we shall see this through. As you say, it's not as if I have much choice anyway. Can you imagine my government's response were I to order everyone to pull out? I'd be lucky to still have an office by the time I flew back home.'

'At least I have the advantage on you there,' April admitted. 'There's nothing my people can threaten me with, I'm long retired. If I walked out of here right now there's not a bloody thing they could do about it.'

'So why do you stay?'

'Free meals and central heating. Never underestimate the draw of luxury to an old woman.'

Tae-young laughed and April leaned over and kissed her hand. 'It'll be fine,' she said, 'probably.'

She got up and left the woman to organise her thoughts.

In the corridor, Clive King was staring up at a particularly bland watercolour hunting scene.

'Afternoon, darling,' said April, standing behind him. 'If you're looking for tips on how to corner prey, I'm happy to guide you.'

He rolled his eyes. 'Impossible woman. I can't believe they let you come. No, actually, I imagine you gave them no choice. I just wish I'd had some warning.'

'Old ghosts chill so deeply, don't they, sweetie? If it's any consolation, I've convinced Miss Son to continue with the talks.'

'I had no doubt you would.' He smiled and nodded towards the door. 'I heard you were in there and thought it best to leave you to it. There's not a man or woman born more capable of persuading someone to do something than you.'

'Why, Clive! I do believe that was a compliment. Or a justification for our brief dalliance in years gone by.'

He shook his head. 'I needed no justification for that. You were impossible to resist then and impossible now.'

'Oh my Lord! Are you flirting?'

He smiled. 'Not really. I'm happily married, a grandfather three times over, my enthusiasm for naughty liaisons in stately homes has long since waned. I was just saying I have no regrets.'

'Nor should you,' she said, taking his arm, 'there are many who would have killed to have spent the night with me.'

He wisely decided not to reply to that, changing the subject onto safer ground. 'Has your brother made any headway?'

April shook her head. 'I don't think so. It's all such a mess. Don't worry, though, he's as shockingly resourceful as me. If anyone can get us out of this place alive, it's August.'

He nodded. 'I'm afraid Rowlands is a little put out that I allowed Section 37 to come.'

'Tough, a bit of healthy competition never hurt anyone. If Mr Rowlands is so convinced he can keep us safe, let him prove as much. Did he get anywhere with his examination of the car?'

'He doesn't really have the expertise. He's convinced that the explosive must have been attached before you came here. But I think that's purely because he doesn't want to admit that someone could have breached his security and planted it.'

'I suppose it's possible,' April admitted. 'It's the work of moments to attach a magnetic charge on the underside of a car. Someone might have thought we made a useful little Trojan Horse, an easy way of sneaking a bomb into the grounds.'

'He has an explosives man on his way who may be able to tell us more. If nothing else, it is at least a physical threat. One we can understand.'

'None of that silly hocus pocus!'

'Exactly. By which I mean no insult to your brother. But I am always going to feel more comfortable if I think we're facing something that is within the realm of my understanding. Bastards throwing bombs at us, that I can deal with. This stuff about curses ...'

'He's talked to you, then?'

'We had a brief chat earlier. I left feeling I had just talked to someone very knowledgeable, even if none of that knowledge had rubbed off.'

'That's August. Leave him to do his thing, it's not for you to worry about. At least not right now.' Her brother's advice occurred to her. 'The important thing to remember is very simple: accept nothing from anyone. If August is right, the curse has to be passed physically to you. If you never take anything from anyone then you should be safe.'

King shook his head. 'It's all beyond me, but yes, he told me much the same thing.' He smiled. 'Which will make passing the port a nightmare at dinner.'

b) Lufford Hall, Alcester, Warwickshire

Toby found Shining in his room on the basement level. He was muttering under his breath and placing a stubby candle on his bedside table. Toby assumed this was the conclusion of their stroll around the gardens earlier. He stayed in the doorway for a moment, not wanting to interrupt. Then, when it appeared that Shining had finished, he stepped inside.

'Well,' he said, 'I believe we've both had annoying afternoons.'

Shining looked up at him and the momentary look of pleasure he saw in the old man's eyes meant the world to him.

'Thought you were going to have to be the only one who remembered to buy milk for the office again, did you?' Toby asked.

'Yes,' Shining admitted. 'But at least I would, once again, have had sole control of the radio.'

'It was a close-run thing,' Toby told him, 'though not for the reasons you thought.' He explained what had happened to him and Fratfield on their way back to the Hall.

'Fascinating,' said Shining.

'Again with the enthusiasm,' Toby replied. 'One day, you'll have the decency not to view my brushes with hell as something to relish.'

'As we've already established,' said Shining with a smile, 'you're still alive so I can enthuse guilt-free. It sounds like some form of reflection spell.'

'Just what I thought.' Toby rolled his eyes.

'Whoever we're dealing with here clearly has a great deal of skill in sorcery,' said Shining.

'And still that sentence makes me feel like I'm chewing tinfoil.'

'Shush, don't make me give you the whole "magic is science" talk again.'

'Heaven forbid.'

'I've never heard of anyone pulling off a reflection spell, it's just one of those things you read about in dusty old books. A way of turning the very worst a person holds inside, all their fears and insecurities, back against them.'

'Been there,' Toby admitted, 'and done that.'

'Lucky for you. Someone who didn't have such a firm grip on their own psychology would no doubt have found it much harder to break free.'

'Fratfield was certainly struggling,' Toby said. 'If I hadn't pulled him out of there, he would have been as dead as the diplomat in our car.'

'Yes, poor Ranesh.' August sighed. 'I hadn't even met him. Whoever's behind this certainly isn't playing the long game.'

'April told me she was going to try and convince the Koreans to stay.'

'I'm sure she'll manage. She's good at that sort of thing. Besides, this would hardly be the first conference besieged by assassination attempts.'

'Surely it would make sense to pack up and move somewhere else, though?'

'Maybe it'll come to that,' Shining conceded. 'Though for now Rowlands is insisting that the bomb must have been brought in by us.'

'How's he come to that conclusion?'

'By a bloody-minded refusal to imagine someone broke in here and planted it. He thinks it was put on the car by someone who knew we were coming.'

'A short list.'

'Indeed, not even Rowlands knew until we were virtually on the doorstep.'

This made Toby think about the fingerprint. He told Shining what he had discovered.

'As you say,' Shining agreed, 'it's more than likely that he tried the light switch when they were giving the room a once-over. Probably covering the original print, the useful print, when he did so.'

'I don't imagine there's much point in asking. He's bound to say yes, even if – and, oh, how I would love this to be the case – he is the man we're after.'

'Yes.' Shining sat down on his bed. 'It's something we have to bear in mind, certainly. There's nothing to say that the assassin isn't one of us. In fact it would make a lot of sense.'

'No problem getting past security.'

'But how to know for sure?' Shining looked at the candle he had placed by his bed. 'I suppose this might help. If it's triggered then we know we've been breached. If it isn't …'

'Then we know they're already here,' said Toby. 'But that doesn't mean it's Rowlands. It's not just the attendees we have to deal with. There's a catering staff, the security people on the perimeter. There must be, what, thirty-odd people to sift through?'

'Thirty-eight. It would be more but they've excluded the ground staff from work for the duration of the conference. They're all security checked. But not by us. Let me have a think …' Shining turned on the bed and lay down, his eyes closed.

After a moment, Toby wondered if he'd fallen asleep. 'Is this the sort of think that makes you snore?' he asked.

'Go away, cheeky staff,' said Shining. 'Get some rest, and a shower. I'll see you at dinner.'

c) Lufford Hall, Alcester, Warwickshire

After a late session within the conference room, dinner was served at eight, by which time all of those gathered beneath the ancient roof of Lufford Hall were more than ready for it. Lemuel Spang in particular was vocal about his hunger while people gathered for drinks in the lounge. He mentioned it frequently while grazing on the platter of petits fours that had been provided by the staff.

'I dislike that man quite intensely,' Tae-young confessed to April.

They had both changed into evening dress. Tae-young's gown was the very epitome of modern class. April had had to spend half an hour brushing plaster dust from hers having last worn it during a Libyan attack on a US embassy back in the 1980s. She was sure nobody would notice the slight tear on the hem from where she had been forced to escape through rubble.

Spang was talking at Man-dae, the young Korean looking desperately around the room, either for someone else to talk to or a blunt object to beat the banker with.

'Should we rescue him, do you think?' April suggested.

'Too risky,' Tae-young replied. 'We might get drawn in. He'll make a break for it when we move through to the dining room.'

Rowlands was stood on his own in the far corner, staring intently at a glass of wine and pretending he didn't mind the fact that nobody wanted to talk to him. His men were absent, working their way in circuits around the grounds, teamed up with the private security staff.

The other two Koreans, Chun-hee and Jae-sung were together, though the latter seemed more interested in the rear of one of the serving staff, April noticed.

'Tell me about those two,' she said to Tae-young.

'Jae-sung can be a bit of a drain,' Tae-young admitted. 'A good man but he has too much of an eye for the ladies.'

'Including you, no doubt?'

'Including me. I spent most of the flight over trying to remove his hand from my thigh. He's not a bad man, though, for all that.'

'And Chun-hee?'

'Who knows? It is so hard to tell with him. He keeps his own counsel. As Minister for Foreign Affairs, you'd think he'd be more outgoing, but he spends most of his time sitting quietly and staring out of the window. He's either perpetually bored or angry, I've never been able to tell which.'

'He sounds an absolute blessing to have onboard.'

'He knows what he's doing, he's conscientious with the work ... I just wish I could read him more as a person, that's all.'

'As long as he's doing his job, I suppose it doesn't matter,' said April.

'His job in this case is rather simple. As you said before, it's not like both our countries don't need this to happen. It shouldn't be a long affair.'

'Good. The sooner papers are signed, the sooner we can get out of here.'

She noticed Clive King walk in, looking every inch the civil servant in strange territory. He was wearing black tie but in the manner of a man who has put it on because he knows it's expected rather than because he could altogether carry it off. His bow tie was crooked, his shirt a fraction too tight. Maybe it wasn't quite so long since King had worn his outfit as it was since April had worn hers but it was certainly a few hearty dinners ago.

He walked up to Spang and Man-dae, the Korean immediately making a run for it.

'Oh dear, poor Clive,' said April. 'That's probably enough to tip him over the edge.'

'You've known him long?'

'Oh yes, many years. We had an affair back in the ... Oh Lord, you know you've lived a sinful life when you can't readily remember which decade it was when you slept with someone.'

Across the room, Clive King heard the sound of Tae-young laughing and looked over at the two women. For a moment he felt a burst of paranoia – what was April saying about him now? Then Spang intruded once more with his seemingly endless stream of inane opinion.

'I just don't see the point,' the man said. 'I mean, what's so bloody amazing about organic, eh? That's all they used to eat two hundred years ago and most of them were dead by the age of forty.'

'True, true,' King replied, not really paying attention.

'Why people have to fight progress I just don't know,' Spang continued. 'Eat your microwave meal and be happy.'

King noticed Rowlands stood on his own and waved him over. Anything was better than suffering Spang alone.

'Gentlemen,' Rowlands greeted them. 'I'm afraid there's still nothing major to go on with regards the bomb. My explosives man says it was a fairly simple device, easy to plant, remote triggered. These days they all are. Once you've got to the point that you can blow something up using your iPhone ...'

'Quite,' said King. 'Well, as long as he does a thorough sweep of the area to ensure there are no other devices to worry about.'

'On it now, sir,' Rowlands said.

'Checked my bedroom myself,' said Spang. 'Learn a few tricks when you're in my game. Nobody loves a banker.'

King didn't think it was Spang's profession that made him eminently explodable.

Toby entered with Fratfield, having bumped into him in the corridor outside.

'You feeling better?' Toby asked him.

'Fine, nothing ibuprofen and wine won't fix.

'How did King take it?'

Fratfield looked uncomfortable. 'Honestly, I didn't know how to explain it so ...'

'You didn't.' Toby sighed.

'I told him we were run off the road by something, and that everything went dark and that you managed to drag me clear. In truth, that pretty much covers it.'

'I suppose.'

'Look, I'm not claiming that there was nothing supernatural at work, I just didn't really know how to explain it. Oh hell, I'm sorry, you must think I've not got your back.'

Toby smiled. 'Honestly, it's fine. I remember what it was like when I had to file my first official paperwork. "Saved the world using time travel" doesn't read well as a summation of an operation. If I'd just left it at "saved the world", it would have been much easier.'

'Now you're just showing off.'

'Absolutely. Now repay me for saving your miserable life by finding the drinks.'

They moved over to the central table, Toby pretending not to have noticed the frown aimed at him by Rowlands. He turned his back to the man, avoiding the need to ignore any further disapproval.

'Can I get you an aperitif, gentlemen?' asked one of the serving staff.

'You certainly can,' said Fratfield. 'What have you got?'

'Pretty much everything, sir,' the young man replied with a faint Polish accent.

'I like it here,' Fratfield said. He looked to Toby. 'What do you fancy?'

'Gin and tonic would be perfect.'

'My friend is wise in the ways of drink. Make that two.'

Shining was the last to arrive. He put that down to two things: firstly the fact that he had spent half an hour preparing what he hoped would be a very useful method for furthering the investigation; secondly, he was probably the only person in the room who had bothered to tie his own bow tie.

'Looking terribly handsome as always, darling brother,' said April, waving him over.

'You're too kind,' he replied, 'and I haven't seen you in evening wear this century, so, well done to you too.'

'One tries to make an effort.'

Shining gave a slight bow towards Tae-young. 'You also look quite wonderful,' he said.

'Charm clearly runs in the family, Mr Shining. Your sister didn't add that to your list of attributes when she explained your work to me earlier.'

'Call me August, please. I hope April hasn't been exaggerating too much.'

'Would that even be possible?' Tae-young wondered.

'Actually,' said Shining after a moment's thought, 'probably not. I'm afraid we weren't supposed to tell you what we do at Section 37.'

'I know. April did explain your presence here has caused some disagreements.'

'Oh, just the usual. I'm quite used to it by now. Though the bedrooms are a new low.'

'I've already upgraded,' said April. 'I'm next to Tae-young. Nobody puts me in the cellar.'

'Toby and I are fine where we are, really,' Shining assured her. 'It's no bad thing to be removed from the rest of the party.'

'At least you'll avoid all the inevitable bedroom-hopping that's bound to happen later.'

Tae-young laughed. 'I can assure you nobody will be coming to my room tonight!'

'That's what you say,' April insisted, 'but I'll need somewhere to hide when they all start pestering me.'

At which point the dinner gong was sounded and she took a still-giggling Tae-young by the arm to lead her through to the dining room.

'A favour,' Shining said, then whispered in April's ear. Once he'd spoken, she nodded and gave him a wink.

'Evening, gentlemen,' said Shining, crossing over to Toby and Fratfield. 'I trust you have both recovered from your ordeal this afternoon?'

'I'm afraid I had difficulty in explaining it to either Rowlands or King,' Fratfield admitted.

'I don't think there was much point in trying,' Shining reassured him, 'although I suppose some form of explanation is needed as we'll both need to put a new car on expenses.'

'At least "car bomb" has previous history on a claims form,' sighed Fratfield. 'I'm not sure "unidentified supernatural force" is likely to swing it.'

'As a man who once lost a Vauxhall Astra to an angry telekinetic from Bath, I think you may be able to argue there's a precedent. Shall we eat?'

The table was ornately laid and Toby wasn't the only one feeling slightly uncomfortable at the idea that they were dining in such splendour given the current situation.

'I feel like I'm sitting down to a slap-up meal at the Captain's table on the *Titanic*,' he whispered to Shining.

'It's always been a peculiarly English habit,' Shining replied, 'polishing the silverware and pressing the shirt collars while the enemy advances.'

Toby was momentarily panicked to note that the seating was labelled. He had rather hoped to hide at the far end with Shining. He found himself seated next to Man-dae on one side and Spang on the other. It was all he could do not to commit suicide with his butter knife. On the far side of Man-dae sat Fratfield, so near and yet so far. He could only hope that the Korean would pass out from boredom before he did, so that he could lean over and have a chat to the SIS officer later. Rowlands, opposite Fratfield, was at least a reassuring distance away.

'You are a secret agent?' Man-dae asked as Toby tried to busy himself with his serviette in the hope that he could discourage conversation by seeming terribly occupied with matters in his lap.

'Not so secret now, eh?' laughed Spang.

'Sort of,' Toby replied with what he hoped was a smile that might also serve as a full stop. 'And you?'

'I am working in my father's businesses,' said Man-dae, 'which means I am doing nothing. I don't think he knows what I am for.'

Toby could relate to that.

'Well, you got a splendid holiday out of it,' suggested Spang.

Toby decided not to point out it was a 'holiday' with a death count.

Man-dae shrugged. 'It is good to travel.'

Opposite them was Jae-sung, who took pity on Toby and began to tell them all about his time in the UK as a student. It mainly involved drinking and girls. At least it gave Toby the opportunity to eat his soup in silence.

He looked over to Shining, who was in heated conversation with Clive King. His situation could have been worse – that certainly didn't look like a conversation he wanted to be in the middle of.

By the time the meal was over, Toby had survived it unscathed. He had managed to avoid the most awkward questions, nod in all the right places and at no point had anyone thrown their drink at him. That counted as a success. He had even managed to attack the cheeseboard and win, no small achievement given its size. A large platter of whittled-away remains sat in the middle of the table with a large knife lying diagonally across the crumbs. It looked like a murder scene in a dairy.

'Well,' announced April at the top of her voice. 'As dinners go, that will certainly do. This time last week I considered a Pot Noodle the height of luxury. Who knew there were meals with several courses?'

'Yes,' said King, 'I must thank the kitchen for a job well done.'

Tae-young gave a very diplomatic smile. 'It was wonderful to enjoy some traditional English food.'

'Oh, English food is lovely once you get the hang of gravy,' April assured her. 'Anyway, what's the point in your being stranded here if we don't throw our customs at you? I think it should be our diplomatic mission. So how about a little entertainment?'

'Entertainment?' King asked, understandably worried about what April might be suggesting.

'Absolutely,' April said. 'What better way to digest our meal than with a little table magic?'

'What is table magic?' asked Chun-hee, trying to keep the scepticism from his voice.

'Oh, you know,' April said, 'a bit of conjuring. August is terribly good at it, aren't you, darling?'

'Well ...' Shining shrugged. 'I'm not too bad but I haven't really prepared anything.'

Liar, Toby thought, knowing a set-up when he saw one being played out.

'I'm not sure we need to see anything like that,' said Rowlands. 'Why don't we just retire through to the other room?' He made to stand up but Toby noticed April giving King a meaningful stare.

'No,' said King, 'why not? Have a seat, Mark. The least you can do is give the chap a chance.'

Rowlands muttered something under his breath but sat back down.

'What about that one with the funny colours?' April said.

'I have no idea which one you mean,' Shining admitted.

'You know, that thing you do with the water and the smoke, that makes people go all green.'

'Oh.' Shining nodded. 'That. Well that's not really conjuring. That's a bit more scientific.'

'I doubt that!' Rowlands scoffed.

Shining looked at him and smiled. 'You have a real issue with the notion of the preternatural, don't you, Mark? What is it about it that makes you so angry?'

'I just don't like people passing themselves off as something they're not,' Rowlands said. 'Fake mediums, Tarot readers, it's all junk.'

Shining nodded. 'Most of it is, yes. In fact, just before I became involved in the conference, it was my job to debunk someone who was, as you say, "passing themselves off" as something they weren't. It's not a big part of my job, but I do occasionally have cause to set the record straight with frauds.'

'So,' said Jae-sung, 'you claim that not all of them are?'

'Frauds? No. Not all of them. Toby gets bored of hearing about my thoughts on this but the important thing to remember about, for the sake of a better word, "magic" is that it is simply another branch of science. It is one that is so old most of us don't use it any more. It is also one that is so advanced we have yet to understand it. It is both future science and old superstition.'

'Science?' Rowlands laughed. 'You can't call it that.'

'Of course I can. Science simply means knowledge. It is the umbrella term we apply to all forms of intellectual and practical study with regards the natural world.'

Man-dae looked towards Tae-young. 'I do not understand.'

April quickly translated for him.

'And science has many branches,' Shining continued, gesturing at one of the waiting staff. 'Could you bring me a large bowl of tap water please?' he asked.

'As I was saying,' he continued, 'there are many branches of science. Chemistry, biology, mathematics. The branch that most seems to be opposed to magic is that of physics. The study of energy and matter. The branch of science we most rely on to explain how the world works around us. The science that explains our fundamental reality. But, like all science, our understanding of physics is constantly changing. It adapts as we understand more. It alters to accommodate new discoveries and theories. When Newton discovered gravity, his notions seemed magical. Now we accept them. It's all just terminology. The miraculous becomes accepted bit by bit. One day, we may even get to the point where there is nothing we deem "magic" – we will just consider it all as part and parcel of our learning as nuclear fission, the speed of light, thermodynamics.'

The waiter had brought a tureen filled with water. He placed it on the table in front of Shining.

'Thank you,' the old man said, 'most kind.' He turned his direction back to the rest of the table. 'In many ways magic and physics are similar. It's all about matter and energy. It has rules. It has structure. It's about cause and effect. Look at the nuclear bomb, something that would have been considered magic two hundred years ago but is really just about the combination of certain types of matter. A potion if you will, with a terrible, devastating effect.' He patted his pockets as if searching for something.

Toby smiled, knowing full well that Shining knew exactly

where he had put whatever he was hunting for, however spontaneous and casual he was trying to be.

'And, much like dealing with radioactive material leaves traces, so too does dealing with magic,' he went on. 'As was proven by a man called Enrique Formosa, a Spanish alchemist who was bending science long before Fermi or Einstein were even born.' He removed a couple of small bottles from his jacket pockets. In one there was a violently pink coloured liquid, in the other a chalky powder.

'Formosa classed these traces as "the devil's fingerprints". There's nothing quite so dramatic as an ancient Spaniard. Ignoring his hyperbole, however, the principle is sound enough and is easily replicated today. Magic lingers, like radiation, on those who have come into contact with it.'

He added some of the pink liquid to the bowl of tap water, then some of the white powder. The bowl of water frothed and sputtered.

'This is the sort of thing I liked doing at school,' Spang enthused, 'like when you put magnesium in a Bunsen burner and it went off like a firework.'

'A process that would – and almost certainly did – appear magical if demonstrated to a person who had no knowledge of chemical reactions,' said Shining.

The bowl of water was now beginning to smoke, faint pink tendrils rising up from the bowl.

'I say,' said King, 'you're not going to make a terrible mess of the place, are you?'

'Not at all,' Shining reassured him. 'The water is changing state, as you can see.'

Slowly a column of smoke was rising from the bowl, much

to the appreciation of all except the ever-miserable Rowlands.

'That is very beautiful,' said Tae-young watching as the smoke rose in a steady pillar, climbing towards the ceiling.

'More than that,' said Shining, 'it's very useful. As you can help me prove.'

'Go on, glamorous assistant,' said April, 'go and help him out.'

Tae-young got to her feet and, rather nervously, stood next to Shining.

'Now,' said Shining, 'to the best of your knowledge, you have never been involved in anything magical have you?'

'No,' Tae-young said, 'not as far as I know.'

'Then stick your hand in the smoke.' She gave him a cautious look. 'It's quite safe,' he assured her.

She stuck her hand in the smoke and it flourished out in thin tendrils as the air from the movement of her hand hit it.

'Gently,' said Shining. 'It's easily displaced.'

Tae-young tried again, sliding her hand into the now reformed column. The smoke pulsed with yellow light around her hand like lightning passing through a storm cloud.

'A negative reaction,' said Shining. 'Whereas when I do it ...'

He stuck his hand in the cloud and it turned a deep green.

'Brilliant!' Spang shouted, clapping his hands like a precocious child at a pantomime.

'Parlour trick,' said Rowlands, who was getting more and more uncomfortable by the moment.

'No,' insisted Shining. 'Future science. Now ...' He turned to Tae-young and whispered in her ear and, after a moment, she nodded. 'Let's see about the rest of you,' said Shining and, together, he and Tae-young blew hard on the pillar of smoke, turning slightly as they did so, in order to aim the resultant wave of smoke across the whole table.

'My God!' said Spang, jumping up in a flash of bright yellow. 'It tingles.'

Indeed it did, Toby realised as it erupted green around him. He noticed a similar effect around Fratfield. *Welcome to the world of Section 37*, he thought. *One mad afternoon and a crashed car and you're marked for life.*

Rowlands jumped to his feet, trying to back away but the smoke ignited green as it touched him.

'Nonsense,' he said.

Then it hit Man-dae and a pulse of brightest emerald shot through it.

'Oh,' said Shining. 'I wasn't expecting that.'

Man-dae jumped to his feet, grabbing the large knife that sat on the cheeseboard. Fratfield was the first to respond, the others still distracted by the smoke. He had his hand inside his jacket, reaching for his gun but Man-dae beat him to it, stabbing the knife into the officer's arm and stealing his gun as his spasming fingers dropped it onto the table.

Man-dae put the gun to Fratfield's head, dragging the man to his feet, the knife still sticking out of his arm, a bloodstain widening on his jacket sleeve.

'Keep back!' Man-dae shouted, dragging Fratfield back towards the door.

Toby saw the look on Shining's face, a momentary calculation on whether he might be able to intervene as the Korean passed him. He made his decision, pulling Tae-young behind him and backing away.

Rowlands had got over his momentary panic, withdrawn his gun and was following Man-dae with it as he backed towards the door. Toby thought he was probably making the same calculation. Could he shoot Man-dae before Man-dae shot Fratfield? More to the point, did it matter? Was it more important to stop the Korean before he could escape than concern himself with Fratfield's safety? Toby was by no means sure he could rely on Rowlands to make the right decision and for a moment he tensed, ready for bullets to start flying.

Then Rowlands lifted his gun up and Man-dae left the room.

'He won't get far,' said Rowlands, 'not with my men outside.'

Then there was the sound of a gunshot and he, Toby and Shining were all running for the door.

Fratfield was in the hall, on his knees. 'Sorry,' he said, clutching his hands to the wound in his lower abdomen. 'Bastard shot me.'

'Get out of the way.' Toby turned to see Chun-hee had joined them. 'I have medical training,' the man said. 'You deal with the traitor.'

Rowlands didn't need telling. He was already running along the corridor towards the rear exit, walkie-talkie in his hand as he barked orders at his men outside.

Toby hesitated but Shining nodded at him. 'You can't help, go.'

Toby followed Rowlands, deciding, as the security officer had before him, that it was unlikely Man-dae would have doubled back towards the front door.

He caught up with him in the conservatory. 'Gun?' he asked.

'You haven't got one of your own?' asked Rowlands.

'I didn't arm myself for dinner, no,' Toby admitted.

'Then you're no use to me.' Rowlands turned to a couple of his men. Toby recognised them as the guards he had talked to earlier, Arnold and Bateman.

Toby pushed past them and ran out into the night. He paused for a moment to listen, hoping to catch the sound of the fleeing man but the three men behind him were making too much noise.

He took another guess. Man-dae wouldn't work his way around the house and aim for the front gate, he'd try and make a break for it over the rear wall. He'd aim for the woods, the one 'weak spot' that Fratfield had identified to them when they had arrived.

Toby ran across the lawns, skirting past the sculpture park and on towards the treeline.

He spiralled around, keeping low in case the Korean opened fire.

There was no sign of him.

He could see Rowlands and his agents spreading out towards him, hoping to cover all the angles but if Man-dae wanted to run, and surely that was his only viable option now, he would be over the wall and gone before any of them could stop him.

Toby ran into the trees, stopping for a moment to listen again. The undergrowth was heavy underfoot; surely if Man-dae was ahead of him he would hear the sounds of the man's running feet?

There was a faint rustle to his left and Toby moved carefully in that direction. If he ran, he would make so much noise himself that he was bound to drive the Korean ahead, like a beater scaring up birds at a country shoot. His only hope was to move quietly, keep his ears peeled and hope he could get the drop on him. After so many months of Shining drumming into him the pointlessness of guns in their line of work, he realised he was no longer prepared for the more traditional side of their job. Perhaps Rowlands had been right to mock him.

Eventually, he reached the far wall. There was no sign of Man-dae and all he could hear was the others running around the grounds.

He sank back against the wall and sighed. They'd brought their assassin out of hiding and now they'd lost him.

CHAPTER TWELVE: THE AGENT

a) Lufford Hall, Alcester, Warwickshire

Chun-hee had done his best to control the bleeding from Fratfield's wound, tearing makeshift bandages from the table-cloth in the dining room.

'The entry wound is low,' he explained. 'With luck it has avoided major organs.'

'With luck,' Fratfield replied, his voice weak.

'You're still breathing, you're still conscious,' said Chun-hee. 'That's as good as it gets right now.' He turned to Shining. 'We need to get him to a hospital right away.'

Keeping one hand applied to the wound, the Korean reached into his jacket pocket, pulled out a phone and threw it to the old man. 'Call an ambulance.'

'Not supposed to still have phone,' Fratfield whispered.

'You're lucky I do not always do what I am told,' Chun-hee replied.

Shining called the emergency services, explaining quickly and concisely. 'They're on their way,' he said, cutting off the call.

Chun-hee held his hand out for the phone. After a momentary pause, Shining gave it to him.

'That phone doesn't leave my side,' he explained, 'whatever your security people say.'

'Because if there's one thing security people don't like to do,' whispered Shining, 'it's listen to other security people.'

Chun-hee narrowed his eyes.

'KCIA?' Shining asked. 'Sorry, I'm old, you call it National Intelligence Service now, don't you?'

Chun-hee smiled but said nothing.

Shining nodded. 'I shall keep it quiet,' he promised, 'on the understanding that we can talk later.'

Behind them, the gathered diners were being kept at a slight distance by Clive King. The last thing the wounded man needed, he had decided, was an audience.

'I can't believe it,' said Tae-young, looking at April. 'All this time it was one of us?'

'Not one of us,' Jae-sung said, 'not if he did this. He must have allegiances with the North.'

Tae-young shook her head. 'He just seemed so ...'

'Innocuous?' asked April.

Tae-young nodded.

'They so often do.'

Toby returned from the gardens, shaking his head. 'It's no use,' he said. 'Rowlands and his men are still searching but if he wanted to escape he'll have done it by now. I ran to the far wall and back but there was no sign of him.'

Shining sighed. 'A final bit of table magic to end the evening. A man vanishes into thin air.'

'The building should be checked,' said Chun-hee.

Toby nodded. 'It will be. First I'm going to head down to the gate and see if they caught anything on the cameras.'

'I'll check my room,' said Shining, taking the key from his pocket. 'The candle.'

Toby squatted down next to Fratfield. 'Still alive?' he asked.

'Just.'

'Good job.' Toby patted him gently on the shoulder and made his way towards the front door.

b) Lufford Hall, Alcester, Warwickshire

Toby ran down the drive to the front gate. The front of the house also featured its fair share of security men poking around in the bushes but Toby was sure they wouldn't find anything. Given the skills Man-dae had already shown, it seemed unlikely that he was a man who would be so easily caught. They were lucky, he thought, that he had retaliated with nothing more dangerous than a knife and a gun. Time and medical care for Fratfield would show how lucky. Given the forces he had to call on, Toby was sure that the evening could have proven more destructive had they not caught him on the back foot.

'Hey,' he shouted, holding his hands in clear sight as he approached the guardhouse. He didn't want whoever had been left on duty to get any worrying ideas and mistake him for the enemy.

'Hey yourself,' came a voice from inside the small building. 'Come on in, you don't look Korean and psychotic.'

It was one of the private security guards. He looked to be in his mid-forties, with the crew-cut hair and build of a man who has known a gym in his time. Toby immediately wrote him off as one of those men who liked to get their knuckles grazed and went into security work hoping to get paid to do so. Then he berated himself for it; he had been the victim of such snap judgements in his time and he didn't know the guy one bit. He could be the best, most conscientious man working in the private sector for all Toby knew.

'Just come from the house,' he said, nodding as the guard shrugged. 'Yeah, fair point, where else would I have come from? Just wanting to know what you picked up on the security system.'

'As I just told your boss,' the guard replied, tapping his walkie-talkie, 'absolutely nothing. He seems to think I've been asleep on the job but I've been paying attention and there's been no movement at all.'

'Rowlands?' Toby asked.

'That's the one.'

'He's not my boss and he's a bit of an arse, sorry.'

'No problem. Bloody government jobs, you never know who's running what.'

'Tell me about it. So anyway, there's been nothing on the cameras ...?'

'And nothing on the fence alarm. I don't know where your bloke's gone to. The camera feeds rotate on the monitors so I might have missed something watching live.'

Toby noted that the guard wasn't taking his eyes off the screens while talking to him. He could see several Box men making their way back towards the Hall.

'But I can control playback,' the guard continued, 'and run the footage back through the spare monitor, bottom right.' He tapped the screen. 'Your man Rowlands thinks the bloke left by the rear.'

Toby watched over the man's shoulder as he ran the footage that covered the conservatory exit. It was clear for a moment and then he saw himself run out of the door.

'That's you,' the guard noted.

'It is.'

They watched Rowlands, Arnold and Bateman emerge next then the guard rewound the footage so Toby could see it all happen in reverse. The guard kept rewinding but the screen showed an empty door. 'Nothing, see?'

The guard shared his attention between the monitors and the control panel, bringing up the archive footage of the front door.

'As for this one,' he let it play and Toby watched an empty door. 'Absolutely nothing. So if your bloke did get out ...'

'He didn't use a door to do it. More likely ...'

'He's still in the house.'

'Good man,' Toby patted him on the shoulder. 'Don't listen to Rowlands, you're doing great.'

'I know,' the guard replied without a hint of arrogance. 'I earn my pay.'

c) Lufford Hall, Alcester, Warwickshire

As Toby made his way back up the drive, he heard the sound of an ambulance approaching, beating its way along the country road with all the sound and fury the emergency services could muster. Toby was relieved. He knew from experience that the odds of Fratfield surviving rested entirely on how quickly he received treatment. Given how soon the ambulance had arrived, his prospects were looking good. By the time Toby reached the front door, he could tell the ambulance was close behind him.

Shining was waiting for him. 'Nothing?' he asked.

'Nothing,' Toby agreed.

'Me neither. So he's still here.'

Rowlands appeared, having heard the sound of the ambulance, with Bateman in tow.

'We need to get our man in and gone as quickly as possible,' Rowlands said. 'If there's a better opportunity for our boy to sneak out of the grounds I don't know of one. Keep your eyes on the vehicle at all times.'

'There's nothing on the camera footage,' Toby told him. 'I checked.'

Rowlands nodded. 'So I'm told. Which means we still have him. So we can still catch him.' He stepped out of the way as the ambulance pulled up in front of them. 'I'll leave you to keep an eye here. I'm sure you can manage that.'

Two paramedics climbed down from the ambulance and fetched a stretcher from the rear of the vehicle. Shining led them inside.

April joined Toby at the front door.

'You think he'll be all right?' Toby asked her.

'From what Chun-hee tells me, he has every chance,' she replied. 'The sooner they can get him into surgery the more likely it is that he'll pull through. He's lost a lot of blood but he's not gone into shock and it doesn't look like the bullet pierced anything vital.'

'How are the Koreans taking it?'

'A mixture of disbelief and righteous anger. South Korea is used to acts of violence against them from the North. I think Tae-young is ashamed, which is silly, but she was feeling guilty about the cost of life these talks had caused as it was, even more so now that one of their party is the culprit.'

'It doesn't matter where the assassin came from.'

'Of course it doesn't. Though I imagine our lot will be breathing a sigh of diplomatic relief. It's easier for our public image if the killer came from their side.'

'Politics,' Toby sighed.

'Of course. But come on, you're a big boy, you know how these things work. Perception is the real power. What we do? Doesn't matter. What we're seen to do is everything. That's precisely why I left active service and went into the more obscure dark arts of politics and diplomacy.'

'I can never get my head around your career,' Toby admitted. 'Nobody can have done half the things you claim to have done.'

'Can't they?' She smiled. 'Perception is everything.'

They stood back as Fratfield was carried past them. Toby raised his hand as the man went past, relieved to see Fratfield nod gently in return.

'He'll be OK,' said one of the paramedics. 'He's a lucky man, the shot couldn't have been more perfectly placed had he tried. Straight through, should be no major complications.'

'Good to hear,' Toby said.

They lifted Fratfield into the back and the ambulance drove away.

'Should we join the search?' Toby asked Shining, the old man having joined them again.

'I think we can leave that to the others,' Shining replied, 'our time would be better served chatting with Chun-hee.'

d) Lufford Hall, Alcester, Warwickshire

They gathered in the drawing room while the security officers continued to search the building.

Shining tapped Chun-hee on the shoulder. 'I think we should pool our resources,' he said.

The Korean looked at him for a moment and then nodded. 'Perhaps that is fair,' he agreed, 'off the record.'

'Oh, naturally.'

Chun-hee picked up a decanter of brandy and some glasses and they made their way to the library in order to find some privacy in which to drink it and talk about what they knew.

'We were aware that this conference was likely to draw unfavourable attention from our enemies in the North,' Chunhee began, sipping at his brandy. 'It was inevitable.

'We received intelligence of a meeting held between representatives of the North Korean government and a private contractor. It took place a month or so ago at Mount Baekdu, close to the Chinese border. We had limited information. All we knew was that someone was being paid a good deal of money to involve themselves in our business. When you hire privately, people hear ...'

'But you are a safe distance away from the incident should the contractor get caught,' said Toby. 'Plausible deniability.'

'Indeed. This has become standard practice of late. As the North attempts to convince the world of its honourable intentions, it turns more and more to others when acting outside its own borders. Perhaps pressure has been put on them by their allies in Russia and China – who wants to be embarrassed by the friend who keeps starting fights, eh?' Chun-hee shrugged. 'It is not important, it is simply the way things are at the moment.

'We attempted to infiltrate the meeting but our agent never reported in. We can only assume he was caught. Our only thread was the contractor. A man some circles refer to as the Magician.'

'An apt name,' said Toby.

'Perhaps,' Chun-hee admitted. 'These people call themselves all kinds of things. Names designed to intimidate or impress. I dedicated my time to tracking him down. He has done work for a handful of people over the years. He works for anyone who can afford his services. He is not as active as most in his line of work but he is expensive and the results are always impressive.'

'The powers he calls on are not to be used lightly,' said Shining. 'The more you rely on them, the more you risk falling prey to them yourself. I'm not surprised he's selective with his contracts.'

Chun-hee nodded. 'I will be honest. I am a rational man. I am not someone inclined to believe in the stories I hear about the Magician and his work. Like all of his kind, he gets work by building a reputation. His is that of an assassin who cannot be traced. He kills in ways that defy explanation. They are deaths that cannot be held accountable to another person.'

'Accidents,' said Toby.

'Just so. Impossible, unexplainable deaths. That makes him sought after. If nobody can even prove that your enemy was murdered, how can the finger of blame ever be pointed?' He took another sip of his drink. 'Perhaps he is as you say. A man who has knowledge of your ...' he reminded himself of Shining's words from earlier, '"future science".'

Shining smiled.

'All I know is that I have traced his movements as far as I

can over the last few years. I have tried to find him. To unmask him.'

'And now you have?' asked Toby.

Chun-hee thought about that for a moment. 'Perhaps.' He shrugged. 'I suppose that is what we must assume.'

'But you're not convinced?' asked Shining.

'The greatest problem in our line of work,' said Chun-hee, 'is that so much of it is about assumption. We pick up tiny clues. We follow the finest threads trying to get at the truth. Along the way we piece those details together. We guess. The best, most logical, guesses but guesses nonetheless. We try and flesh out the invisible.'

Chun-hee paused again. Toby thought he was probably trying to decide how much he should say.

'I had made my guesses,' he continued. 'I thought I was close to the Magician. I thought I knew who he was. And now ...'

'It wasn't who you thought?' asked Toby.

'No. I had been following a man's trail. A ...' He scratched at his face, becoming more and more reluctant to talk. 'It is not fair to say. Because now the evidence goes against me. But I thought he was one of your men. I had traced his route around the world and found that he could often be placed near confirmed sightings of the Magician. This was too much of a coincidence, I had decided, these men are too often in the same place at the same time. But now ... now I know that I cannot have been right. I cannot. And yet, this young man? This wealthy little fool? He is the man who has terrified client and victim alike for the last few years? I find it hard to accept.'

He drained his drink and topped it back up.

'You think we may have been misled?' asked Shining.

'I do not see how,' Chun-hee admitted. 'Kim Man-dae has broken cover. Sometimes it is difficult to admit you have been wrong. And yet now I feel I must. The Magician is not who I thought it was, and I have been made to look a fool.

'I was here to keep an eye on the delegates, to protect them from harm. I have been looking in the wrong direction and it is only good fortune that the killer has been unmasked. We must hope that, exposed as he now is, hunting him down and putting an end to this is within our grasp.'

'Who did you think it was?' asked Toby, looking towards Shining. 'Now you know you were wrong surely there's no harm in saying?'

'There is every harm. I do not intend to allow a shadow to fall over a man who is clearly innocent. There is no chance it is the man I believed. That is now clear to me. I have been poor in my work. I shall not continue to be so.' He got to his feet, abandoning his drink. 'Now I must try and make up for it. The traitor Kim must still be in the building somewhere. We should not be sat here talking, we should be helping the others find him.'

'Absolutely,' Shining agreed. 'You go ahead, we'll see you shortly.'

The Korean left and Shining and Toby regarded what was left of their drinks.

'I wish he would tell us,' said Toby. 'You saw what happened when the smoke touched Rowlands. It went green. He's not the innocent he appears.'

'Perhaps not,' Shining agreed.

'Why would it have turned green if he wasn't hiding something?'

'The experiment proved nothing except for the fact that he's had some exposure to magic. If Man-dae hadn't been such an impetuous little idiot, he could have easily brazened it out. Why run?'

'Because he thought we'd exposed him.'

'Chun-hee is right to be suspicious. Are we really supposed to believe that the Magician, a man who has earned a reputation as a terrifying assassin, is spooked by a parlour trick?' Shining sighed and slammed his glass on the table next to him. 'It doesn't fit. It's nonsense and, deep down, if he could just get beyond his overinflated sense of damaged honour, Chun-hee knows it.'

'So we need to keep working on him?'

'We need to keep working on everything, yes.'

e) Lufford Hall, Alcester, Warwickshire

The Hall was searched from top to bottom. It was gone midnight by the time that Mark Rowlands was forced to angrily admit, 'He's not bloody here.'

Revising security details to patrol the building and grounds throughout the night, he went outside to smoke a cigarette and swear at shadows.

Those who had remained gathered in the drawing room were forced to retire to their bedrooms, locking their doors and lying uncertainly in their beds, wondering over each creak they heard in the old building.

None were more uncertain than Ryu Chun-hee, who ignored his bed in favour of the armchair by his bedroom window. He stared out at the night and tried to reconcile his chaotic thoughts.

He was certain that his initial suspicions as to the identity of the Magician had been wrong. He was not so old and stuck in his ways that he couldn't admit failure. Still, he couldn't believe Man-dae was the assassin either. Which only left one alternative: a third, hitherto unknown possibility. But who?

He watched as one of Rowlands' security officers crossed the lawn outside his window, quartering the grounds, hunting for ghosts.

Eventually, he fell asleep, slumping in his chair.

When he woke it was still dark, his neck cricked from the uncomfortable position he had been sitting in. This was ridiculous, he decided, he should go to bed, get some proper sleep, then maybe, in the morning, once his head was clear, he might be able to piece things together.

He got to his feet, holding on to the back of the chair as pins and needles coursed through his legs.

Only then did he notice the shadow stood in front of his window.

Was this what had woken him? The awareness that he was no longer alone in his room? Once upon a time he had prided himself on his alertness. Nobody could get the jump on Ryu Chun-hee, he had said; even when sleeping, his senses were alert.

He thought about that as the shadow bore down on him, a hand clamped across his mouth and a sudden burning sensation in the back of his neck.

'No dark theatre for you, I'm afraid,' said a voice in his ear. 'Your medical report tells me you've been having a little heart trouble. The good news is: you won't be having it again.'

Chun-hee fought against his attacker, even as he realised the burning sensation for what it was, the dissipation of poison in his system from the point of a hypodermic syringe.

He struggled for another twenty seconds and then his fight was over.

f) Lufford Hall, Alcester, Warwickshire

Bateman walked out into the night and tried to let the cold wind blow the stuffiness from him. God, how he hated these diplomatic affairs. Just when it had looked like there was going to be an end to the pacing up and down and poking around in bushes, the little bastard had gone to ground and it was back to going over the place with a fine-tooth comb.

If you asked him – and of course nobody would – the Korean was in the wind. Why would he hang around? So the perimeter alarm hadn't been triggered, who cared? That just meant the man had known what he was doing. But no, it had been decided he must still be on the property so now he had to forgo a few hours' sleep in order to walk around in the bloody cold for a bit.

It was operations like this that made him wish he was back in the Middle East when it was still an interesting place to be.

His girlfriend disagreed but then she didn't really understand the way your attitudes changed after you'd been shot at a few times. Not that she'd known what he was up to, of course. She thought he'd been embassy staff, filing paperwork and arranging cultural exchanges. Still, she had fretted.

'I just never know if you're going to come back in one piece,' she had said to him one night when he had been home on a few days' leave. 'You hear stories of what it's like over there.'

'People exaggerate,' he'd assured her, and that was true.

He'd been known to do it himself when swapping stories in the barracks. 'I've never seen a single bullet fired.'

Which certainly wasn't true. He'd fired plenty himself.

Then he'd been sent back home and life had become dull. She couldn't have been happier. She kept talking about kids. He'd nod and smile as they looked at colour schemes for converting the spare bedroom into a nursery but inside he was rotting. Everything was just so safe. It felt oppressive.

He knew he wasn't alone in the way his time under fire had affected him. He talked with a few of the old boys. They got together once in a while. Shared a few drinks, relived both the good times and the bad.

'Well,' one of his old lieutenants had said one night, 'I'm glad to be out of it. I sit out on my back porch and look up at the sky and I know that nobody's going to fill it with incendiaries. What's the point in fighting if you're not trying to find peace, eh?'

Bateman hadn't seen him again. Knew that they would never see eye to eye.

For him, the danger had become vital. It had been what made him feel alive. Now, when he really was doing paperwork and sitting in a claustrophobic office he felt himself withering away to nothing.

He kept fit. He'd taken up hang-gliding, surfing, climbing. He'd go away for the weekend with a couple of the old crew and they'd have a few beers and have a crack at one of the Cornish sea cliffs or, on one particularly brilliant trip, Dumbarton Rock. Hanging there, fingertips bleeding as he forced them into tiny handholds, he came close to the sense of being alive he had otherwise lost.

Then he went back home and looked at baby-wear catalogues.

Now this, knocking about a stately home on the off-chance someone wanted to have a pop.

He patted his pockets, hunting for the couple of cigarettes he'd cadged earlier. He was supposed to have quit – preparation for the theoretical bloody baby again – but he'd felt the urge tonight and decided to hell with it.

He still carried his old Zippo, smoker or not. It had been a companion ever since his training days and his pocket felt too empty without it.

He put one of the cigarettes in his mouth and squinted at the sudden burst of light from the zippo flame as he ignited it with his thumb.

The cigarette tasted strange. Like burning wood. It hadn't been that long, surely? He coughed and took it from his mouth.

It flared, a bright yellow flame working its way down its length.

'Cheap shit,' he said, sneering at the way it burned down like a fuse. Bloody typical. He'd only cadged a couple and there was something bloody wrong with one of them.

As the flame reached the filter there was a small pop and a flare of blue light, like a Chinese firework. The light left a coloured after-image in his eyes. It looked like a string of pictograms. It made him think of the Cyrillic alphabet. He blinked a few times and then it was gone.

Hoping he'd have better luck the second time, he put the other cigarette in his mouth and – cautiously – lit it. There was a pleasing crunch of combusting tobacco and he took a lungful. Job done.

He walked away from the building, cutting towards the woods at the rear.

The air seemed to grow colder as he moved away from the building and he briefly wondered if he should have gone back to his room for a coat. Then, angry at himself for what he perceived as proof of having gone soft, he turned up his suit jacket collar and walked quicker, getting a good lick on.

There was a distant rumble of what sounded like thunder and he turned to see if there was any sign of lightning.

The sky was clear, the stars bright.

Maybe someone was letting off fireworks somewhere.

He cut through the sculpture park, trying to make out the shapes in the half-light. He'd taken a look around the place the previous morning. All the usual modern crap, weird figures made out of bent wire and steel. Like a junkyard filled with the offcuts of a trainee welder. Now, as they became little more than silhouettes against the night sky, they somehow seemed more impressive. Strange, unfathomable shapes made out of darkness. One looked like a sailing ship, he thought, with a billowing, triangular sail. Another was a five-pointed star, its points tapering out into corkscrew shapes. Another was a see-saw, a long pole tipping to and fro on a circular fulcrum. He touched the end, snatching his finger away at the sharpness of its point. 'Have someone's eye out with that,' he muttered. 'They not heard of bloody Health and Safety?'

He touched it more carefully, smiling to see that it was perfectly balanced, one gentle push from his finger was enough to tip the pole towards the opposite side.

Well made, he admitted. Clever if you liked that kind of thing.

He kept going, heading towards the woods.

Halfway there, he heard the sound of thunder again. He looked around but, as before, saw no sign of cloud. Which made the rain, when it came, all the more unexpected.

He cupped the little that remained of his cigarette in his hand and made a run for the trees. It could hardly be more than a shower and he was likely to get wetter trying to get back to the house than taking cover there.

The rain seemed to follow him into the dense canopy of the trees. Their winter branches offering little in the way of protection.

'Ah,' he sighed, 'fuck it.'

It was only water, he'd just have to hope his suit jacket had dried by the morning, he'd only brought the one.

Christ but it was hammering it down!

He flung the stub of the cigarette away and hung close to the trunk of a large tree, getting some small cover from a fat branch directly over his head.

He looked back towards the house and thought he saw someone walking through the sculpture park. Just a shadow. One of the others caught out in the bloody rain, he thought.

There was the snap of dry twigs behind him and, instinctively, he spun around, reaching for the gun in his holster. You could take the man out of the hot zone but you'd never really change him, wasn't that the story of his life?

There was no sign of anyone. He listened hard but it was difficult over the sound of the rain hitting the carpet of dead leaves all around him.

Was it worth investigating? Probably just a fox or badger.

He turned back towards the Hall and gave a short cry at the sight of the woman stood only a couple of feet away. The embarrassment of this coursed through him. The idea of her sneaking up on him was one thing, crying out like a girl as a result was beyond mortifying.

'All right love?' he asked. 'Not a good night to be out, eh?'

The moon reflected off the white dress she was wearing and she looked soaked to the skin. He should probably offer her his jacket, he thought, then decided it was so sodden it was hardly likely to help.

He tried to place who she might be. It didn't help that he couldn't see her face, her black hair covering it like a hood.

'You one of the kitchen lot?' he asked, walking up to her. 'Should be tucked up, yeah? Don't you know there's a buzz on? Shouldn't be wandering around out here, could get yourself shot at.'

She didn't speak. She didn't move.

As he drew close, the stink of the rotten leaves around them seemed to multiply. Either that or he was catching a whiff of some bit of wildlife that had died out here.

'Speak up, girl,' he said. 'It's not a good idea creeping up on people tonight.'

She inclined her head slightly but he still couldn't see her face. It was pissing him off as much as the rain. Did these civilians not know a bloody thing?

'Let's have a look at you,' he said, reaching out to pull the hair away from her face.

Bateman had thought it was impossible to put a scare on him. Sometimes a man sees so much that the part of him that feels fear just falls away like a vestigial limb. What he revealed, pulling the clammy hair to one side, proved him wrong.

He ran, purely on instinct, not fully processing the face – or, more accurately, lack of one – he had seen, just leaping into fight or flight mode.

The rain continued to pelt down as he ran out into the open. His feet slid out from underneath him and he spun on the wet grass as he heard a deafening crack. Not thunder this time, he knew, this was closer and sharper. He kept trying to get to his feet but the rain-soaked grass fought back, and he slid like he was oiled.

Instead of fighting it, he rolled, sliding across the ground, only just aware of the crashing sound from behind him where one of the trees on the edge of the woods had somehow come down, landing in the spot where he had fallen. It had missed him by inches.

He finally got a grip on the wet ground and got to his feet, running more carefully this time. He thought about firing his gun, just to get a bit of help out here but then it occurred to him that he wouldn't have the first idea how to express what it was he was running from.

He turned then, running backwards as his rational mind rose up and began to question. The woman was no longer there. Had she ever been? Yes. Of course she had. He wasn't the sort of man who imagined things. She must have vanished into the woods, though how she could have walked anywhere when she didn't have any ...

He turned back towards the house, just in time to spot the stone bench and table he had been about to run into. Stupid! Look where you're bloody going, man!

He collided with the bench and fell to the ground, his body hitting one of the lose plinths that held up the solid stone top of the table. It wobbled above him and he shifted away, just managing to avoid its heavy edge landing on his head. It rolled along the grass for a few feet, like a wheel come loose from a prehistoric car and he got to his feet, not quite able to believe how narrowly he had managed to avoid being brained by the thing as it fell. He needed to stop this useless panicking, that was twice now that he had nearly blundered into something that could have killed him.

He looked around, there was still no sign of the girl. He shouldn't be running. He needed to walk back to the Hall, check in with the guardhouse and see if anything had triggered the alarms and then play it from there.

He entered the sculpture park, trying to rub away some of the rainwater from his face. The path through the exhibits was lined with stone edging. As he brushed water from his head he stepped awkwardly, his left foot tripping on a loose stone in the path border. He cried out as he fell to the ground. What was wrong with him? He was a bloody disaster area! Could he not keep his feet for two bloody minutes?

He pushed himself up and found himself face-to-face with the girl again. She gave a dry cough and he tasted the stench of rot in his mouth.

Panicking again, he turned and ran. He pulled his gun from his holster, turned and shot a couple of rounds at the girl. There was no discernible effect bar the fact that, for those few seconds he was running blind. When he turned around it was to suddenly register the see-saw sculpture in front of him. The sharpened end of the pole punched right into his belly, the other end of the pole dipping down towards the ground, hitting it and then bouncing back to embed itself into his gut another half-inch or so.

'Ah fuck,' he coughed, 'fucking thing.'

He grabbed at the pole, hoping he hadn't done himself mortal damage. He still had his gun in his hand and, thinking only of the bit of ironwork sticking out of himself, he dropped it to free up both hands.

The gun hit the stone edge of the path. All modern pistols are designed to weather such treatment. They contain drop-safety features, firing pin blocks that are there to prevent accidental discharge. Even if such a thing should fail, the impact strength needed to cause a misfire is considerable. Add to that the odds against the gun being pointed at anything when dropped. Yes, Bateman would have had to be exceptionally unlucky for it to be a problem.

The gun fired, the 9mm bullet entering Bateman's mouth and exiting from the top of his head. He slumped forward, his weight against the pole slowly working it deeper into the stomach wound.

When he was found, two minutes later, by a couple of men who had been alerted by the shots, he presented quite the work of art.

CHAPTER THIRTEEN: THE FAIR

a) Lufford Hall, Alcester, Warwickshire

Toby was shaken awake by Shining. The old man was standing in the faint light of the corridor.

'Room service?' Toby asked.

'Morning news,' Shining replied. 'One of Rowlands' men was found dead in the sculpture park last night. He was soaked to the skin, impaled on a piece of modern art, having accidentally shot himself in the face.'

Toby groaned and rubbed at his tired face.

'Personally,' Shining continued, 'I'm inclined to suggest death by supernatural means. Naturally, after last night's excitement the usual cynicism seems surprisingly absent. In further news: the perimeter alarm was triggered by someone leaving the property.'

'Which way?'

'Through the woods, naturally, so the cameras show us nothing. All we have to go on is a blip on a computer display.'

'And your candle?'

'Not triggered.'

'Which means?'

'Well, that *was* open to cynicism from the others I'm afraid, purely because they don't want to believe the possible implications. They think that our assassin made a break for it in the night, killing the officer en route. They think that means we're safe again. At least for now.'

'Whereas you think that's just what someone wants us to believe?'

'Precisely.'

Toby swung his legs out of the bed. 'What time is it?'

'Half past eight. I let you sleep in.'

'You're very kind.'

'No I'm not. Today is going to be hard and I need you sharp. I need to pop out, do a little research, but I'll be back in an hour and a half or so. Until then, Section 37 is all yours. Maybe it would be worth your hunting down Chun-hee and seeing if you could get him to be a bit more forward.'

'Where are you going?'

'Alcester. It's only twenty minutes' walk over the fields. I need to think.'

'Good luck.'

b) Alcester, Warwickshire

The walk to Alcester gave Shining exactly the space he needed.

As much as he enjoyed the fact that Section 37 was no longer the one-man band it had been for so many years, the habit of spending all that time alone was hard to break. Over the decades, he had become used to a singular life. Now, effectively trapped in a building crammed full of people, all pulling in different directions, he found himself suffocated. As much as he had tried to preach the positive to Toby, the fact that he was relegated to a dark basement room didn't help either. He just wasn't used to being so confined, so restricted.

Being out in the open, buffeted with the winter air, he could feel the oppressive atmosphere of the last twenty-four hours fall away. It was like rinsing off grime beneath an aggressive shower.

Soon he would stroll the quaint streets of what he was sure would be a lovely little market town, the sort of place that had become filled with charity shops, designer pottery outlets and pubs draped in so many hanging baskets they looked like they were growing mould. There would be black and white Tudor buildings and the kind of ancient church that Dennis Wheatley would have had his villains sacrifice virgins and livestock in. It would all be a perfect change of environment that would allow his head to chatter away, processing what it knew and then positing new ideas and plans. Perhaps there would even be an estate agents or three so that he could look in the window, as all British people must when in a strange town.

By the time he reached the outskirts of Alcester, his idyllic plans were already beginning to look fragile. The traffic was heavy and the pavements filled with people.

Instead of the quiet of a winter morning far away from the city's assault on the senses, he found the streets were filled with dance music, the whoop and holler of fairground rides and a constant undercurrent hum of countless electric generators.

As he walked along the high street, he watched as a giant metal octopus, covered in pulsing light bulbs and filled with screaming children, spun its way between Georgian buildings.

A ghost train screamed and cackled through crunchy speakers. Dodgems fizzed and crashed in front of the old church. The air dripped with fried onions and burned sugar.

'Well,' he said, to nobody in particular, 'the quaint English countryside has changed since I last clapped eyes on it.'

'Mop Fair, innit?' said a woman trying to force a pushchair through the crowd. 'Does your head in.'

'Mop fair?' he asked, but she'd already gone, fighting her way past the crowds, one bruised ankle at a time.

He looked around, trying to get his bearings. This was hard to do when someone had seen fit to dump a fairground into the mix.

A man was struggling to herd a group of children whose faces were buried in clouds of pink candyfloss.

'Hope your bloody teeth rot,' he muttered as he tried to keep them moving.

'Excuse me?' Shining asked him. 'Could you point me towards the Swan Hotel?'

The man sighed as if this really was the last straw, then gestured towards the end of the street. 'End of the road there. Have a large one for me, would you? I bloody need it.'

'Bit early for me,' Shining admitted and began to negotiate his way through the crowds and noise.

By the time he was stood outside the hotel he had 'accidentally' found himself in complete ownership of a couple of toffee apples and was trying to get into one of them without showering the pavement with tooth fragments. This was proving beyond him. He was sure that good times lay ahead between him and the treat but in these initial, awkward stages, it was rather like trying to bite a chunk out of a bedpost. He decided to give up for now, promising himself that he would sneak up on it later; hopefully, if he could just catch the damn thing unawares, he might be able to grab an edible chunk. If all else failed, he was fairly sure there was a toolkit in the boot of the car.

The Swan Hotel was a large pub with a couple of rooms to let. Shining walked up to the bar where a jaded-looking woman was trying to make it look like she was wiping the beer pumps. In reality, Shining suspected she was holding on to them to stop the pub spinning too quickly.

'Busy night?' he asked.

She looked at him as if he was the first human being she had ever seen. 'Mad,' she admitted. 'I don't know why we do it. Pinot Grigio and Waltzers just don't mix.'

'Yes, I noticed someone appears to have opened a carnival in your high street.'

'Mop Fair,' she said. 'Happens every year.'

'And the mops are?'

'No idea. Never understood it. Years ago it used to be a market for hiring staff. Now we celebrate that glorious tradition with rollercoasters and burgers in polystyrene boxes. World's gone mad. I've got a ghost train outside my bedroom window. A tatty skeleton stares at me while I undress.'

'Charming. I'd draw the curtains if I were you.'

'Doesn't help, the damn thing's lit up like it's on fire. I'm hoping it'll get quiet this afternoon so I can have a kip on the pool table.'

'Here's hoping.'

'Get you a drink?'

'I'll have a tomato juice, if I may. I'm actually here to see one of your guests.'

'No problem, the rooms are up the stairs that way,' she gestured towards a pair of double doors in the far corner. 'Just don't let the landlord see you, he gets funny about visitors.'

'Oh, it's nothing like that,' he assured her.

'Nah,' she chuckled, handing him his drink, 'that's not what I meant. He charges per person, that's all, always thinks people are going to ram themselves in his poky little rooms without paying.'

'Oh no, I won't be staying long.'

'Don't blame you. If I hear that ghost train scream once more, I'll give them some real dead people to worry about. There's two rooms and only one's occupied, you can't go wrong.'

He paid her for the tomato juice and headed upstairs.

The two rooms faced one another across a wide landing. The door to one was wide open so he knocked on the door of the other. After a moment it opened.

'Is you,' said Tamar, stepping aside to let him in. 'I am thinking you send me to wrong town.'

'Don't tell me you haven't been playing on the hoopla, I won't believe you.'

'Hoopla? What is a hoopla?'

'A peculiarly English method of distributing cuddly toys, don't worry about it. Here,' he reached into his pocket, 'I bought you a toffee apple.'

She unwrapped it and sniffed at it. 'It is like a club made of sugar.'

'Precisely, you lucky thing. Have you brought the netbook?'

She nodded to where it sat on the bedside table. 'Is fully charged.'

'That's splendid. Sorry to be rude but bear with me while I check my emails, would you?'

Tamar shrugged. 'I will eat my sugar club for breakfast.'

'Good-o.' He logged on to his mail client and scanned through the inbox. There was one from Cassandra:

Hello Charles!

Who isn't even called Charles but never mind. I think your name is probably Algernon, I don't know why, you just look like one. An Algernon that is. Don't tell me if I'm right or not because I won't even believe you, whatever you say, BECAUSE YOU ARE FULL OF LIES!! But in a really nice way :-)

So, anyway, to business! How is Timothy Who Is Not Timothy? (I think he is called Gary because I once knew a Gary that looked just like him). Has he been talking about me all the time? I bet he has. Poor love. I feel bad for him but he'll get over me. Until then ...

(There followed a gif of a sad-looking kitten.)

August, distracted by a sudden crashing sound, looked up to see Tamar was beating the toffee apple with the butt of her pistol.

'Do try not to blow your head off for the sake of sweets, old thing,' he said. 'I know a man who had a rotten accident with an accidental discharge last night.'

She held up the gun to show she had removed the cartridge. There was a pleasing crack followed by a soft squishing sound. 'I've won your challenge of rock fruits,' she said with a smile, popping a piece of splintered red toffee into her mouth.

'Good for you,' he said, returning his attention to the email.

'I'll let you have a pop at mine in a minute, it was quite beyond me.'

In other news!

The email continued.

Guess who's the cleverest girl you know? No! Not her! Me! I've found a likely candidate for your curse. It sounds like The Rain-Soaked Bride (cool name for a band, when I finally get this guitar to behave I may use it). It's Japanese, like all the really fruity stuff. I've scanned the relevant pages from a book I found containing the legend (it's an English translation, don't worry!). It's attached. Go and read it now, I'll still be here when you get back. :P

August opened the attachment, a slightly yellow scan of old pages, and began to read:

Many years ago in the Shinano Province there lived Kōsaka, a girl of great beauty. Her skin was like snow and her hair like woven night with the light from the stars put aside for her eyes. It shone whenever she smiled and all who saw her fell in love.

She was the daughter of a proud but poor family and she spent her days working in the fields, gathering food for the village.

While she worked she sang and those who heard the sound said it was the most beautiful thing they had ever heard.

For all those who loved her, there was only one she loved. Takeda, the son of a neighbouring farmer. They had played since they were children and the older women of the village had known then what the future would hold. Sometimes love is always there.

Kōsaka and Takeda were to get married at the end of the season, once the crops were gathered and the grain stored. They would let their love grow over the winter to keep them warm. In the spring they hoped to make fruit of their own.

The elders of the village warned them that it would be better to marry in spring. Autumn was when the rains came and the plains flooded. The dry riverbeds filled and the waters raged. Autumn was no time for celebration. But Kōsaka and Takeda knew what they wanted: the rain could not wash away their ambitions.

Then, one day, a week before the wedding, a nobleman from Ueda rode through the village on his way to Komoro. He was travelling with only a handful of his retinue, but the villagers recognised the flags that hung about his caravan and bowed their heads as he passed. All except Kōsaka who was singing by the well, the sound of her song and the rushing of the water meant she did not hear the horses.

The nobleman heard her voice and was not angry at her lack of respect. Like all who had seen Kōsaka he found his heart grow hot, like the sun, as he watched her pump the water. He fell in love.

The nobleman was used to having the things he wanted in life. When he saw a painting he liked, he bought it and hung it on his wall. When he heard a Koto player who made him smile, he hired that musician and made them part of his ever-growing ensemble of musicians and entertainers. The nobleman had never once heard the word 'no'. It was a word that meant nothing to him. It was a word he gave but never received.

That is why, when he told Kōsaka he wished to marry her, he could not understand her reply.

'But I am rich,' he told her. 'I live in the best castles, I eat the finest foods, my life is a paradise and I wish to share it with you. You are lucky to be asked.'

'I thank you,'Kōsaka told him, 'but I am already to be married.'

'But you are not yet so,' the nobleman explained, 'and it is impossible that he could give you a life such as I offer.'

'Nonetheless,' she insisted, 'it is him I wish to marry.'

The nobleman did not understand. He could not see why anyone would choose another over him. Did he not have the best of everything? Was he not an attractive man?

He asked her again. And again. And every time the answer was the same.

In time he grew angry. 'If this other man was not here,' he told Kōsaka, 'you would marry me then, I think.'

'Maybe so,' she replied, 'but he is so I will not.'

Kōsaka was a beautiful soul, she did not understand the effect her words had on the nobleman. She did not know the things that greed and jealousy will make a man do.

He left the village only to return three days later, bringing with him his finest soldiers.

'Now,' he told her, 'I have the strength to make you do as you are told.'

He set his soldiers loose on the village and they bloodied their swords and set fires to burn in the homes of the people who lived there.

Finally, they came for Takeda, who fought to protect both the woman he loved and the people of his village. But eventually he could fight no more.

'And this is the man you wish to marry?' asked the nobleman. 'A man whom I have beaten so easily?'

'I do not marry him because he is a warrior,' explained Kōsaka. 'I marry him because we are in love.'

The nobleman was angered further and ordered Takeda to be

staked down in the hard earth of the dry riverbed.

'He is lucky to have your love,' the nobleman said, 'but let's see how lucky he really is.'

The nobleman made plans for their marriage. A lavish affair that would take place right there in the ruins of Kōsaka's village. He invited his wealthy and powerful friends from all over the province. He promised a celebration the like of which had never been seen before. He ordered dancers, musicians, performing animals and actors. The entertainment would last for days.

And if the rains came, as they always did at this time of the year? Then they would be safe within their tents, though the same would not be said of Takeda in the dry riverbed. 'Perhaps he will be lucky,' the nobleman said to Kōsaka. 'Perhaps.'

The rains did not come the next day, though many guests did. The tents were erected, the music began to play and crowds of people gathered on the plains, beneath the creeping dark clouds of autumn.

The rains did not come the day after that. Though a troupe of actors did, who performed a new play written in honour of the nobleman and his wife-to-be. It was a story of young love, of beautiful poetry and happy endings. It was, as all plays must be, a pretty little lie.

In the dry riverbed, Takeda pulled at the ropes that bound his wrists. But his body was weak from the cold and the lack of food or drink. The rope cut into his wrists but the heavy wooden spikes that the soldiers had hammered into the dry earth held fast. Takeda could not escape.

On the third day, the rains came. They fell from a sky that had promised for so long, their water hitting the dry earth and rolling off it. The earth is like a man who is dying of thirst. It gets so dry it cannot drink easily.

The riverbed began to fill and Takeda shouted curses at the

nobleman and his soldiers as the water rushed over him, getting higher and higher.

Kōsaka's tears were almost as heavy as the rain itself as she heard the cries of the man she loved coming up from the dry riverbed. She fought to go to his aid but the nobleman's soldiers held her tightly.

'But the young man should certainly see the happy occasion,' the nobleman told her.

He ordered everyone to stand at the side of the dry riverbed, with himself and Kōsaka close to the bank so that they could see Takeda as the waters rose around him.

Kōsaka promised the nobleman that he would die for what he had done to Takeda and her. She swore it as an oath.

The nobleman simply laughed. 'He was not lucky, my dear,' he told her, 'that is all. Unlike you. For now the rest of your life will be a dream of pleasure. You will have everything you ever wanted.'

And, as the waters rose over Takeda and he breathed his last, Kōsaka sobbed and her tears were such that even the rains could not match them.

They washed away the tents and the dancers. They drowned the actors and the performing animals. They swept every single guest across the plains, lost in a sea of saltwater, an ocean of Kōsaka's misery.

The nobleman tried to fight for his life, desperately swimming up through the tears but Kōsaka would not let him.

'A husband and wife should stay together for ever,' she told him. 'You married a woman of faith and honour. Aren't you lucky?'

And she clung around his neck, dragging him down and down into the water where, finally, he drowned.

'Charming,' said August, closing the attachment and returning to the original email.

Brilliant, eh? A load of old nonsense of course. I don't think they even had marriage ceremonies back then. They had a much simpler system, if you shagged a woman three times the family considered you her husband and that was that! (I've had SO many husbands!).

Still, like all these things I bet there's a little bit of truth in it. Whatever actually happened to Kosaka (where do you find squibbly 'o's to put in emails? Never mind ...) she seems to be the curse spirit you're after.

She's like a patron saint of ill-fortune. A bad-luck spirit. Like I said to Tim/Gary, she's the very epitome of curse spirits, because she does nothing *herself* but if you see her then your luck changes. It becomes the sort of miserable luck that will likely be the death of you. Brilliant eh?

As far as I can tell, she conforms to the standard rules: once the curse has been passed to its victim, the only escape is to pass it back. There's no time limit (don't imagine she needs one, you ain't going to last long once she's on your back) and the person who casts the curse has to be present.

So, no help whatsoever really but at least you got a cool creepy story out of it.

Try not to die of anything, I'm doing a pub theatre run of my Phase IV adaptation after Christmas. It's going to be full length this time and I plan on training up REAL ANTS!!! So you and Tim/Gary need to be there or I'll put a curse on you myself.

Lots of love!

XXCXX

Shining closed the email and thought for a moment. Cassandra was right, she hadn't told him anything that helped. It wasn't the weapon that mattered, it was the person holding it.

'You have finished?' Tamar asked him.

Shining closed the netbook and nodded. 'Things are getting more and more dangerous,' he said.

'That usually means they are nearly over.'

'Yes,' Shining agreed. 'It does.'

'Do you need me?'

'For now I'd rather you stayed here. You're my little wild card. My backup. But be ready, I have a feeling that today ...' His voice faded away. 'Backup,' he repeated.

'You are not making sense.'

'Because it doesn't,' he closed his eyes, thinking hard, 'or does it? It would explain ...' He opened his eyes again. 'Did you bring that spare phone?'

She dug inside a small holdall and held it out to him. 'It is program with my number, nothing else.'

'Good, and I will only call you. No texts or emails. If anything like that comes through ...'

'Don't open it.'

'Exactly. I need to get back.' He got to his feet.

'Before you go ...' She looked awkward. 'Is Toby ...?'

'He's fine.' Shining smiled.

The words 'for now' popped into his head but he chose not to say them out loud.

CHAPTER FOURTEEN: THE MAGICIAN

a) Lufford Hall, Alcester, Warwickshire

Toby got dressed and grabbed some breakfast. He was rather hoping he would bump into Chun-hee in the dining room, where he could make their conversation seem casual. He knew the Korean was keen on keeping his true occupation secret, and the last thing Toby wanted to do was make that difficult for him by making a big deal of seeking him out. Working his way through the heated salvers of food, he noticed April enter and decided he could at least get some idea of what the morning's schedule would be.

'Morning,' he said as she scowled at him.

'The one thing I really don't miss about working for a living,' she told him, 'is the mornings. When you get to my age you don't use alarm clocks any more, you simply wait for brittle life to resurrect you for one more day. They're disgusting.'

'Alarm clocks?'

'Devices designed to interfere with a natural function. They are the contraceptives of sleep.'

'Right. Bacon?'

'And with that, the morning just seems that little bit better.' She grabbed a plate and held it out to him so he could fill it. 'Where's my brother?'

'Walking to Alcester.'

'Walking? At this time of day? Why didn't he drive, the idiot?'

'Our car was blown up, remember?'

'So it was. Silly bugger would probably have done it anyway, he doesn't realise your legs are just things to look at while you're sitting down.'

'Have you seen Chun-hee this morning?'

'No, but we're supposed to start at nine-thirty so he'll be around somewhere. Why?'

'Secret,' Toby whispered with a grin.

'Oh, shut up, silly boy, what are you talking about?' He whispered in her ear. 'Oh!' she said, grabbing a sausage with her fingers and biting the end off it. 'Well, that makes things a little clearer.'

'But Shining promised he wouldn't blow his cover.'

'Of course he did, he's nice like that. Well, hang around, he'll appear soon.'

But he didn't. Tae-Young, Jae-sung, Clive King and Lemuel Spang had all gathered in the conference room and Chun-hee's absence was being noted as the clock clicked past the half hour.

'I'll go and see if I can find him,' suggested Toby, happy for the excuse but only too aware that the man's absence, given recent circumstances, did not bode well.

He walked up to the West Wing, having got directions to the man's room and knocked on his door. Silence.

Toby sighed. He had little doubt that he would find nothing good on the other side of the door.

He tried the handle. Locked. Which, annoyingly meant that he either had to find someone who had access to the key, probably Rowlands, or break it down. He knew which route would be the most professional.

He lined himself up with the door and kicked just below the handle. There was a crunch of wood around the lock. He kicked once more and the door opened.

Toby went inside, aware that his time was short as the noise would probably bring others running. He squatted and touched the carpet. It was dry. Chun-hee was sat in an armchair by the window, his eyes staring out into the room, unblinking, dead.

Toby checked for a pulse, through thoroughness rather than expectation. There was none.

Looking around the room, there was no sign of a struggle. Indeed, there was no sign of foul play whatsoever. This didn't mean much, Toby knew, though he was all but sure it would be used to argue that Chun-hee had not been another victim of the assassin.

'What's going on?' Rowlands had appeared in the doorway.

'He didn't appear for the morning session so I agreed to come and find him,' Toby explained. 'I just did.'

Rowlands looked at the door. 'Did you really need to kick the door in?'

'I was worried for his safety.'

Rowlands mirrored Toby's actions, checking for a pulse. 'Too late for all that,' he said. 'He's been dead some time, I'd say. Heart attack, probably.'

'A bold diagnosis considering all you've done is check his pulse.'

Rowlands stared at him. 'Unlike you, I believe in preparation. I familiarised myself with his file, as I did with everyone else who was attending.'

I bet it didn't tell you everything about him, Toby thought.

'He had a history of heart complications,' Rowlands continued, gesturing towards the door. 'Perhaps you would like to call an ambulance? If you're wanting to be of use?'

'Shouldn't we check the room?'

'Obviously. But as there's two of us, don't you think someone should call an ambulance as well?'

'Fine.' Toby didn't really see what else he could do. He could hardly insist on being there while Rowlands checked the room – if, indeed, he intended doing any such thing – not, at least, without making his suspicions embarrassingly clear.

He descended to the entrance hall, put through an emergency call on the landline and then returned upstairs as quickly as he could.

Rowlands was pulling the broken door closed.

'Finished already?' Toby asked.

'What do you expect?' Rowlands replied. 'I gave the place a quick once-over but there's no evidence of foul play. I imagine last night just got the better of him.'

'So much so he had a heart attack later while sitting quietly in his room?'

'Look,' Rowlands squared up to him, 'what is your problem? Ever since you got here, you and the old man have been obstructive and threatening.'

Toby tried to think of a way of saying 'you started it' that didn't make him sound like a petulant schoolboy. 'We would have been only too happy to work alongside you,' he said, 'but you made it clear from the moment we arrived that we were unwanted.'

'You were unnecessary. And forced on me at the last minute, I barely had time to read up on you before you walked in the door! Running an operation like this takes preparation, it's not how I like things done.'

'No, the way you like things done is—' A thought suddenly popped into Toby's head. 'You didn't know we were coming.'

'If I had, I'd certainly have complained in no uncertain terms.'

'And that's the main problem you have with us?'

'I dislike your section and everything it stands for. It's a waste of resources, a dumping ground for the ineffectual.'

Toby nodded. 'We'll see about that.'

He turned and walked away. Arguing further with Rowlands was hardly helpful. Besides, he needed to think. He needed to try and get things straight in his head.

b) Lufford Hall, Alcester, Warwickshire

As Shining walked up the driveway, he found Toby sat by the decorative fountain, looking up at the Hall. It was a calm and pleasant place to sit, though the helicopter still embedding itself in the lawn was unlikely to be an addition the garden designers would have approved of. Perhaps, if the staff had still been in residence, they could have strung hanging baskets from the rotor blades.

'They kick you out?' the older man asked.

'Rowlands would love to, given half a chance. But no, I was doing the same as you. Thinking.'

Shining sat down next to him. 'Yes, I've been doing plenty of that. What have you come up with?'

'Rowlands isn't the assassin.'

'No,' Shining agreed, 'I don't think he is. What's made you come to that conclusion?'

'He didn't know we were coming. He could be lying, I know that, it's hardly conclusive but ... I believe him. He was surprised to see us.'

'And that rules him out because?'

'Because of what I saw in the motorway services. The curse spirit. We were expected.'

'Yes, we were.'

'But the smoke turned green when it touched him.'

'Faintly, yes. But having been exposed to some form of magic makes him the culprit no more than we are. At some point, he has experienced something that was more our remit than his. Something, I would suggest, that helped foster this attitude he has of dismissing the subject entirely.'

'He caught a peek of something strange and it didn't sit well with him.'

'It rarely does. Having checked into his history there's a possible explanation from his time with the Serious Organised Crime Agency. He was beaten to within an inch of his life while working a human trafficking case.'

'Doesn't sound particularly magical.'

'An initial statement, taken from the paramedics who got him to hospital, says that Rowlands claimed his attackers were invisible.'

'Ah.'

'Indeed. I imagine he bit off more than he could chew. Then, once recovered, he decided a bit of self-editing was in order. His official report states that he was set upon by a gang of men. He claims they got the jump on him and that he was swiftly subdued.'

'OK, so maybe that explains the smoke. Not that it matters.'

'Not really, no. It could have been anything. As you and I know, the preternatural is not as rare as some would like to believe.'

'So, we ignore Rowlands. I presume we're also not seriously considering Man-dae?'

'Not really. He didn't know we were coming either.'

'Which leaves us ...?'

'With two people.' Shining smiled. 'And the only one who really fits is never going to be suspected by anyone other than us.'

'No.' Toby sighed. 'He's not. So what do we do now?'

'We go and get him.'

c) Lufford Hall, Alcester, Warwickshire

'Do you think we should get some backup?' Toby asked as they stopped off in his room to fetch his gun.

'I can't see the point in the inevitable argument,' said Shining, hoisting the small bag of tools they had collected from the groundskeeper's store onto his shoulder. 'We always knew this was likely to be the way things would play out. Nobody is going to believe us for one minute when we tell them what's been going on.'

'Nobody would have ever put it together,' Toby agreed, 'because the only way it all fits is to allow for possibilities that others wouldn't consider.'

'Precisely.'

'Story of our lives.'

They stepped out of Toby's room and moved past the clatter and chaos of the kitchens.

'Can I help you?' one of the waiting staff asked, having noticed them.

'Just taking a look in the cellar,' said Toby.

'Cellar?' the man asked. 'It's all locked. Your lot sealed it up when they first got here.'

'I know,' said Shining, 'which is precisely why we're taking a look at it.'

'I don't know how you'll get in, I'm afraid.'

'We'll manage,' Toby assured him as he and Shining continued away from the kitchens and along a gloomy corridor towards a further flight of stairs.

Toby removed the small torch he kept on his key ring and shone the light towards the foot of the stairs. There was a heavy-looking door, bolted and chained, a heavy padlock hanging from it. Shining put the bag of tools down, unzipped it and lifted out a bolt cutter.

'I can't believe Rowlands' men didn't check here already,' said Toby.

'Why would they? There was no way Man-dae could have had access. It was sealed up before he even arrived.'

Shining cut through the chain and, as quickly as he could, opened the door.

Toby moved past him, handing Shining the torch as he did so. Shining swept the torch beam around the room, keeping behind the jamb of the door in case the light made him a target. Toby, crouched low, moved inside, his gun held out. It was a jumble of dusty metal shelves, packing cases and furniture buried beneath protective sheeting.

The torch beam fell onto the face of Man-dae, and Toby aimed his gun on reflex. The Korean was staring, eyes wide open and it took Toby a second to realise he was dead. As the torch continued to pass through the darkness, it fell on another door on the far side of the room.

'You can come in,' he whispered to Shining. 'Unless our man enjoys sitting in the dark, I think he's next door.'

Shining joined Toby and the younger man switched off the torch for a moment. A thin sliver of light was visible beneath the other door.

Turning the torch back on, Shining made a quick examination of Man-dae. There was no pulse.

'Served his purpose,' whispered Toby.

Shining nodded. 'A puppet, his strings now cut. This man is powerful indeed. It beggars belief ... If he's this powerful, it's amazing any of us are still alive. Be careful.'

They made their way towards the other door.

Standing outside, Shining switched off the torch and took hold of the handle. Toby dropped to his haunches and aimed his gun.

Shining pushed open the door.

Bill Fratfield was sat in an ageing armchair eating an apple. As the door swung open, he swallowed in surprise, jumping forward in his chair. Then, when the penny dropped that there was little he could do, he fell back again and sighed.

'Well,' he said, 'that's annoying.'

'For you and me both,' Toby replied. 'You made me look a right idiot.'

Fratfield shrugged. 'Hardly. You caught me. Which is extremely surprising.'

'Your little piece of theatre with Man-dae was pretty watertight,' Shining admitted.

'If you were dealing with someone that wasn't familiar with the notion of a Doppelgänger Contract,' said Toby, 'then nobody would have figured a way past it.'

Fratfield offered Toby a begrudging smile. 'You're well informed.'

'I think we occasionally move in the same circles,' Toby admitted.

The 'higher presence' had mentioned the principle of the Doppelgänger Contract when it had taken over Tamar's body. A service it had offered to Toby, duplicating him so that he could be in two places at once. He wouldn't be in the least bit surprised if it had mentioned it intentionally. Had it seen this moment coming?

'When you work from the principle that there were two of you,' said Shining, 'you were really the only obvious suspect. Of the party here, so few knew we were even coming. Certainly only one of them was in a position to overhear Chun-hee admit he was working for the National Intelligence Service.'

'More than that,' Fratfield admitted. 'He even apologised for having suspected me in the first place! Shoving me onto the ambulance with an honourable bow!'

'He wouldn't give us your name but it was obvious he suspected an intelligence officer who had travelled extensively.'

'Which rules out Rowlands of course,' added Toby, 'being Box.'

'Bet you still tried to make him fit, though,' said Fratfield. 'You really don't like him very much.'

'No,' Toby admitted, 'though I like him a damn sight more than I like you.'

'Fair enough. You've got to admit we had fun on our trip to Stratford, though.'

'Yes, another excellent bit of theatre,' said Shining. 'Your first attempt to deflect attention by making yourself out to be the victim. Even that stood out as strange, though. Bit of a change of MO, wasn't it?'

'Yeah, well, I was hardly going to curse myself was I? Besides, it's all been theatre, hasn't it? That's my job. That's what I get the big money for.' He grinned. 'Grotesque set pieces, major panic and a lot of scratched heads.'

'Hasn't worked, though, has it?' asked Toby.

'If the bloody Koreans had asked me my opinion rather than just forced me under contract,' Fratfield admitted, 'I might have told them they were asking for the impossible. Both sides need the money too much to give up. Still,' he leaned forward, 'you never know. One last push might do it.'

'We'll never know,' said Toby gesturing with his gun. 'Get up and turn around.'

Fratfield did just that. 'If you'll allow me,' he said, reaching gently beneath his jacket with extended fingers to pull out a gun. He moved quickly and yet made it clear he had no intention of firing it. Dangling the gun from his fingers, he handed it to Toby.

A suspicion hit Shining, just as Toby's hand closed on the gun. 'Don't!' he shouted but it was too late. The gun was in Toby's hand and Fratfield's smile was widening.

'Never accept anything from anyone,' he said. 'Wasn't that the advice?'

A crack of thunder echoed inside the room behind them. As Toby spun towards the noise, he found the barrel of another gun pressed to the back of his head, and Fratfield relieved him of his own pistol.

'You can keep mine,' Fratfield told him. 'It isn't loaded.' There was another crack of thunder. 'Well, not in the conventional sense at least.'

Toby pulled the magazine from the grip of the weapon, a piece of paper was wedged where the cartridges should be.

'Be careful with that,' said Shining, even as a gust of wind added to the impossible weather patterns forming in the basement of Lufford Hall, snatching the paper from Toby's hand.

Shining ran after it, moving back into the main room. He hit a light switch next to the door, flooding the storage room with neon light. He chased after the paper, even as he felt rain beginning to fall. It poured, splashing off the relics, dripping down the walls and soaking into the pages of old books and the upholstered cushions of ancient furniture.

Toby made to grab Fratfield but the man kept the gun aimed squarely at his face as he inched past him and after Shining. 'Two choices, Toby,' he said. 'Quick or slow?'

Toby let him go. However slim his chances might be of avoiding the curse, they had to be marginally better than avoiding a bullet fired from inches away.

'Grab it!' shouted Shining, snatching at the piece of paper as he barrelled into a set of shelves, sending stacks of old china tumbling to the floor.

Toby was right behind him, plucking the paper from the air. 'Fratfield's on the run.'

'And so should you be,' said Shining closing Toby's hand around the curse. 'You're only hope is to outpace him. I'll deal with Fratfield, you get out of here.'

Toby rubbed the rainwater from his eyes and turned as he heard the creak of another set of shelves behind him.

'Move!' Shining shouted, pulling Toby out of the way as the shelves collapsed, pounding into the floor inches from Toby.

Where the shelves had been, the Rain-Soaked Bride was now revealed, her long, dark hair covering the little she could call a face.

Toby darted back and felt his feet slip on the wet floor. Shining was there again, grabbing him just as he had been about to fall on a stuffed deer's head, its antlers inches away from his face as the older man lifted him back onto his feet.

'Everything is out to get you,' said Shining, 'remember that. The world will take any opportunity to end you. You need to be careful. Be aware. Most of all, you need to be out of range. If you put enough space between you and him, the curse won't work. We need room to breathe.'

'But Fratfield's already on the run, surely he's doing the job for me?'

'He's not going to go far,' said Shining. 'He wants to finish his contract and he's not going to do that by leaving the building. Please, trust me, you need to get out of here. That's the only chance you have. Get to the Swan Hotel in Alcester, I'll come and find you there.'

Shining neglected to mention Toby would find Tamar

there. He thought the young man would probably avoid the place if he thought he might be bringing danger her way.

Toby looked towards the Bride, her crumbling fingers extended towards him as he slowly sidestepped her and made his way towards the door. With every step, his feet skated on the wet floor. As he backed away from the curse spirit, he heard another set of shelves creak. He turned to face them, slamming his hands into them as they toppled towards him and shoving them backwards. Their contents smashed against the floor and he just managed to get his hand up in time as half a broken plate shot towards his face. The sharp ceramic cut into his palm, drawing blood.

He grunted and clenched his fist, continuing to navigate past the toppled shelving towards the open door. The rain poured down on him as he made it to the stairway and ran up towards the staff quarters, his soles slipping so that he fell, taking the last few steps on his hands and knees.

The rain followed him along the corridor past the kitchen.

'Careful!' someone shouted, and Toby dropped on instinct, a large carving knife bouncing off the wall of the corridor next to him. 'You could have had my bloody head off with that!' said one of the kitchen staff. 'What were you thinking?'

'I just slipped,' came the reply, 'here, what's going on with the sprinklers?'

Toby was already on the move again, leaving the confused conversation behind as he aimed for the next flight of stairs that would lead him up and out of the building.

He reached the main entrance hall and ran across the chessboard floor, his wet soles once again slipping from beneath him and sending him crashing to the floor. He lay there for a moment, dazed, until the splashing of rain on his face brought him to his senses and his feet. From above him there was a sharp crack and he threw himself towards the back of the room, sliding across the tiles and hitting the far wall as the air filled with the sound of the massive chandelier shattering on the ground. He covered his head with his hands as the glass shards pelted at him, stinging his exposed skin as they peppered him with cuts.

He took no time to check the damage, just got to his feet and ran towards the rear exit.

d) Lufford Hall, Alcester, Warwickshire

Shining watched Toby go then turned his attention to the Bride.

'I'm sorry,' he said, 'if the myth about you is even half true. But, be warned, I won't let that get in my way when it comes to stopping you.' She inclined her head as he walked past her. He paused in the doorway and turned back towards her even as she began to fade from view. 'If only you could choose the company you keep,' he said, turning back around and making his way upstairs.

He heard the crash of the chandelier as he passed the kitchen and broke into a run.

He was quite convinced he'd see the broken body of Toby beneath its twisted arms as he entered the entrance hall, and the relief when he realised the young man must have avoided it momentarily stopped him in his tracks. He could only hope that Toby would make it far enough away to be safe. It was hard to specify how far that would be, but, as long as Fratfield stayed here, Toby should be clear.

'What the hell's going on?' asked Clive King, having stepped out of the conference room, followed by the rest of the delegates.

'I've found our assassin,' said Shining, 'and we've got him on the run.'

'What's that?' Rowlands asked, entering from the front door. 'I've had my men covering the grounds all morning but *you've* found him?'

'Yes,' Shining agreed. 'It was Bill Fratfield.'

'Bill?' April couldn't believe it. 'But he's ...'

'In a hospital miles away,' said Rowlands. 'The codger's finally flipped.'

'I wish I had,' Shining replied, looking around the room. 'Is it just me or is it getting dark in here?'

The windows began to darken and Shining thought back to what Toby had told him about his experience in the car coming back from Stratford. 'We need to stay close together,' he said, 'things are about to get very dangerous indeed.'

Slowly, inevitably, the room was plunged into total darkness.

CHAPTER FIFTEEN: THE FEAR

a) Lufford Hall, Alcester, Warwickshire

Barry Steelhorn had been working private security for eight years and while it had its ups and downs, it beat the prison service hands down. These days he was paid decent cash to keep an eye on men in suits. They didn't kick off when the mood took them. They had nothing to say on the sexual habits of your wife. They didn't try and score points off you as you went about your duties. They just sat in their little meetings, and acted like you didn't exist. That was fine as far as Barry was concerned. He had no real interest in them either. They were just the people who signed his cheques. If they were in trouble then he'd do his bit, that was the job and he wasn't afraid to throw his weight around if the need arose. Most of the time, though, it was about sitting around, keeping your eyes peeled and your mind alert.

Sat in the guardhouse at the perimeter of Lufford Hall, he poured himself a cup of tea from his flask and sat sipping it while keeping his eye on the CCTV monitors.

There was nothing to see. Just an empty road and open fields. As the camera feeds rotated, the screens featured footage of the Hall itself from the three cameras placed in trees surrounding the property. They were no more eventful as a rule. This morning they had offered him pairs of security officers wandering around the garden in a bored grump.

Barry wasn't bored. That was the key to a job like this. Boredom got you in trouble, it made you sloppy. He kept his mind active by thinking through the plot of an adventure novel he kept planning to write. It was going to be about a brilliant young soldier who solved an international conspiracy by shooting things. One day he'd write it. Until then he kept working over different chapters in his head, adding more car chases and explosions. It was going to be the best book ever.

He had finished his tea and was rooting around in his backpack for a packet of chocolate biscuits when he noticed one of the monitors go blank. Then another. Then one more. They were the feeds for the Hall itself. Everything on the wall was fine but he could bring up no footage of inside the building.

Giving up on the chocolate biscuits, he reached for his walkie-talkie and tried to contact someone in the Hall. There was no reply. The SIS boys were supposed to be the click of a call button away. He knew they looked down on the private staff but couldn't believe they would be so stupid as to ignore him. Something must be going on.

'Oi,' he shouted through the window to his shift partner, Luis, who was walking up and down the road outside because he'd got a bit stir crazy from sitting in the guardhouse all morning. 'Something's up.'

Luis came jogging over, a look of excitement on his face. He was only a kid, Barry thought, barely out of school. One day he'd learn that you didn't get excited about trouble.

'What is it?'

'Cameras on the house have all gone down. I need you to sit here and mind the gate while I go and have a look.'

'Shit, can't I go?'

'No, you bloody can't. Do as you're told.'

Luis slunk inside and dumped himself on the chair in front of the monitors.

Barry didn't blame him for wanting to go but the kid was too wet behind the ears. If there was something wrong up there then he wasn't going to be the one to send him running off into it.

'I'll keep in touch on the radio,' he told Luis. 'It's probably just a technical problem.'

He didn't believe that for a moment, but it would keep Luis happy. If it had only been one camera that had packed up, then fine, maybe a loose wire or something, but all three?

He jogged up the road, trying to think of a reasonable explanation for the outage. He couldn't see how someone had got past the wall in order to interfere with the cameras. He'd been on the ball and had seen nothing on the perimeter footage. Nor had any of the alarms tripped. Maybe it was a technical fault somehow – did all three feeds join at some point? Maybe that was where the problem lay?

As he crested the hill so that he could look down on the Hall itself, such simple thoughts as a severed cable vanished. He stood there for a moment, staring ahead, not having the first idea what to think.

His walkie-talkie crackled. 'Barry?' came Luis' voice. 'See anything yet?'

Barry pulled the walkie-talkie out of its holster and wondered exactly how to explain what his eyes were telling him in a way that didn't sound completely mental.

There was nothing wrong with the cameras. The black screens in the guardhouse were only showing precisely what lay in front of them. The entire Hall was covered in a dome of darkness. Like an uneven, black pudding bowl had been flipped upside down and placed over the building.

'Just hold on a minute, Luis,' he said. 'I'm still checking.'

He began to make his way down towards the front of the Hall. As he drew closer, he could see that the surface of the darkness wasn't smooth. It rippled as if it were made of smoke. Maybe the whole thing was some kind of gas?

He approached via the front lawn. From close up, the darkness appeared like a liquid wall, bubbling and shifting. It cut right through the large urn water feature at the centre of the lawn.

He walked right up to it, holding his hand in front of his mouth in case it was something poisonous. It didn't smell. He didn't taste anything as he breathed. Neither of which meant much, he knew, but it didn't look like gas. It was too thick, too glutinous.

He looked around for some sort of tool, snapping a branch off a bush from one of the flower beds.

He stepped up towards the wall of darkness and slowly poked at it with the branch. As the tip entered the darkness, his walkie-talkie barked into life once more, Luis' voice coming out through the speaker.

'You must be there by now, Barry. What's up?'

Barry dropped the stick in surprise, swearing and yanking the walkie-talkie free.

'I'm there, Luis,' he said, 'and it's really weird so bear with me for a minute, will you?'

'Weird how?'

'Jesus ...' Barry reached down to retrieve the dropped stick. 'Weird as in ... I don't know, "weird".'

He picked the stick up and carefully stirred the surface of the darkness. Tendrils of it seemed to chase the tip of the stick around.

'Fuck it,' said Barry, pressing down the call button on the walkie-talkie. 'Just get over here, will you? I need you to see this.'

b) Lufford Hall, Alcester, Warwickshire

'What the hell is going on?' Clive King shouted, his voice echoing around the darkness of the entrance hall. 'I can't see a thing.'

'Just stay calm,' said Shining. 'We need to keep our heads.'

'Says the man who is out of his.' This was Rowlands, somewhere off to Shining's left.

'There's no time for arguing,' Shining insisted. 'You're not an idiot. Stop pretending to be one.' He turned towards where he thought Rowlands was standing. 'This is obviously something from outside your experience so let me do my damn job.'

He tried to move towards where he thought Rowlands had been standing. It was so disorientating, nothing but panicked voices in the dark.

'Rubbish,' Rowlands replied. 'There's a perfectly rational explanation for this.'

'I wish someone would tell me what it is,' said Tae-young.

'This is not rational,' Jae-sung added, his voice close to Shining. The old man reached out a hand, hoping to touch the Korean.

'I think you're right next to me, Jae-sung,' he said. 'Keep talking.'

'I can't believe you're all playing into this!' shouted Rowlands. 'Wandering around like idiots. We need to find the door and get out of here.'

There was a crackle of static from Rowlands' walkie-talkie as he tried to contact the rest of his men. 'No signal,' he muttered. 'Something must be jamming it.'

'No shit,' whined Spang. 'As far as we know, the whole world's vanished. We're probably on Mars!'

'We're exactly where we were,' Shining said, 'more or less. Just try and stay calm.'

Shining heard Rowland's footsteps on the tiles, some distance away, the man pacing up and down in frustration and panic.

'I'm here,' said Jae-sung, doing as Shining had asked. 'You are close. I can hear you moving. Very close.'

Shining swung his arms around, hoping to connect with the man.

There was a crashing sound as Rowlands tripped over something. 'Jesus,' the SIS man shouted. 'Ridiculous. Utterly ridiculous.'

'I have a light,' said April, and there was the sound of her Zippo bursting into life. 'There. It's not really helping ... I can see the flame but it's not lighting up the room.'

'I can't see any flame,' said King. 'I can hear your voice, I know you're close. But I can't see any flame!'

'Please try not to panic!' said Shining. 'If we panic then we're lost. We need to find one another.'

'How can we find one another when we can't see?' said King. 'What's happened to us? Have we all gone blind?'

'No,' said April. 'I can see the flame, I'm not blind, it's just that ...'

'We can't see it,' said Tae-young. 'It's like we're all in our own darkness.'

'Rubbish,' said Rowlands. 'Some sort of chemical agent. A nerve gas, maybe.'

'Mars!' Spang shouted.

'That doesn't even make sense,' insisted April. 'Please listen to August.'

'Not a chance,' Rowlands replied, banging around at the far end of the room. 'The man's mad. If we listened to him, we'd be – the door! I've got the door.'

'Don't open it!' Shining shouted, not really knowing why, just a gut instinct that overtook him.

'Oh shut up,' Rowlands replied. There was the sound of a door opening and then silence.

'Rowlands?' King shouted. 'Rowlands?'

Silence.

'Where has he gone?' asked Jae-sung, his voice almost right in Shining's ear. He reached out and put his hands on the man's shoulders.

'I've got you,' he said.

'Who?' Tae-young asked.

'Jae-sung,' said Shining.

'Yes?' Jae-sung's voice was now some distance away. Shining held on to the pair of shoulders in front of him and squeezed.

'Who am I touching?' he asked. 'I have my hands on your shoulders. Who is it?'

'I'll give you three guesses,' came Fratfield's voice in his ear.

c) *Lufford Hall, Alcester, Warwickshire*

Toby cut across the sculpture park aiming for the rear wall.

How far was far enough to be safe? Nothing seemed out to kill him right now. His balance was steady, his footing sound. Most importantly: there was no rain. He was soaked to the skin but the air around him was now dry. Surely that meant he was beyond the curse's range?

He looked back over his shoulder and what he saw stopped him for a moment. The entirety of Lufford Hall had vanished from view, a wall of darkness surrounding it. It was the same as he had experienced in the car. What horror show would be playing out for those inside even now? Shouldn't he try and get them out?

'Oi!' a voice shouted and he looked over towards the left-hand side of the wall and saw one of Rowlands' men, obviously working his way around the perimeter, trying to understand what had happened. *Good luck on that one*, Toby thought, *I've seen my fair share of the impossible, and all of this is beyond me.*

'Keep your distance,' Toby shouted, moving back towards the Hall and the security officer. 'Don't cross the threshold.'

Then he felt the air change. The faint sound of thunder. A couple of raindrops fell on his head and, to his right, moving amongst the metal sculptures, he saw the Bride.

Too close, he was still too close.

A shot rang out and Toby let himself fall backwards. The security officer was firing at him! Why the hell was he firing at him?

Because you're cursed, he thought, and because it wants you dead.

He scrambled to his feet, turned back in the direction he had been aiming and made a zig-zagged run towards the far wall.

Another shot. Toby moved into the cover of the forest, taking the opportunity to turn and look.

He saw the officer, aiming towards him, but that wasn't all. Behind the officer, stepping out of the darkness, like a man rising up through marshy water, Fratfield appeared.

The rogue agent reached for the security officer who was completely unaware that there was someone behind him.

'Behind you!' Toby shouted but the officer just took another badly aimed shot in his direction.

Fratfield grabbed the officer. He gripped the hand that was holding the gun and threw the man down onto the ground, wrestling the gun from his grip.

The man turned to try and defend himself but Fratfield shot him at point-blank range and then continued to walk away from the Hall, in Toby's direction.

The sound of thunder increased and Toby saw the Bride, still moving amongst the sculptures, her white dress flitting in and out from between the sharp iron structures.

'You said it yourself,' Fratfield shouted. 'Doppelgänger contract. There can be as many of me as I like. One to play with the old man and one to play with you. So, let's have a little fun. I'll give you a head start.' He held his hands up to his face covering his eyes, the gun barrel sticking up like a strange antenna. 'A count of twenty. One ... two ...'

Toby turned and ran towards the wall.

d) *Lufford Hall, Alcester, Warwickshire*

Shining let go of Fratfield's shoulders but not before something struck him in his midriff and sent him skating across the tile floor.

'August?' April shouted. 'Are you all right?'

That's a good question, he thought as he got to his feet, spinning around, trying to get a sense of whether whatever had attacked him was still close.

'I'm fine,' he replied, then felt the air around him shift as if something massive was surging towards him. He doubled over, trying to make himself a smaller target. Perhaps it helped, though he was still sent tumbling backwards, colliding with what felt like a chaise longue and falling behind it.

The room is still here, he thought, *we can still interact with it. We can't see it, but it's physically here. Along with something else, something dangerous.*

And what had happened to Rowlands? What had he found on the other side of the door?

e) *Who knows?*

Mark Rowlands stepped through the door only to find himself facing more darkness.

'It's the same out here,' he shouted.

Out here? It didn't feel very much like outside. The sound of his voice was muffled as if he were stood in a small room.

'Did you hear me?' he shouted, still holding the door handle. He turned to step back into the room. 'I said it's ...'

He was suddenly flooded by light as he stepped back inside. He momentarily screwed up his eyes in shock, opening them to find himself on a city street.

'Impossible,' he muttered to himself, even as the warmth of sunlight fell on his face, as real as anything he had ever experienced.

He squatted down and touched the tarmac beneath his feet, rough grit pressing into the tips of his fingers.

'Impossible,' he said again.

He turned around to find the street continuing behind him with no sign of the door he had just stepped through.

He rubbed at his face, unable to process what was happening to him.

He stared up and down the street. A familiar street. Very familiar.

A car drove past him. He watched it pass, a red sports car. He knew the car. He knew all of this.

The car parked up a short distance ahead and he watched a familiar man step out, look around and then cross the street.

The man, Rowlands knew, was called Napoleon Ayoade. Nigerian by descent, he had been in the UK for four years, part of a criminal chain running a network in human trafficking. He ruled an army of street kids through a mixture of fear and cash. The rod and the carrot. He claimed voodoo ancestry. He said he had demons on his side, the Devil watching his back. Rowlands hadn't believed a word of it, of course. An opinion that had only slightly wavered when the man had nearly been the death of him.

All of this was years ago. What was he doing here now? It must be, as he had said before, some form of gas. He was lying on his back in Lufford Hall, dreaming everything.

He watched as Ayoade paused outside a large, red door, the staff access to a nightclub called Revolutions that the man used as cover.

Unable to restrain himself from mirroring the actions of the past, Rowlands waited until the man had entered the building then slowly followed after him.

He listened at the door, as he had all those years ago, then looked over to a tatty hatchback parked a couple of doors away where two of his fellow SOCA officers were sat observing the building. The one in the passenger seat, a middle-aged man called Philips that Rowlands had always looked up to, nodded. They had his back. Or at least, that was the plan; Rowlands knew they would arrive too late to save him a savage beating because he had the advantage of hindsight. He also knew that Philips would be dead of bowel cancer in three years' time. History was where ghosts really lived. They filled it to the brim.

Rowlands opened the door and walked quietly up the dark stairwell that led to the offices above the club. His job was to check the location of Ayoade's prisoners. The first thing Ayoade and his men would do on SOCA storming the building would be to kill them. These were men who left no wagging tongues. The powers that be were not willing to risk such a potential media shit-storm so it had been decided that Rowlands would enter the building first, the rest of the team on standby. He would locate the prisoners, if possible free them, if not then do his best to provide protection while the others came in from the front, all guns blazing. It was a mess. Badly conceived and barely planned.

Rowlands was sticking his head in the lion's mouth and he knew it. Their intelligence suggested that there were only three of the slavers in the building: Ayoade himself and two of his men. Still, the risk was higher than should have been countenanced.

But this time Rowlands had an advantage. He knew what was going to happen.

f) Fields outside Lufford Hall, Alcester, Warwickshire

Toby had gone over the wall, imagining the security system lighting up in the guardhouse, and dropped down into the open fields on the other side. Looking around for potential cover, he was forced to accept there was none until he got to a hedge that lined the far side of the field. He could run along the wall that lined the house, but that would still leave him exposed by the time Fratfield appeared. The far hedge was the only viable option.

He ran, aiming for the shortest line between the wall and the hedge. He forced himself to sprint as fast as he could, trying to control his breathing as he pushed his speed faster and faster across the cold, hard earth beneath his feet.

As he drew close to the hedge, he scanned along it, trying to find a break that he could force himself through to reach the relative safety of the other side. The foliage was dense, an advantage if he could only get through it. It was too high to jump and, by now, Fratfield must have reached the wall of Lufford Hall; Toby would be an obvious and easy target as he tried to throw himself over the top of some bushes. Spotting a small gap a few feet to his right, he changed direction and, squinting his eyes shut against the sharp branches, dived at it, hoping his momentum would help carry him part of the way through. He became wedged against the thick branches and they hooked and tore at his suit as he pulled himself through, adding countless new scratches and cuts to the mess the shower of glass from the chandelier had made of him. For one awful moment he thought he was going to be stuck, hanging there, unable to turn or defend himself as Fratfield and the curse he brought with him approached from behind. Then, with an almighty shake, he pierced the hedge, pulling himself along the ground on the other side until his legs were free. He turned to look through the hole he had left behind. Fratfield was stood on the far side of the field; there was no sign of the curse spirit.

Toby ran along the hedge. A few hundred yards away there was the cover of trees that ran along the road to Alcester. Once there he would be relatively safe from gunfire at least.

His skin was burning as sweat poured into open wounds. His muscles were already cramping after having to force himself so hard. Bruises were erupting at every point he had fallen or been hit by the various inanimate objects that had been aimed at him. He was already struggling and the pursuit had only just begun.

g) Lufford Hall, Alcester, Warwickshire

Shining reached out to the chaise longue next to him, rubbing his hand against its upholstery, trying to ground himself in the reality of it.

'There's something else in here with us,' he said. 'It just sent me flying. I'm OK but you need to prepare yourselves for it. I don't think it's the major threat but it—'

'What sort of something?' Spang cried. 'What is it? What is it going to do to us?'

Then he screamed, the little reserve he had maintained completely gone now as the presence in the dark came for him.

'It's got me!' he shouted. 'It's got me!' As he continued to scream, the sound soared above them, as if the banker was being dragged through the air. Then, with a finality that chilled Shining, the sound cut off, replaced by a faint gurgling sound and then a rush of air and a crash as Spang's body was dropped onto the remains of the chandelier.

The whole room erupted in panicked shouting, and Shining felt the force well up around them as, one by one, the panicked sounds were cut off in the dark.

'Shut up!' he roared. 'For the sake of your lives, shut up!'

Silence fell once more. Though whether through his advice or simply because there was nobody left to make a noise, Shining couldn't tell.

'I think it tracks sound,' he whispered, proven accurate as something collided with the chaise longue and sent him back against the far wall where, blacking out, he slumped to the floor, unconscious.

h) Who knows?

Rowlands moved quietly through his memory of the rooms above the nightclub. He held the layout of the building in his mind. It was easy enough, he would never forget this place for as long as he lived. There was a main room at the rear which Ayoade used partly as an office and partly as a recreational room. It had a large TV, games console and bar. They had found a cabinet filled with coke and pills. It was here that Ayoade like to entertain. Sometimes he would invite girls up from the club, sometimes he would just drag one of the slaves out from the cells he kept them in, waiting to have them shipped out to clients. Those cells were to Rowlands' left at the top of the stairs, Ayoade and his men would be to his right.

Last time he had moved towards the cells, determined to fulfil his mission. That was where – *the things, the invisible things* – the gang had set on him. Men they hadn't accounted for. He had only just survived, his backup arriving, storming the building and dragging him to safety. They had managed to save some of the prisoners. The gang that attacked Rowlands – *not a gang, something in the air* – had made their presence felt there too. They had torn into the captives with animalistic violence.

This time he went to the right.

He pulled out his firearm and walked quietly but purposefully towards Ayoade's room.

Outside the door, he could hear the three men inside, laughing over the sound of a driving game on the console.

He took a measured breath, turned the handle on the door and burst inside.

He fired as soon as he had the target, taking out both of Ayoade's men first then the man himself. The slaver slumped back in his leather sofa, a bullet wound like a third eye, weeping red into the thick curls of his beard.

'Job done,' Rowlands said, turning to leave the room as something unseen rushed along the corridor at him, the air whipping through his hair like the sign of an oncoming train.

'Not again!' Rowlands shouted. 'Not again!' Firing his gun at nothing even as he felt himself lifted up from the floor and forced back along the corridor towards a window that, he remembered, looked down on the delivery access for the club.

His back collided with the frame and it cracked beneath his weight. But he was damned if he was going to go down so easily. You could do as you liked in dreams, he thought, grabbing at the edges of the window and pushing himself against the pressure of whatever it was that was attacking him. It was as if someone had aimed an aeroplane engine along the hallway, the wind forcing the skin on his face to peel back, tugging his mouth into a distorted rictus.

But it's a dream, he insisted to himself, and I'm damned if I'm going to give in to dreams.

He imagined his fingers digging into the frame of the window, nails piercing wood and plaster. He lowered his centre of gravity, bending his legs and summoning all the strength he could muster (which was infinite, he decided; how could you have limits in your own head?) and forced himself forward, straightening his legs and jumping back into the corridor.

He swung his arms against the wind, stamping his feet down with every step, imagining he was an immovable object, a rock around which the river of air would be forced to flow. It was easy enough. After all, hadn't he been accused of having just such an attitude before now? He was the man who would not be moved.

Then the air began to alter its density. The steady flow shifted around him, forming dense bands that buffeted against him, trying to make him lose his balance, to push him back.

He roared with the effort, desperately trying to visualise his feet as concrete or iron, anchors against the flow. He turned on his side, making himself a smaller obstruction, cutting down resistance.

The pockets of denser air continued to come at him and he pushed the memories of his original beating from his mind. There was no way that, in the real world, you could be beaten up by wind. Ayoade had been full of shit. He had been a showman, like all gangsters, spreading lies about his abilities, encouraging fear. You couldn't summon spirits from the air. Rowlands wouldn't accept it. He believed in the solid. In the real. In an enemy he could see. An enemy he could shoot.

He cried out as an invisible fist hit him low in his abdomen. It wasn't real, he repeated. It was a dream. It was just fantasies from his mind.

Another blow, this time to the side of his head and he spun back a few feet, losing ground he had fought hard to gain.

This was ridiculous. He couldn't feel pain, he couldn't reel from fantasy. He forced himself to push on. He focused his eyes, now streaming, on the end of the corridor. If he could just get there, he would be by the cells in which Ayoade kept his prisoners. Two rooms rammed full with people who had been lifted out of their lives, forced to sleep like animals on the floor with an overflowing bucket of waste in the corner. That had been real, he told himself. Pain, misery and shit. They were constants in this world.

He. Would. Not. Give. In.

Another blow, this time hitting his leg and he heard it crack, a bone in his thigh splintering as if it had been pounded on by a hammer.

A hammer that did not exist.

He screamed and continued to force his weight onto the broken leg, pain pulsing up through him, nausea and delirium.

No pain. No sickness.

One more step.

No stopping. No giving in.

One more step.

Another blow, this one to his shoulder and he ignored the way the joint twisted in its socket. It wasn't real. It didn't hurt.

One more step.

Another blow and his nose erupted in twin streams of blood that curled around his cheeks and trailed in perpendicular lines behind him.

One more step.

The stairs were now just in front of him. If he pushed just a little further he could turn down them, away from the force of the wind. He could walk back down onto the street of his past. He could tug Philips out of the surveillance car and take the man for a drink. He could end this pointless memory of the day he failed. He could submit to pleasure.

One more step.

But then he would be leaving Ayoade's prisoners and, real or not, that was something he could never do.

Another blow, this one only glancing off his left hand.

Real or not he would be the man he prided himself on being. He would be the one who walked the right path. He knew some people thought he was just a career officer, keeping his nose clean and looking for the promotion. Working his way from one desk to the next. They didn't understand him at all.

One more step.

He was opposite the stairway now but he ignored it.

On. And on. There was no pain. There was no wind. Just imaginary roadblocks set up by his own insecurities and fears.

One more step.

A blow to the face again and he felt himself gag as his throat was showered with tooth fragments. He spat blood and bone but it splattered back into his face.

A blow to the chest and the breathing that had already been difficult was, for a moment, halted altogether.

No giving in. It was all in his mind.

One.

More.

Ste ...

A final blow, once more to the head, and the disorientation was total. His feet lifted from the ground and he spun, his slack mouth ballooning out, his arms and legs splayed as he turned in the air, a leaf caught in a storm. He sailed back along the corridor, bouncing off one wall and then the other, leaving a smudged, red kiss on each as he went on towards the window. The air was filled with glass and splinters as he exploded through the remains of the frame.

No more. No pain.

He felt the sun hitting his wet face, his ears deaf to anything but the roar of wind as he became a thing of the air. Dust. A ghost. Gone.

Then the ground, the final sensation of the tiled floor of the entrance hall. A cold stone kiss to his raw wounds.

Then nothing.

i) Who knows?

Shining lay on his back, his cheeks cooled by flakes of snow that fell from the night sky above.

He tried to move his legs, but the thought left his brain only to dissipate somewhere along the way. His limbs were dead to him. Soon the rest would follow.

'This,' said a voice beside him, 'is not your best day. I

suppose that much is obvious. You would hardly be here again otherwise.'

Shining didn't have to incline his head to know who was speaking. He remembered the night well enough. The night he should have died. Certainly, he would have done were it not for the presence, the higher power that squatted next to him in the building snow. If he looked at the person speaking, he knew he would only be seeing a shell, a borrowed host. To anyone who hadn't experienced the curious habits of the speaker, it would seem as if Shining were having a deathbed conversation with a homeless man, an ageing king of public parks and open spaces, who ruled from a bench not four feet away, swathed in his royal vestments of yesterday's news.

'Am I supposed to crumple?' Shining asked. 'Faced with the memory of my darkest hour? If so I wouldn't hold whatever you possess by way of breath. I have known far too many dark hours over the years. I am numb to them.'

'I'm sure. As it happens, I decided I would take this opportunity to have a little chat. This is not your memory talking. No phantoms here. This is a live broadcast, if you will.'

'Charming.'

'I thought so. It's been a while. I thought it time we caught up.'

Shining heard the body of the homeless man settle down next to him, cross-legged on the ground.

'Of course,' the voice continued, 'I haven't been entirely ignoring you. Congratulations on Toby, he's quite the bright spark.'

'Stay away from him.'

The homeless man chuckled. 'Let's not waste time with posturing, August. I'll do as I wish. Anyway, you know me, I'm not one to force these things. Toby and I have only chatted, I've laid no claim to him. He's his own man. Unlike you.'

'Free for now.'

'Well, that rather depends on how the day pans out, doesn't it? It's not looking particularly hopeful is it? Young Toby on the run, the old man and his charges under siege, fighting for their lives. Mr Fratfield is quite a scamp. A potent fellow.'

'With friends in low places?'

'Well, yes, I may have lent him a little assistance here and there. You know me, I do like to sponsor potential. He was doing very well for himself but he does have a habit of overstretching. You know the rules, magic isn't something you should fling about willy-nilly, it's like splashing around in an ocean full of sharks. Sooner or later, one is bound to get one's legs bitten off. I've boosted his abilities a little, kept him hidden.'

Shining scoffed at that. 'You're the worst shark of all! I, of all people, know that. Once you've sunk your teeth into him, there's not much hope for him, is there?'

'But I haven't! Unlike you, Mr Fratfield wasn't quite so desperate. I'm afraid he is still his own man.'

'That must be frustrating.'

'A little, but even I have rules. He has to come willingly. You remember, I'm sure.' The homeless man gestured around them where the snow was beginning to settle on the bushes and trees. 'For now I hover and wait. I have him in my sights and one day, I'm sure, he'll have no choice but to offer himself to me.'

'Always the games.'

'Of course! We all have our structures. Our natures. Some of us simply embrace the fact and take pleasure in them. I have allowed Fratfield to flourish. In my experience, that inevitably leads to a fall. Look at you! If you have some terribly clever plan that will get you out of your current situation then you're keeping it remarkably quiet. I rather think you'll be mine soon enough. A debt collected. We made a pact, did we not? Here in this very park, as your life trickled out, blood turning to ice, you made a promise to me if I helped you.'

'I didn't have a choice.'

'Of course you did! You could simply have slipped away!'

'If I had died then countless others would have died with me. I needed to keep going.'

'And now you're facing the same situation all over again.' The homeless man gestured in the air and, one by one, Shining could see figures projected against the night sky. First there was Tae-young, running with a crowd of young people as soldiers circled them, clubs raised.

'Ah,' said the homeless man, 'Geumnamno. The people are revolting and the forces of Chun Doo-hwan are closing in. Over one hundred people will be dead by the time the demonstrations are crushed. Perhaps, among them, a young student who might otherwise have grown up to be a woman of politics?'

Then Jae-sung appeared, crawling along in the darkness of a Manchester alleyway.

'How he loves to go on about his happy youth in England! In truth he never quite fitted in. And one night he found himself mugged for his wallet, bleeding and battered by the bins of a takeaway. He would have died had he not been found by one of the staff. Perhaps, this time, that member of staff will be just too late?'

These images stayed and were then added to by Clive King, staring into a tumbler of scotch in his hand.

'His daughter has just been killed in a hit and run,' explained the homeless man. 'At this point, he doesn't know his wife is pregnant again. All he knows is that there is a bottle of antidepressants in the bathroom cabinet and the temptation to mix them into his drink is almost impossible to ignore. You ephemeral humans have such a limited tolerance for pain. A bad year culminating in a loss he thinks he will never be able to bear. The urge to simply die is so strong he will hold the pills in his hand for an hour before finally throwing them away. Maybe this time the decision will be different?'

Finally, Shining saw his sister, face grim as it stared out of the windscreen of her car, chin resting against the steering wheel.

'And what about dearest April?' Shining heard the man ask. 'She gives off the impression of impregnability doesn't she? But we know better.'

j) Who knows?

April Shining stared out of the windscreen and wondered what had brought her to this point. Her life had always been an impenetrable network of cause and effect. Hadn't Toby joked about his inability to piece it all together? She might have told him he wasn't alone. Many was the time she looked back over her life and lost her grip on it all. Now, somehow back behind the wheel of her old Mini, the clock of years turned back to – oh Lord, who knew? Sometimes it felt as if this night had been a lifetime ago, sometimes she felt it hung over her as if it were only hours gone.

She had been at Lufford Hall. Yes. She was certain of that, despite how real the steering wheel felt beneath her fingers, how clear the rain was as it burst and diffused over the dirty windscreen. Looking through the glass was like peering back into her past, a distorted place of bright colours and barely comprehensible shapes.

Ahead of her, of course, was Jeffery's house. She could see the lights burning in his bedroom window.

That light was blessed. As long as it burned she knew that he had yet to begin. Jeffery was not a man who made love with the lights on. He felt some things belonged to the darkness. As long as it stayed on, April could imagine that nothing more painful was happening than conversation. Perhaps he was showing Valerie the new bathroom, the en suite so recently installed.

April had been telling him for months he should spend the money. The adjoining dressing room was never used, little more than a box room, how much better would it be to have the place fitted out with a bath and toilet? No more stubbed toes in the dark, working their way along the landing to the rear of the house. Now they could lie together and soak, towel off and be between the sheets within moments. When he had told her he'd contracted the builders to do it she had felt absurdly pleased, as if it were somehow a sign of togetherness. An act of putting her into his life. Obviously, a bathroom suite was not a wedding ring but it had been good enough. He wanted her to be happy in his home. Didn't that mean something?

The bedroom light turned off.

She had been in Lufford Hall, she reminded herself. None of this was actually happening. It was over and done with. She was staring up at a house of ghosts. It couldn't hurt her any more. She should just close her eyes and dream herself back to the present. Back onto that chessboard floor. She definitely shouldn't repeat her idiocy of the past, acting like a stupid, lovesick idiot over a man who had got under her skin. She had been old enough to know better for God's sake, a middle-aged woman who had played the game for all of her life. Of course Jeffery hadn't really wanted her. Of course he had never intended to be faithful. As always, she had been a weekend distraction, office work he brought home. That she could have ever thought it was something more, something she could actually pin her heart to, was so embarrassingly naive she cringed to remember it. How could she have been so ridiculous as to fall in love?

She should close her eyes and leave. She didn't need to go through all this again.

She reached over to the glove box, pulled out her revolver and climbed out of the car and into the rain.

This was ridiculous. It had been excruciating enough the first time. The Ice Queen brought so low, reduced to a jealous girl with violence on her mind. Hadn't she spent the rest of her years making sure she never made herself so vulnerable again? Hadn't she closed that weak heart away in a box for good? Why was she going through these pathetic motions again? Jeffery hadn't been worth it. He had just been another lying player.

She walked up his front path, assuring herself that she had no intention of knocking on the door.

She knocked on the door.

As his front garden flooded with the light cast down once more from the bedroom, she assured herself she had no intention of waiting for him to angrily descend.

She knocked again, watching as the landing light came on and a shadow appeared at the top of the stairs.

Fine. She'd look at her memory of him once more. Maybe you

never really laid such ghosts to rest. But she certainly wouldn't repeat the childish actions of her past. She wouldn't use the gun.

The door opened and she pointed the revolver at him. Watched that handsome face, initially distorted by anger become distorted even further by fear.

'April!' he said. 'What the hell are you doing here? I thought you were in Prague until Friday?'

'Clearly,' she heard herself say, stepping forward and forcing him back into the hall. 'Or you wouldn't be fucking your secretary tonight.'

'I don't know what you're talking about!' he insisted, his eyes glancing towards the stairs, no doubt worried that Valerie would suddenly appear. 'Now let's not be stupid about this. What do you think you're doing?' He reached for the gun in her hand and she pressed the trigger, putting a bullet in the wall of the hall.

'Jesus!' he shouted. 'You could have hit me!'

'Yes,' she said, turning the gun on him. 'I could.'

Stupid. Stupid. Stupid. *You're embarrassing yourself*, she thought. *You're making him more powerful, not less. Just walk away. Get out! Get out!*

She stormed out of the house, hoping he didn't see her start to cry as she turned out of his front door and stepped out into the rain.

She shoved the gun into her coat pocket and ran back to the car, climbing in, turning over the engine and pulling out onto the wet road.

Don't drive so fast! she tried to tell herself. *Get back in control! Is that what you want to let him do to you? To turn you into this? To make you this weak?*

She pressed down on the accelerator.

k) *B49, Alcester, Warwickshire*

Toby was flagging. Moving through the trees by the side of the road, he was aware that Fratfield and the curse he brought with him were closing in. As he stopped to catch his breath, Toby heard the sound of the rainfall hitting the undergrowth; fat, impossible raindrops beating out a rhythm on fallen winter leaves. In the end, they would catch up with him and then he would be too weak to defend himself. He had taken too much of a beating, his skin covered in wounds, his body bruised, to keep up the speed he needed in order to get ahead on foot.

He looked to the road as he heard the sound of a car approaching. Here was a chance. The way he looked, he was under no illusion that he presented an attractive prospect but the possibility of a ride out of there was the only way he could imagine surviving the day.

He stumbled out onto the road as the car turned the corner ahead of him, waving his arms and doing his best to block its chances of avoiding him.

It occurred to him that, if he wasn't a safe distance away from Fratfield, he might be offering himself up to a perfect way of resolving the curse. He looked beyond the car and, absurdly, saw the rain in the distance, flowing towards him in a barely visible wall. If that was too close then no doubt the car wouldn't stop, or its brakes would fail, or its tyres skid. Any moment now it would collide with him and send him broken, to the verge, where the Bride would finally have snared her victim.

The quiet road filled with the sound of squealing brakes and the car came to a halt a few feet away.

'What the hell are you playing at?' came a voice from the driver's seat. 'I could have had you over.'

The driver was a man in his late fifties, and the look on his face as he took note of the state of Toby could only be the precursor to a hasty U-turn.

Toby looked to the wall of rain as it crept ever closer.

'Please,' he begged, 'I desperately need your help.' He walked towards the car, being careful to stay in front of it, hopefully stopping the driver from being able to just drive off.

'You been in an accident, lad?' the man asked. 'You look like you've been beaten from here to next week.'

'Can you give me a lift?' Toby asked. 'I really need to get to town.'

The rain crept ever closer, and with it, Toby knew, the odds of the man saying 'yes' diminished.

The driver scratched at his face, clearly undecided. 'What happened to you?' he asked.

Trying to explain now would only take up time Toby didn't have. He decided to take a risk, stepping out of the way of the car and moving towards the passenger door.

'You wouldn't believe it,' he said. 'I'm lucky to be alive.'

He pulled at the door handle. The door was locked. 'Please?' he asked again. 'I really need to hurry. Just wait until I tell you all about it!'

The rain was now only feet away. The surface of the road changed colour where the water rushed across it, a line of dark grey that crept closer and closer. In the distance, just at the corner the car had recently taken, he caught a flash of movement in the tree line.

The driver reached over and unlocked the door. 'Get in then,' he said. 'Can't rightly leave you here, can I? I don't make a habit of picking people up, though.'

'Don't blame you,' Toby told him, climbing in. 'But I can assure you I'm in no fit state to cause trouble. I just really need to get to town.'

'Aye.' The driver looked at him and Toby glanced at the rearview mirror where the rain was now almost touching the car. He was aware that he had now endangered the driver if they didn't get moving. What would happen if they drove away once the rain was touching them? Would the car slip off the road, killing them both?

The driver put the car in gear and pulled forward, just as the first few drops hit the rear window.

Toby watched in relief as the wet road receded in the rearview mirror with every second.

'Thank you so much,' said Toby. 'You're a lifesaver.'

l) Who Knows?

April felt the wheels lose traction on the road and, for a moment, the car was out of control.

Ahead, the traffic on the Euston Road was a mess of lights distorted in the rain and she lifted her hands from the steering wheel, feeling an absurd relief in the notion of sailing out of control. Hadn't she spent her whole life with her knuckles clenched? Desperately fighting for control and authority, kicking against the pricks? How wonderful to just let go for once. To throw up her hands and slide into the dark.

It felt like freedom.

m) Who knows?

'What do you want?' Shining asked, trying to focus his thoughts away from the images that flickered in the sky above him.

'What do I always want?' the voice asked. 'Amusement. It's a simple enough goal in life.'

'And the current situation pleases you?'

'It's approaching fun, yes. You have to admit he's good value. Most of you lot are terribly dour and functional. Fratfield is employed to be excessive. He's a theatrical event! Curses, bombs and daggers in the night! I would have sold tickets if I weren't so terribly possessive. At least I was able to make a small cameo.'

'Controlling Man-dae ... Of course ...'

'Puppeteering is rather my specialty.'

'Did you have to cut the strings so brutally?'

'Well, Fratfield could hardly leave him wandering around the garden, could he? Straight down to the cellar.'

'A bit obvious that, as a hiding place. Fratfield went to such lengths to cover the fact that he'd checked it and sealed it up. He'd have been better off just keeping his mouth shut. But then, that's the problem with theatrical types, always showing off.'

'Intellectuals, too – they always have to show their workings, just in case we missed how clever they were.'

Shining looked at his sister, watching through her mind's eye as she threatened a man with a gun. He needed to bring this to a close before there were any more casualties.

'But it could be better, couldn't it?' he said. 'As diverting as it's been for you, playing alongside Fratfield, you've missed a trick rather.'

'Tell me more.'

Shining smiled. 'You already have me. You'll always have me. But if you played your cards right, you could have Fratfield too. Wouldn't that be better?'

'Oh, August.' The homeless man leaned into Shining's eyeline. 'Have you become so cold that you would trade your own life at the expense of someone else's?'

'It's called espionage. We do it every day. You said yourself that Fratfield isn't desperate enough to give himself up to you.'

'He's not. I've been offering my services free of charge. It seemed worthwhile, considering the pleasure of taking part. He's a professional but he's not an idiot. He's been very careful not to be indebted to me. He wouldn't risk that for the sake of completing the contract.'

'And it's paid off for him, hasn't it?' asked Shining. 'He's got everything he wants. We'll all be dead, he'll be the sorry hero, a couple of months on sick leave and he'll be back on form. The double agent with tricks up his sleeve that only one department would ever suspect. A department that will have vanished as a threat.'

'When you put it like that, I'm quite sickened at his good fortune.'

'So why not do something about it? If you were to offer a little assistance to me, I could ensure that his fortunes take a turn for the bleak. Then, he would have no choice but to accept whatever deal you might offer.'

'Oh, but that would be so traitorous. I'm not sure I could live with myself.'

'Don't give me that. It's exactly what you've wanted all along. I know you well enough. You've been planting seeds from the first, telling Toby about the Doppelgänger Contract –' A thought

284

suddenly occurred to Shining. 'And that little floor show in the motorway services that helped us identify the Bride.'

'Not that you've used the information. I don't know why I bother sometimes ...'

Shining laughed. 'Would you believe that was a main part of our suspecting Fratfield? And it wasn't even him, it was you all along ...' He got back to his point. 'So what's it to be?' he said. 'A little trade? You help me deal with this mess and I'll deliver Fratfield up to you.'

'Are you quite sure you know what you're offering? In my care, he could become quite intolerable, you know.'

'I'll cross that bridge when I come to it. Espionage is all about the long game.'

'It's tempting ...'

Shining watched his sister climb into her car, eyes full of angry tears. 'Enough games!' he shouted. 'Stop pretending this isn't exactly what you wanted in the first place.'

The homeless man laughed. 'Oh, very well, you've got yourself a deal. But I'm not going to solve everything for you. I'll help you, here and now, but Toby's on his own.'

'No. You reverse his curse too.'

'I couldn't even if I wanted to. Which I don't. I mean, obviously, if he asked me for help *himself*, I might consider it.'

'No! You'll keep your claws out of him. Fine. Deal, give me the strength I need now and I'll get you Fratfield.'

'So nice doing business with you.'

n) Who knows?

Tae-young screamed as the body of one of the protesters fell past her, a dead look in his eyes. A soldier turned towards her, his baton raised. There was no point in trying to reason with him, she knew. Now that the violence had erupted it wouldn't be contained. Fires burned until all the fuel was gone. She put her arms above her head, hoping at least that she could limit the damage as he swung the baton towards her.

It took her a second to understand why the blow didn't connect. The baton was frozen in mid-air, a hand gripping its tip and holding it in place.

August Shining stepped out from behind the soldier, the baton still held in his grip.

'Give me your hand,' he said to Tae-young. 'We're leaving.'

o) Who knows?

Clive King looked down at the pills in his hand and imagined the warm blessing of a sleep that would never end. What was the point in fighting on when none of it ever really mattered? Best just to call it a day.

He lifted his hand to his mouth but another hand closed firmly over it.

'Never think you know what the future holds, Clive,' said August. 'You'll always be wrong.'

He turned King's hand over and the pills tumbled to the floor.

'Though you may as well neck the scotch because that's rarely a bad idea.'

p) Who knows?

Jae-sung tried to drag himself into the light, his fingers slipping in the oily slick of refuse and rain that covered the ground. His head was a white-light of agony, his vision so blurred he could no longer separate the blur at the end of the alley into shop fronts and pedestrians. It was a tumble of noise and colour that was as remote to him as his home.

He knew he would probably never make it as far as the light, and the temptation to just roll over and let the darkness settle over him was extreme. He had no idea how badly wounded he was – after the first couple of kicks he had lost count of the actual effects. All he knew was that he no longer functioned. Perhaps, if he just rested for a while, he would come to with a little more clarity.

The floor smelt of vinegar and rot but he let his cheek press down into it, closing his eyes.

'No time for that, old thing,' came a voice and he felt arms lift him up as if he weighed nothing.

Draped over the shoulder of August Shining he looked up and smiled as the pain in his head faded away and they both stepped out into the light.

q) Who knows?

April's hands hovered above the steering wheel as the car continued to skid. She shifted her foot away from the brake and leaned back in her seat. Let her fly wherever fate took her. She had no fight left in her. She wasn't sure she could halt the car now even if she tried and why should she? To hell with it, why struggle for ever?

She looked on through the windscreen, as the car veered towards the busy road. She saw the red of a bus looming towards her. *That would do it*, she thought, *this little sardine can would be no competition*. Let her be folded into the metal of her silly little car, a footnote in the newspapers, a tatty bouquet left to wilt in the exhaust fumes.

There was a sudden movement and she saw August appear in the windscreen, running, stupidly, impossibly, towards the car. He collided with it, his hands slamming into the bonnet as he continued to run, pushing the car back just as the bus soared past, oblivious to how close it had come to a collision.

April just stared out into the rain and the face of her brother as he lifted his hands from the bonnet of the car, leaving two deep indentations from the impact.

He walked around to the driver's door, opened it and she tumbled out and into his arms.

Silly old woman, she thought as the tears flooded out of her and onto the lapel of his jacket. *He'll never let you hear the end of this.*

'Oh shush,' he said, as if she had spoken aloud. 'What are we for if not for each other?'

He held her close as she dug her fingers into his thin shoulders and the rain was burnt away to steam as the night street was flooded with light.

r) Lufford Hall, Alcester, Warwickshire

Shining snapped awake as the light began to return to the entrance hall. He sat up.

Backing away in confusion, Fratfield was looking around trying to gauge his best route of escape. He turned and made a break for the rear exit, but his leading foot skidded in the shards of glass from the shattered chandelier and he flipped backwards, crashing to the floor with a bone-aching thud.

'Unlucky,' said Shining, looming over him. 'Perhaps you've spread yourself a little thin?'

As the traitor moved to get to his feet, Shining kicked out with his right foot, sending the man's head snapping back. Fratfield slumped back to the floor.

Shining looked towards the centre of the room where the body of Lemuel Spang lay twisted amongst the ruins of the chandelier, his legs bent back on themselves. Over by the door, Mark Rowlands looked even worse, folded almost in half, his jaw hanging loose, his arms clearly broken. All of a sudden, his walkie-talkie burst into life, filled with the urgent calls of his men outside. Calls he would never answer.

Fratfield had left a litter of dead behind him. In the last forty-eight hours he had been responsible for the deaths of seven people.

'No more,' said Shining. 'Not one more.'

'What's going on?' asked Clive King, rubbing at his face as the light continued to flood back into the entrance hall, the darkness dissipating beyond the window.

'Car keys,' said Shining, holding out his hand. 'I need to get after my man.'

He looked to April who was wiping her eyes, trying to remove the signs of tears. She nodded at him and he nodded back.

'Wait,' said Tae-young, as she slowly regained her senses. 'A car? I think I can help with that.'

CHAPTER SIXTEEN: THE SWITCH

a) Alcester, Warwickshire

The driver's name was Bellamy, and Toby's concerns that he was unlikely to believe the truth of his situation turned out to have been misguided. Having underestimated the man's credulity, he had constructed a fictitious story about being driven off the road by two men in a van who had proceeded to drag him from his car and steal his belongings. Bellamy's response to this had been unexpected.

'Probably the additives in the food,' he said. 'The stuff these kids are eating these days beggars belief. I've seen studies.'

'Right,' Toby had said. 'I think they just wanted the car and my wallet.'

'But it's the chemicals that drive them to it. All these conditions they have these days, HD and what have you, the next generation are growing up to be animals and it's all because we've driven them doolally with Tartrazine. You are what you eat, isn't that what they say? I'm only going as far as Alcester.'

The fact that Bellamy had changed the direction of the conversation so rapidly threw Toby for a moment.

'That's fine,' he said. 'I need to go to somewhere called the Swan Hotel, know it?'

'You need to get to the police station, more like.'

'After, I have a friend staying at the Swan.'

'If you're sure.'

Toby hoped Bellamy didn't press the issue, or, even worse, insist on following him inside the hotel. Not knowing that he did, indeed, have a friend there, Toby had visions of an awkward confrontation as he was proven to be a liar.

He needn't have worried, Bellamy just shrugged.

'Here,' he said, as a few drops of rain hit the windscreen, 'weather's changing.'

Two words that had Toby looking around in a panic.

'Weather said it was going to stay dry all week,' Bellamy continued. 'Don't know what they're doing. 'Course, it's the Yanks isn't it? And the Japs. Broken the clouds with their experiments.'

Toby saw a car gaining on them from behind as, slowly, the rain increased.

'You need to go faster,' he told Bellamy, 'for both our sakes.'

'Not with these brakes, I don't,' said Bellamy. 'They're a bit overdue. I know what you mean, though, I haven't felt happy since they invented acid rain.'

On the grass verge ahead, Toby saw the Rain-Soaked Bride emerge from the foliage.

'It's not the rain,' Toby said, twisting in his seat so he could see the car behind them. 'It's her.' He pointed his finger towards the Bride.

'Friend of yours, is she?' said Bellamy. 'If she'll cross the road, I'll pick her up for you.'

'No!' Toby shouted as Bellamy lifted his foot from the accelerator. 'We need to get out of here.' He grabbed Bellamy's knee and forced his leg down on the accelerator pedal making the car jerk forward with a rush of speed.

'Oi!' Bellamy shouted. 'You'll be the bloody death of us.'

That was possibly true, Toby thought.

'The brakes!' Bellamy said, pumping ineffectually at the brake pedal. 'I knew they were on the way out but they're not responding at all.'

'Bad luck,' Toby said as they soared past the Bride. He looked at the rear-view mirror and saw the pursuing car was now right behind them. Through the pursuing car's windscreen he saw Fratfield's grinning face. In the passenger seat a young man lolled against his seat belt, dead or just unconscious, Toby couldn't tell.

'I can't slow down!' said Bellamy. 'The accelerator's stuck and the roundabout's just ahead.' The man was pulling at the accelerator pedal with his foot, trying to lift it up from its depressed position. 'I don't know what's wrong with it!'

Toby didn't think there was much point in explaining that it was all down to his presence.

He looked ahead to where the road split as it approached the roundabout. The sign showed that Alcester was reached from the middle exit, directly across the roundabout. The crossing traffic was heavy, the roundabout acting as a junction with a busier thoroughfare.

'I'll drop the gears and hope for the best,' said Bellamy. 'I won't be able to turn at this speed so we'll just have to hope

I can slow us down enough to use the handbrake without flipping the car.'

Toby knew the odds weren't in their favour. The car would probably turn over at the first opportunity.

'Leave the gears and hit the horn,' he told Bellamy, knocking the man's hand away from the gearstick. He looked ahead at the roundabout. It was fairly flat, just grass with few barriers.

'That's not going to do much bloody good, is it?'

'It'll give the rest of the traffic warning. Do it.'

'I'm going too fast.'

'Do it!' Toby shouted. 'I'm trying to save your life.' *And mine for that matter*, he thought.

'But what about the roundabout?'

'You said yourself,' Toby replied, 'there's no way we can turn at this speed.'

'Bloody hell!' Bellamy screamed as the car sailed out of the junction, straight in front of an approaching lorry and on over the roundabout in a shower of turf and a roar of horns. Toby grabbed the steering wheel, avoiding a large sign and aiming the car directly down the road to Alcester. The road veered gradually and he was able to keep control of the car as it sped along it. He slapped at the hazard lights, only fair to give other drivers as much warning as possible. Their best bet was to keep their speed up and try and get ahead of the curse.

He glanced at the rear-view mirror and was relieved not to see Fratfield. Their manoeuvre across the roundabout would have caused obstructions that should delay him. He looked at the window. There was no rain.

'Try the brake pedal again,' he said. 'Pump it.'

Bellamy did so. 'It's working,' he said unnecessarily as Toby was forced to slap his hands on the dashboard in order to stop his face from slamming into it.

'The accelerator's lifted,' Bellamy said. 'I don't know what it was playing at.'

He dropped through the gears and pulled the car into the forecourt of a petrol station. 'What the hell was all that about?'

'You've been targeted by Big Pharma,' said Toby, undoing his seat belt and getting out.

'Dave Roberts from Evesham?' Bellamy asked, having misunderstood. 'I only told him not to spray his corn so much.'

But Toby was already gone, running away from the petrol station and along the main road.

b) Alcester, Warwickshire

Toby looked from one side of the road to the other, trying to find cover. Fratfield couldn't be far behind him. Even if the near pile-up he and Bellamy had caused on the roundabout had held the man back for a few minutes it was obvious where Toby had gone and the road to the centre of town was long and straight, with little opportunity for his changing direction.

There was no sign of the rain, his only reliable method of knowing when Fratfield was close, but it could only be a matter of time.

The few minutes in the car had, despite the manner in which the journey had ended, given him an opportunity to get his breath back. Nonetheless, sprinting down the road and trying to figure out a way off it, he soon began to tire.

Finally, he was able to cut right, getting off the main road and into a rabbit warren of residential streets.

He could hear the sound of the nearby fair. Like Shining before him, he thought it seemed an absurd presence in this quaint old town. In normal circumstances he might have been glad of it as it would certainly provide him with cover. His concern now was the risk he might put others under should he suddenly become the focal point for disaster. The curse seemed to have reasonable aim for the most part – the majority of its victims had died alone, not in a great wave of collateral damage – but what had happened in the car went to show that it wasn't always precise. Bellamy had nearly joined Rachel Holley as an innocent caught up in its net.

Shining had told him to get himself to the Swan Hotel. If he could get himself there unseen he could hide from Fratfield but could he ever hide from the Bride herself? Once he was within her sphere of influence, she would find him anywhere. He had to figure out a way of putting proper distance between them. Maybe the town had a train station? But then, if he was on the train by the time the curse struck he could take a lot of passengers with him. Perhaps it would be better to just steal a car? If he was caught behind the wheel then at least it was only himself he had to worry about. Unless of course the car crashed into others.

The only way to keep others safe was to go somewhere remote. That opportunity was hardly open to him now – quite the reverse, he realised, as he stepped out of a side street and into the main street running through the centre of town. Crowds of people pushed in all directions as they moved between the rides. Music pounded, the ghost train screamed and Toby was at a loss as to what he should do.

His only option was to get through the crowds as quickly as

possible. Maybe, on the other side of town, he would find a car he could steal that might put him some distance away. It would be a risk but the only sure-fire way of protecting innocents was to put a gun to his head and he wasn't inclined to do that.

As he moved through the fair, constantly zig-zagging from one tight space to another, he suddenly became aware of the air growing colder. If there was the tell-tale sound of thunder, he certainly couldn't hear it above the row on either side but, still only halfway through the fair, he felt a couple of raindrops land on his head.

He tried to break into a run but, hemmed in on either side, it was all he could do to keep moving. As people began to shout and shove trying to get out of the sudden downpour, he found himself knocked to the ground. Putting his hands up to protect his head, he tried to get to his feet but was knocked again and again as people rushed past him. It was the curse, he knew, more than simple impatience on the part of the crowds. The Bride would be just as happy to have him trampled to death as anything else.

He fell forward, scuffing his hands on the road and someone from behind caught him hard enough to send him face-first to the ground, a pair of heavy black boots zooming into his eye-line.

'Get up,' said a voice he recognised and he looked up as a woman's hands gripped him beneath the arms.

'Tamar?'

'August did not tell you I was here?'

'No.' And instantly he realised why. He was risking the lives of everyone around him, and now that included the woman he cared for more than anything else. 'He knew I wouldn't have come.'

'You are that happy to see me?'

'Everywhere I go I bring trouble,' he explained. 'I'm cursed. The world's out to get me.'

She raised her eyebrow. 'I know that feeling. So we need to get away from crowd?'

He nodded, looking around for sign of Fratfield or the Bride. He found the latter atop the ghost train, squatting down on the brightly coloured 'T' of the sign and looking right at him.

'She's there,' Toby said, pointing. 'We need to get clear – if these people get caught in the crossfire ...'

Tamar pulled her gun from under her jacket, pointed it in the air and fired twice. Even over the noise of the fair rides it had an immediate effect.

There was a scream from a woman stood next to them and the mass exodus of the crowds increased its panicked speed. Parents grabbed children and hoisted them onto their shoulders, everyone running to get beyond the rides and off the street.

The ghost train screamed, the large mechanical skeleton that straddled it clicking to and fro like a pendulum. There was a high-pitched whistle from the waltzers as the cars collided and spun. The spinning octopus above them built to a climax, flashing in purple and green light as it tipped one way and then the other. The large speakers crunched out a bass-distorted dance tune.

At the far end of the street, revealed by the parting crowds stood Fratfield.

'He is our man?' Tamar asked.

Toby nodded.

Tamar raised her gun but Toby shouted at her to stop. 'The only way I can get rid of the curse is to pass it on,' he said. 'Those are the rules.'

'And how do you do that?'

But before Toby could answer there was a loud cracking sound and the octopus ride tipped towards them. Toby pushed Tamar to one side, the spinning cars narrowly missing him as they carved through the air. There were screams from the people trapped inside, convinced they were about to be flung into the air.

Toby made a run for it, wanting to put distance between himself, the ride and Tamar.

There was another sound of grinding gears and a waltzer, thankfully empty, left its platform and sailed through the air, clipping Tamar as she tried to run after Toby.

'Tamar!' he shouted, running towards her.

She got to her feet, cradling a broken arm. 'I am all right,' she insisted. 'It barely touch me.'

But that was enough for Toby. He ran towards the ghost train, waving at the Bride who still stood on top of it.

'I'm here!' he shouted. 'No need for anyone else to get hurt.'

'No Toby.' Tamar ran after him, grabbing at his shoulder with her uninjured arm.

'Get away!' Toby begged her. 'Please. I couldn't bear it if I ended up ... not after everything else.'

'I am not your responsibility,' she told him. 'You do not own me.'

'It's not about owning you!' he told her. 'It's about loving you. Now, for God's sake, keep back, it's me she wants.'

Tamar pushed in front of him. 'Then she'll have to go through me.'

'Stupid!' Toby moved to the side, calling up at the Bride. 'Quickly, please, do it! Just don't hurt her!'

The skeleton cracked to and fro, the Bride inclined her head.

'I am not stupid.' Tamar grabbed him and pulled him back. 'I am doing what is right.'

'You don't owe me anything!' Toby said. 'Please understand that. It's not about debts. It's not about being owned.'

'I know,' she told him. 'But I am not going to leave you.'

The rain stopped, frozen in mid-air around them.

'What are you doing?' Fratfield shouted. He had kept his distance up until now, happy to watch but not wanting to risk being hurt himself. Now, frustrated, he walked between the rides, pulling his own gun out of its holster. 'Finish the job, damn you, that's what you're for!'

Tamar fired first, hitting Fratfield in the shoulder. He spun on the spot, his gun flying out of his hand.

'Don't kill him,' Toby insisted, grabbing the gun.

He looked up again at the Bride. 'I don't know how this works,' he said, 'but that woman means the world to me. She's ... well, she's just amazing. I'm no good at explaining that sort of thing. I'm not very ... I can't find the words. She'll only shout at me if I try. Doesn't matter. The point is, I won't stand by and risk her dying too.' He put the gun to his head. 'If I pull the trigger are we all square? Are we done?'

'No, Toby!' Tamar tried to wrestle the gun from him but he pushed her back.

'Do it!' Fratfield shouted. 'It's good enough for me!'

'It's not about you,' Toby replied. 'It's about her.' He pointed to the Bride. 'Are we done?' he asked again, pressing the barrel of the gun to his head. The Bride inclined her head again. Saying nothing.

Was that an answer? It must be. Surely if he was dead then the curse was satisfied. He closed his eyes and tightened his finger on the trigger.

Above them, there was a sudden roar of rotor blades as a helicopter carved its way through the air above the street. For a moment Toby was distracted, looking up and recognising the helicopter from Lufford Hall.

The downdraft from the rotor blades sent the frozen rain spiralling around them, Fratfield fighting to keep to his feet as the helicopter hovered just a few feet above them.

In the cabin there were four people: the pilot, Tae-young, Clive King and Shining.

'It's unbelievable,' said King. 'You can actually see where the rain begins, appearing as if out of thin air.'

'With all due respect, Mr King,' said Shining, 'the rain is the least of my concerns.' He tapped the pilot on the shoulder who handed him the microphone handset that was connected to a speaker on the underside of the helicopter.

'Toby,' said Shining, his voice echoing off the buildings around them, 'you need to be careful. It's not just Fratfield. An old friend is involved, too. That enemy agent we discussed before. The higher power. He's been playing this whole situation to his own advantage. He's been working with Fratfield. Be aware. He could be anyone at any time. Understand? He could be anyone!'

'Are you sure we wouldn't be of more help trying to attack Fratfield?' asked King. 'He's the threat here.'

'No he isn't,' said Tae-young, looking at the Bride who returned her gaze, her wet hair rippling in the wind caused by the rotor blades.

'Toby will understand,' said Shining. 'I trust him. He'll know what to do.'

Toby's finger held fast. His eyes stayed closed. Then something popped into his head.

He turned the gun towards the helicopter and fired two shots. One clipping the left-hand landing skid, the other going wide.

'Take us up!' Shining demanded. 'Quickly!'

Toby's aim followed the helicopter as it sailed skywards but he didn't take another shot. He sighed and lowered the gun.

'What are you doing?' Tamar asked.

He turned to her and, with terrifying speed, slapped her across the face. 'Do shut up, you whining sow.'

Then he turned and walked towards Fratfield, shaking his head.

'This is just a mess,' he said, but the voice did not sound a bit like Toby's. It was cold and dismissive. It was the voice of the 'enemy agent' to which Shining had referred. He didn't even walk the same, a swagger, an insouciance that belied the young officer's situation. 'All you had to do,' he said to Fratfield, 'was kill a few people. Now I like a bit of spectacle but this is ridiculous. What's your problem?'

'Is that . . .?' Fratfield's eyes narrowed.

'Who do you think it is? Thanks to your handling of this, my cover's blown. Do you want me to clear up your mess?'

'I'm perfectly capable of handling this on my own,' Fratfield replied. 'As I told you before, I don't intend to become indebted to you.'

'Fine.' The rain began to fall again, the Bride turning to face the two men, her momentary indecision gone. Toby held the gun out, grip first, to Fratfield and tapped at his own forehead. 'Then let's get this done with. One shot and we can get on with more interesting things.'

Fratfield gritted his teeth, not comfortable with this thing ordering him around. 'Fine,' he said, snatching the gun. 'I'd make yourself scarce if I were you, otherwise this might hurt.'

He pointed the gun towards Toby whose face suddenly changed. 'Oh,' he said, his voice normal again. 'Hang on. I think there's something in the barrel that shouldn't be there.'

'What?' Fratfield's face fell as the penny dropped and he turned the gun around to look at the barrel. Stuck in the end was a rolled-up piece of paper. He plucked it out. The curse.

'Gotcha!' said Toby. Then, in the voice he had used while pretending to be controlled by the other presence: 'Never take anything from anybody. Remember?'

Fratfield turned the gun back towards Toby and pressed the trigger. It jammed.

'Bad luck,' Toby said, turning his back on the man and walking back to Tamar.

The Bride leapt from the ghost train, the mechanical skeleton clicking forward one last time, then, with a squeal of shearing metal, the whole thing came loose and tumbled forward.

Fratfield was staring at the Bride, at what was left of her face, revealed as the wind pulled her hair apart. She opened her mouth and a jet of brackish water sprayed out, hitting Fratfield in the eyes. He put up his hands, unaware of the skeleton's head scything down until it hit him square-on. There was the crash of metal, the popping of light bulbs, the splitting of fibreglass and the crack of bone.

'You hit me,' said Tamar, staring at Toby.

'Yes, sorry, I was trying to be convincing, you see, and I thought ...' She slapped him hard and he shut up.

'You will not do it again. Stupid man.'

'No.'

With an angry sigh, she hugged him. 'I am glad you are not dead.'

The Bride stood up from the ruin of meat and bone that had been Bill Fratfield, looked at the two of them and, beneath her black hair, what was left of her lips turned into a smile. Then she was gone and the rain went with her.

a) Warwick Hospital, Lakin Road, Warwickshire

Fratfield cried out as a bolt of pain lanced through him. He sat up in his hospital bed, his hand moving to the dressed bullet wound in his abdomen.

'Are you all right?' asked the nurse who had been adjusting his drip.

'No,' Fratfield replied. 'I ...' he couldn't explain the pain. He caught the vague smell of candy floss and burned electrics. 'There was something ...' One of his other selves, he realised. Something had happened to one of the duplicates.

'I'm all right,' he said, lying back down, the pain still crackling through his body.

'Actually,' said the nurse, her voice taking on a distinctly different tone, 'you're not. In fact you've made a right mess of things.'

'Excuse me?' it took Fratfield a few seconds to realise he was no longer talking to the nurse.

'In fact, you're about …' the nurse inclined her head as if listening to something, 'three minutes away from being surrounded by security officers. You're blown. They're coming for you.'

Fratfield made to get out of the bed but the drugs in his system and the pain from his wound threw his balance and he slid to the floor.

'Not in a good state, are we?' the nurse asked, tugging playfully at the plastic tubes that still connected Fratfield to the drip behind his bed. 'Let's be honest, you're going nowhere. You're trapped. You're done.'

Fratfield tried to stand up but his head was swimming and he couldn't get his thoughts straight.

'Unless of course,' the nurse said, squatting down next to him, 'you'd like a bit of help? It'll come at a price, naturally, but I imagine you'd rather pay it than face what Her Majesty's Government has in store?'

Fratfield looked at her and knew that he was lost.

A few minutes later, the hospital ward was in chaos as a team of Rowlands' men entered, pushing their way past complaining staff and into Fratfield's room.

By then, of course, it was empty.

b) Section 37, Wood Green, London

August Shining put down the phone and settled back into his office chair.

'Nothing?' asked Toby.

'He's in the wind,' admitted Shining. 'Last seen approaching Dover. Anyone else and I'd hold out a chance of them picking him up at passport control, but not him. He's too good. They found the owner of the car he stole dumped in a layby. One more dead body added to the list.'

'It could have been more.'

'Yes,' Shining admitted, 'it could have been. I'm afraid I can hardly look on this as our brightest day, though. We caught him as much by luck as judgement.'

Toby got up from his desk, moving slowly, still aching from his experiences of the last few days.

'Well,' he said, 'at least we still have one of them.'

Shining nodded. 'And that's sent the powers that be into freefall. King has worked wonders backing up our story, but there are still those who refuse to believe we've caught a double agent as well as killing him and letting him escape.'

'It does get confusing.'

'Hello, boys.' April entered in her usual excitable manner. 'Just wondered if you wanted to pop out for lunch. I'm taking Tae-young and Jae-sung to an all-you-can-eat buffet before they have to fly home.'

'Too much to do here, I'm afraid,' said Shining, 'but give them our best.'

'Darling boy,' she said, kissing him on the cheek, 'I think you both already did that.'

She stood next to Toby. 'And how is ...?' She pointed upstairs.

'Fine,' he said, smiling. 'Actually, we're going out tonight.'

'A date!' she screamed and then buried her face in his shoulder as if embarrassed by her outburst, something Toby knew she never could be.

'We're just going for a drink,' he said. 'It's no big deal. It doesn't mean anything.'

'Nonsense,' she said, 'you never know what these things lead to.'

SIX MONTHS LATER

From the other side of Little Green, a driver beats his horn twice in quick succession. It echoes like a musical sting from a trumpet, bouncing around the buildings of Richmond. Toby Greene, a man who is doing his very best to appear relaxed, nearly jumps out of his skin at the sound.

'A little on edge, old thing?' asks the voice in his ear. 'Do try not to scream in panic at every bit of traffic noise.'

'It's all right for you,' Toby mutters, keeping his lips still and his voice only just loud enough for the small mic in his bow tie to pick up. 'The worst thing that can go wrong for you this afternoon is that your sister embarrasses you. Again.'

August Shining leans back against the wrought-iron gate where he's waiting and smiles. 'True. Now get a move on or the whole thing's blown.'

'What do you think I'm trying to do?' Toby replies, breaking into a run.

He glances at his watch. The clock is indeed ticking and he

has only minutes left in which to pull this off. Failure, as is so often the way in his life these days, will mean the threat of a sound beating, maybe even death.

He breaks across the road, narrowly avoiding the path of a motorbike whose slipstream tugs at his jacket.

'Careful,' says Shining. 'That sounded too close for comfort.'

'Yes, yes.' Toby sighs, wondering if having his superior commenting on his every move isn't a distraction too far. 'You just be ready your end and let me worry about what I'm doing.'

Out of the corner of his eye he suddenly spots his target. The car is pulling past the train station and heading in his direction.

'The car's coming!' he says.

'Well, move then! You mustn't let her see you!'

Toby darts through the door of a nearby pub. 'A taste of Ireland', it promises. Looking around, it only seems to offer a taste of sullen misery.

'There ain't a fucking dress code,' says an old man sat by the door, eyeing up Toby's suit as he works his way through an apple juice and vodka.

'Obviously not,' Toby replies, noting the old man's combination of stained anorak and tracksuit bottoms.

He watches the car pull past the front of the pub, gives it a couple of seconds to make sure the traffic will have moved on a little way and then steps back out onto the street. He can see the car a short way in the distance. He hangs back a little, wanting to make sure he's not spotted in the rear-view mirror.

'OK,' he says into the microphone, 'I need a quicker route. I need to steer clear of the main road but somehow get ahead of them.'

'Already on it,' Shining replies. He's scrolling through the maps app on his phone. 'Right ... You feeling fit?'

'Just do it.'

'Then get across the road.'

Toby runs between the traffic, following his superior's instructions all the way.

'The street you're now on runs parallel with the main road,' Shining tells him, 'but when you get to the end you're going to run into them again so you need to be a little more creative. You need to be heading north.'

'North,' Toby replies. 'Great.'

He cuts into the central courtyard of a block of flats and looks around. No rear exit. 'Creative,' he sighs.

An old woman is manhandling her shopping through the pass-coded entrance door to the flats beyond. He tries to look casual – an almost impossible task given the suit he's wearing – coming up behind her and helping her lift the wheeled trolley through.

'Thank you, dear,' she says.

'My pleasure,' he replies. 'I don't suppose you live in one of the flats over there, do you?' he asks pointing in the direction he needs to go.

'Number 12a,' she replies. 'Just there.' She points directly opposite them.

'That'll do,' he replies. 'I need a massive favour.'

'Toby,' Shining asks, sighing at the flurry of negotiation going on in his earpiece, 'I hate to rush you ...'

'I'm on it!' Toby replies.

'Who are you talking to now?' the old woman asks. 'God?'

'He would love to think so. Which way?'

She points along the poky entrance hall. 'Bathroom's at the back there. Second on the left.'

'You're a wonder,' Toby replies, kissing her on her forehead.

'Well,' she shrugs, 'when you've got to go ...'

He dashes into the bathroom, relieved at the sight of the window that looks out over the road behind. He opens it and drags himself through. It's tight, and there's a moment when the latch catches on his belt, but with a little wriggling he manages to get through, hanging by his fingers from the sill. He's looking out over the green. The car should now be approaching from his left. All he has to do is get ahead of it.

He drops to the ground, keeping his legs loose so that he rolls.

Brushing the dust from his suit as he runs, he crosses into the park and begins to sprint. The car will have to drive along the road he has just crossed, then turn the corner and drive up the far side. If he can just get to the far corner before the car does, he'll cross the road before them.

'I can see you!' says Shining. 'You're going to make it. Keep running, they're just behind you.'

Toby doesn't bother to reply, saving his breath as he tries to move even faster. He risks one quick glance behind him and he can see the car moving along the road he just crossed. He just has to complete the diagonal before they turn the corner. He can see Shining now, beckoning to him from a few yards away. There's a hedge at chest-height, bordering the edge of the green, but it's dense and he vaults it, springing down on the other side in a shower of leaves and a pair of slightly scratched palms.

'Made it!' Shining laughs, beckoning for Toby to move ahead of him through the gate.

Toby notices the car turning onto the road just behind them.

He walks ahead of Shining and past the ornately painted sign declaring the place to be the 'Church of the Sacred Mind'. The curly letters that make up these words are surrounded by stylised pictures of brains.

'I can't believe you convinced us to use this place,' he says, trying to catch his breath.

'Nonsense, it's perfect, a solid humanist ceremony and a cracking buffet lunch. As well as being a legally ordained minister and demonologist, Pleasance is a cracking cook.'

The car that Toby was avoiding pulls up in front of the building and April gets out.

'See, darling?' she says to the car's other passenger, 'I told you he wouldn't be late.'

Tamar steps out and smiles at the man who is about to become her husband. 'He does not dare,' she says. 'He knows I would kill him.'

'Ah,' Shining sighs, 'young love.'

'Here they are!' shouts Pleasance Bellvue, minister of the Church of the Sacred Mind and occasional agent for Section 37. 'Everything's ready for you in the garden, my loves, you've a splendid turnout.'

She is a giant of a woman, six and a half foot of Jamaican descent. When she offers enthusiasm, the world can be in no doubt of the fact.

She takes Toby and Tamar's hands and then wraps them both in a bear hug that leaves an already slightly breathless Toby feeling unconsciousness can only be seconds away.

'Go through,' Pleasance tells them, finally releasing them, 'have a mingle. I've just got to turn the samosas over.'

Toby takes Tamar's hand and they step out through a large pair of patio doors into the garden.

It's a massive courtyard, its walls lined with ivy that has been threaded with fairy lights. Against the far wall, there is a small raised dais, surrounded by white drapes and sprinkled with petals. A banner above it reads 'Tamar and Toby, The First Day Of The Rest Of Their Lives.'

'There's a thought,' says Toby.

'She puts my name in front,' says Tamar, squeezing his hand. 'She is a wise woman.'

As they step out, the small group of people gathered around a central buffet table turn and give an enthusiastic round of applause. Someone wolf whistles. Toby notices it's Cassandra, who is wearing a dress that appears to have been constructed out of bomb-damaged net curtains.

'You're finally here, then,' says a voice to Toby's right. It's his father, staying as close to the exit as possible. 'Trust you to know so many mentals. I dread to think what your mother, God rest her soul, would have said.'

'Congratulations?' Toby suggests, before quickly changing the subject. Today was going to be a happy day, he was damned if he'd let it be otherwise. 'Thank you for coming.'

'Aye, well, I was down anyway. Couldn't miss this, could I? Never thought I'd see the day.'

'Hello, Roger,' says Tamar, taking his hand. 'It is nice to see you again.'

Toby smiles. She's a better liar than he is. When he'd first introduced them six weeks earlier, during a torturous weekend at his father's cottage in Wales, he had suspected it had taken a considerable effort on her part not to break Roger Greene's neck. He had found her several times hiding in the bathroom and pulling faces in the mirror.

'Sure you don't mind inheriting such a father-in-law?' he had asked.

'Death comes to us all in the end,' she had replied with a smile.

'Nice to see you, too,' says Roger to Tamar, speaking slowly and loudly as if to an idiot. Toby has tried to explain that, however strangled her English occasionally sounds, she can understand him just fine. Roger is clearly not yet convinced. 'I hope you know what you are doing? Not too late to back out you know ...'

'Thanks, Dad,' says Toby.

'You know what they say,' Roger sighs. 'Marry in haste ...'

'Before the baby arrives?'

Roger Greene turns to see the glamorous figure who has joined them and his eyes light up. Toby smiles, his father always has had an uncontrollable libido.

'Well, hello,' he purrs, making no attempt to hide his appreciation of the new arrival. 'The afternoon's looking up.'

'Oh, you charmer,' the new arrival replies.

'Dad,' says Toby, 'this is—' but a raised hand stops him.

'Don't spoil the surprise,' insists Alasdair Forge, white witch and female impersonator. 'I'm sure your father will find out in good time once we've got to know each other a little better.'

Alasdair puts his arm around Roger Greene and leads him towards the buffet table. He doesn't attempt to stop the old man's hand as it makes its slow way down his back before coming to rest on his left buttock.

'I think your father will be angry,' says Tamar.

'Won't he just? Don't worry about it.'

'I wasn't.' She kisses him on the cheek.

'You sure you want to go through with this?' Toby asks her. It is not the first time he's asked the question.

'I would not be here if I did not,' she replies. 'You are a good man and you make me laugh. I could do worse.'

'So romantic. You didn't mention your uncontrollable lust for me.'

She smiles at him. 'See? You are always funny.'

She takes his arm and drags him over to where Jamie Goss is trying the punch.

'The wonderful thing about punch,' he says, 'is that it's both food and drink in one bowl. I can get charmingly wasted and also keep up with my five-a-day.' He pops a segment of apple in his mouth and grins at Toby. 'Not that you're probably familiar with fruit.'

'What do you mean?'

'Oh, nothing, I just didn't imagine you eat a lot of it.' Goss pats him on the stomach.

'Jamie is trying to infer I'm fat,' explains Toby.

'No I'm not!' Goss insists. 'I'm implying it. It's you that's doing the inferring. Anyway, I'm allowed to be a bit mean, you've made me bring Alasdair to a wedding. It'll give him ideas.'

'You should be so lucky,' Toby tells him, looking over to where Alasdair is laughing loudly at something deeply unfunny that Roger Greene has just said. 'Anyway, he'll probably end up marrying my father.'

'As long as he doesn't try and bring him home.' Goss turns to Tamar. 'I presume he's paying you to marry him?'

'No, I no longer sleep with men for money, thank you.'

Goss's face falls. 'Oh. I didn't mean to ... I mean, it was supposed to be a joke.'

'Wonderful,' says Toby. 'You've actually made him stuck for words.'

Tamar picks a piece of orange from Goss's punch glass and pops it in her mouth. 'I win,' she says. 'Always.'

'Can I push in?' Toby thinks that Derek Lime, ex-wrestler and physicist can push in anywhere he damn well likes. 'Good to see you again,' he says to Toby, shaking his hand carefully so as not to break it. 'I knew your name wasn't Charlie,' he says, nodding at the banner.

'Or Keith,' says Goss.

'Or Gary,' says Cassandra, having joined them.

'Terry,' Toby corrects her.

'You were always Gary to me.'

'It's all right,' says Shining, joining them. 'I have a friend called Leonard who will be wiping your memories before you leave the building.'

Derek laughs.

Goss takes another mouthful of his punch.

Shining takes Toby by the shoulder. 'Can I borrow him for a moment?'

'Is Len all set?' Toby asks.

'By the time they get home, they won't have the first idea what they've been doing all day. The only exception is Pleasance. After all, she does have to file the paperwork.'

Shining looks at Toby's father who is trying to dance with Alasdair despite the fact that there's no music playing. 'What about Roger?'

'He's not cleared to know any of these people.'

'Oh, I know, but he easily could be.'

'No. Let him forget the same as everyone else. I'll tell him I'm married the next time we see him. Which I hope won't be too soon.'

'Certainly not for a couple of weeks.' Shining pats his jacket pocket. 'I've printed off your boarding passes. You're all set.'

'Thank you. I do hope we don't miss the Apocalypse or anything while we're away.'

'If you do you do, I managed on my own for long enough. Although ...' Shining takes Toby's arm. 'It won't be the same. You know that, yes? The difference you've made ... not just to the Section ... you've given an old man a spring in his step.'

'I suspect it to be arthritis.'

'I hope your plane crashes.'

'If it does, I'll haunt you.'

'You'd better.'

Shining gives him a hug, but Pleasance has appeared and that means it's time for Toby to get married.

Throughout the ceremony, all he can do is stare at the woman he loves, still not quite able to believe it. A couple of times Pleasance has to nudge him to give his responses because at that moment he is all but lost, amazed at the life that now lies in front of him.

They kiss and there is a shower of confetti. Some of it appears to sparkle and pop as it descends around them.

'Just a little extra I threw in,' says Cassandra to April who is stood next to her. 'I don't think it's dangerous.'

'My darling,' says April, 'what in this life of worth isn't?'

Arrábida Natural Park, Setubal, Portugal

'There's a phone.'

Toby pulls the hire car in to the small layby, kisses his wife and looks out of the windscreen at the small roadside stall set up next to the callbox.

'I think,' he says, 'that if we want a bunch of flowers, some overpriced honey or jars of fruit, we're in luck.'

'It is not far until we are at Setubal,' says Tamar. 'I'll let you buy me dinner there.'

'Fair enough. I'll be quick.'

He takes his mobile phone out of his pocket and holds it up, still not able to find a signal. Normally, he'd be glad of the fact, but he wants to reply to a panicked text from Shining that slipped through during some magical moment of network coverage on the drive through the park.

Looking over at the stall he sees another tourist browsing the bouquets, the owner of the small Seat parked further along, he assumes. He is all but hidden in baseball cap and sunglasses, scratching at his short beard as he tries to make his choice. Toby mocks himself for paying such close attention, even on holiday – no, honeymoon! – he's on the lookout for trouble.

It's the text, he tells himself. Shining wouldn't disturb them unless it was important.

'Good price for roses,' says the stall owner as Toby passes, offering him a smile of tobacco-yellow teeth.

'No, thank you,' Toby replies. 'I'm just after the phone.'

The owner shrugs, returning his attention to the man in the baseball cap who has chosen a bouquet of red roses.

Toby steps into the callbox, inserts some change and dials the number for the office.

After a few moments, Shining answers. 'Dark Spectre publishing,' he says. Only Section 37 would choose a small-press horror publishing company as a cover. It does the job but Shining has threatened to start actually publishing some submissions which has Toby wondering when the little free time he does enjoy is likely to vanish.

'It's me,' he says.

'Toby? The line's awful. What are you doing ringing me? If it's advice you're after, I'm afraid you've pegged the wrong man.'

Toby watches as the man in the baseball cap walks away from the roadside stall carrying his bouquet of flowers.

'You sent me a text,' he says, 'saying something serious had cropped up and you needed to speak to me.'

'I didn't, you know ... unless it was April, she keeps stealing my phone. I can't imagine she'd have wanted to interrupt the two of you, though.'

Tamar is getting out of the car, stretching her legs and lifting her face up to the sun.

The man in the baseball cap stops walking and hands her the bouquet of flowers.

'For you,' he says, 'as a sign of thanks.'

He walks away, leaving her holding the bouquet and looking confused.

Toby is already running, the phone dangling from the callbox as he chases after the man.

He is too quick, the car engine is already running and the Seat pulls away just as Toby reaches the driver's door. He catches a glimpse of the driver, and now he sees something he recognises beyond the beard, cap and glasses.

Fratfield.

The car drives off, and Toby turns to Tamar who is still holding the bouquet.

'Why did he do this?' she asks, picking at the flowers. She gives an angry shout as the thorn on one of the roses pricks her and she drops the bouquet.

From between the blooms, a small piece of paper tumbles onto the ground, is caught by the breeze and spirals up into the air above them.

Toby watches it go and, in the distance he sees dark shapes forming.

'Come on,' he says, pushing Tamar back towards the car. 'We need to get out of here now.'

'What is it?' she asks, getting into the passenger seat as he moves around to the driver's side.

He looks out across the open country. What looks like a tornado is heading their way, a pillar of dust curling towards them.

He doesn't answer her, just climbs in the car, turns it in the opposite direction to that taken by the Seat and, in a roar of an over-revved engine, tears off up the road.

'Young people,' says the stall owner, watching them go. 'Always in such a hurry. When will they learn? They have all the time in the world.'

ACKNOWLEDGEMENTS

As always, my team of operatives worked hard behind enemy lines to make this book happen:

At mission control, Agent Macbook led the way and offered vital input on the details of the mission while Agent Greased Lightning handled special weapons and wetwork. At our Andover office, Agent Aladdin Sane handled decryption and clarified the mission reports.

In the field, Agents Moose and Sloth received initial mission orders and checked for hotspots.

I'd have had a bullet in the back without each and every one of them.

Also by Guy Adams:

THE CLOWN SERVICE

Toby Greene has been reassigned.

The Department: Section 37 Station Office, Wood Green.

The Boss: August Shining, an ex-Cambridge,
Cold War-era spy.

The Mission: Charged with protecting Great Britain and its
interests from paranormal terrorism.

The Threat: An old enemy has returned, and with him
Operation Black Earth, a Soviet plan to create the ultimate
insurgents by re-animating the dead.

DEL REY

THE SUICIDE EXHIBITION

By Justin Richards

WEWELSBURG CASTLE, 1940.

The German war machine has woken an ancient threat – the alien Vril and their Ubermensch have returned. Ultimate Victory in the war for Europe is now within the Nazis' grasp.

ENGLAND, 1941

Foreign Office trouble shooter Guy Pentecross has stumbled into a conspiracy beyond his imagining – a secret war being waged in the shadows against a terrible enemy.

The battle for Europe has just become the war for humanity.

**This is *The Thirty-Nine Steps* crossed with
Indiana Jones and *Quatermass*. Justin Richards
has an extremely credible grasp of the period's
history and has transformed it into a ground-
breaking alternate reality thriller.**

DEL REY

Also available from Del Rey:

THE BLOOD RED CITY

By Justin Richards

The alien Vril are waking, and the Never War is heating up. Colonel Brinkman and his team at Station Z desperately need answers – they have to discover exactly what they are facing and how the attack will come. But the information doesn't come easily. With a major Vril offensive imminent, the Nazis step up their own project to exploit Vril weapons and technology.

Leo Davenport finds himself fighting with the Greek resistance as he struggles to solve an ancient mystery. Major Guy Pentecross must travel to the ruined deathtrap of the most dangerous city in the world to track down the one man who can help.

From a spaceship crash in Bavaria in 1934 to the rat-infested devastation of Stalingrad, from the ancient ruins of occupied Greece to the bombed-out streets of London, the second book of the Never War series continues a secret history of the Second World War in which humanity itself is fighting for survival...

DEL REY

Also available from Del Rey:

OSIRIS

By E. J. Swift

Nobody leaves Osiris.

Adelaide Rechnov

Wealthy socialite and granddaughter of the Architect, she spends her time in pointless luxury, rebelling against her family in a series of jaded social extravagances and scandals until her twin brother disappears in mysterious circumstances.

Vikram Bai

He lives in the Western Quarter, home to the poor descendants of storm refugees and effectively quarantined from the wealthy elite. His people live with cold and starvation, but the coming brutal winter promises civil unrest, and a return to the riots of previous years.

As tensions rise in the city, can Adelaide and Vikram bridge the divide at the heart of Osiris before conspiracies bring them to the edge of disaster?

DEL REY

Also available from Del Rey:

CATAVEIRO

By E. J. Swift

A shipwreck. And one lone survivor.

For political exile Taeo Ybanez, this could be his ticket home.
Relations between the Antarcticans and the Patagonians are
worse than ever, and to be caught on the wrong side could
prove deadly.

For pilot and cartographer Ramona Callejas, the presence of
the mysterious stranger is one more thing in the way of her
saving her mother from a deadly disease.

All roads lead to Cataveiro, the city of fate and fortune, where
their destinies will become intertwined and their futures
cemented for ever...

DEL REY

Also available from Del Rey:

THE MARTIAN
By Andy Weir

I'm stranded on Mars.

I have no way to communicate with Earth.

I'm in a Habitat designed to last 31 days.

If the Oxygenator breaks down, I'll suffocate. If the Water Reclaimer breaks down, I'll die of thirst. If the Hab breaches, I'll just kind of explode. If none of those things happen, I'll eventually run out of food and starve to death.

So yeah. I'm screwed.

DEL REY